The Curse of the Frost King

THE FAE SPARK TRILOGY
BOOK ONE

JEN L. GREY

CHAPTER 1

Hannah

Sometimes I thought someone up above had a sick sense of humor.

I was in the one spot I'd avoided my entire life. My skin was crawling, and my head was screaming, *Hannah, run away*! But my body wouldn't let me leave. Some sort of... *whisper* kept repeating in my ear: *Open the box.*

It had been rolling through my head nonstop since the moment my great-aunt Maureen had passed away. Every dream I'd had since then was of my memory of the night my mother had died, and Aunt Maureen had buried this big iron box in the ground close to this freaky-ass rowan tree that had spread its roots over this spot during the past twenty years.

I hated this tree as much as Aunt Maureen had loved it. Rowans typically grew only in Ireland, but my great-grand-mother had managed to find one to plant here and had kept it alive against all odds. The damn thing hadn't just survived—it had thrived, and now it towered over me, full of red berries with branches and leaves that sounded like hissing murmurs were coming from their depths in the wind. No matter how hard I listened, true words never formed, but I always sensed that the tree wanted *something*.

Even when I was a child, this place hadn't felt right and had kept me unsettled. I'd seen shadows and heard sounds that I could never explain even to this day. Now I was drenched in sweat, digging up soil and hacking at the roots of the very tree I'd tried to stay the hell away from, in a pink shirt that said *I'm with Stupid*. It hadn't been intentional, but it was damn fitting.

I attacked one of the big branching roots, my arm muscles burning. Blowing out a breath, I set the axe next to the crowbar and once again jammed the shovel into the earth with a sharp *crack* that jolted up my arms. I froze, breath catching as if someone had just caught me doing something terrible.

Part of me expected to see Aunt Maureen looming over me, hands on her hips, deciding what item she should steal from me to teach me a lesson about disobeying. The metallic taste of nerves coated my tongue as I remembered the last time. I'd been running late to my tanning session before my shift at the tanning salon started, and I'd run outside only to find that my car was missing. I could only imagine what she'd steal from me for doing this—if she were still alive.

Knock it off. I huffed a strand of honey blonde hair out of my face, then stomped my foot on the step of the shovel to drive it deeper. A warm, earthy scent engulfed me, contrasting sharply with the usual crisp scents of autumn in eastern Tennessee.

The late afternoon light stretched the shadows of the tree long and painted everything in gold. I needed to finish this up because there was no way in hell I was going to be out here at night. With the way the whispers and bad signs had amplified since my aunt passed, I wouldn't be surprised if Michael Myers or Freddy Krueger came chasing after me. I didn't need that.

Determination fueled me even more. I *knew* what I'd seen

that night. "Bullshit I saw nothing, Aunt Maureen. What were you hiding?" She'd insisted I'd dreamed it, and she'd even said I could check. But when I'd marched outside to find my proof, the grass had grown over this spot like nothing had happened. I'd believed her—believed I'd imagined it, or dreamed it—for a time. But one night, when the whispers entered my head, I'd headed out here, hoping to dig up the box while she slept. She'd caught me red-handed and had insisted she just didn't want the tree hurt.

I hadn't believed her, even though I gave up searching for the box. But ever since she'd passed, the memory of her burying it had continually shown up, to the point that I couldn't think about anything else... not even when I was tanning. The memory of the iron box gnawed at my mind, urging me to settle this once and for all.

The metal of the shovel hit something solid with a *clang*. Definitely not a rock because the sound was more hollow and metallic.

My heart leaped into my throat, and cold tendrils of fear clawed my chest.

"See, I knew I wasn't crazy, Aunt Maureen! Finally!" I dropped to my knees and scraped away soil with my hands. My fingernails filled with dirt as I uncovered a dark metal edge.

I worked faster, ignoring the sweat trickling down my spine and the trembling of my fingers. The rowan tree seemed to lean closer, its branches casting strange patterns over me. The red berries resembled drops of blood in the fading light.

Great. Maybe that was a sign of what was to come if I didn't get my ass out of here.

I cleared off the top and found parts of the sides, fighting the roots that had pushed into the weak spots in the metal. The box was just as I remembered it: black iron with brown copper reinforcements and a heavy padlock with metal handles on the sides.

As if that higher power wanted to remind me I was their bitch, a raven cawed from somewhere overhead, making me jump. The fast-sinking sun and the golden light giving way to purple shadows confirmed I needed to get the box to the car and get my happy ass to my cheap apartment and away from the horror. I grabbed the box and tried to lift it, but it was heavier than it looked.

Of course it was.

"Dammit, come on," I grunted, bracing myself to heave it up and out of the hole. Still, the damn thing didn't budge. Then I noticed the problem. I hadn't cleared away enough of the roots. Some still held the sides, embedded securely in the metal. They'd probably even worked their way into the bottom as well. The box might as well have been sewn into the ground. Well, I'd be a monkey's uncle... someone *did* hate me.

The temperature dropped at least ten degrees as the wind picked up, making me shiver. The branches rustled, and a few berries dropped around me, bouncing on the ground. And the whispering clawed at the back of my mind, indistinct words that made me want to jump out of my skin.

With a quick glance at the sky, I sucked in a breath. How the hell was the sun already disappearing? The last rays of light bled across the horizon, clawing at the clouds like dying embers.

Well, there was no chance I'd be able to dig the box out before night came, so I'd just have to open the damn thing here and now.

I picked up the crowbar and wedged it into the space between the lock and the shackle. This was the moment of truth. I'd finally see what was so important that Aunt Maureen had lied to me about it for all these years. I picked up the axe, turned it so the axe head faced the trunk, and struck it against the crowbar. After three strikes, the metal shackle gave way.

The rowan tree shuddered above me, and a chill ran through me. I looked upward, scowling, and the hissing murmurs intensified. They were no longer just in my head but seemed to come from the box itself.

"Shut up," I gritted out. My mind had to be playing tricks on me.

My hands shook as I pulled the shackle free. "Let's get this over with."

With a deep breath, I tried lifting the lid, but it wouldn't budge, as if something was holding it down.

Nope. Not today, box. I was going to get my answer after all these years. I shoved it harder, and then it gave way with a loud *creak* that echoed down the hillside. A musty, metallic scent hit me—like dried blood and something I couldn't quite place.

Inside lay an ornate gold table mirror with full sunbursts at the top and bottom and golden strands weaving down the frame. Clouds and winged horses had been carved into the top and bottom, flanking the sunbursts.

My attention slid to the dagger beside the mirror... and time seemed to freeze. It was a golden tri-sided spiral dagger with an elegant handle and ridged leather grip. I'd seen one similar to this before, when a horrible ex who'd been obsessed with knives had shown it to me. He'd called it a tri dagger and said it was the deadliest knife in the world and it would take three surgeons to stitch a man up if he were stabbed with one —if he could even be saved. Fuck, the guy had been creepy.

He'd disappeared after he'd shown up here, and Aunt Maureen had hobbled out with her cane, threatening to put it where the sun didn't shine.

Tears burned the backs of my eyes, and grief struck, hollowing me out deep inside. I missed her, and I'd be willing to have my car stolen again just to have her back. She was the only family I'd had in the world, and even though she'd been eccentric, grumpy, and stubborn and had refused to move, no matter how many plans I'd made, she'd loved me as much as I loved her.

She'd been good to me. Fed me, clothed me, and always listened with tenderness and concern. When Mom and I hadn't had anywhere to go, she'd given us a place to stay. And she'd taught me how to defend myself and how to fight as best she knew how.

When Mom died, there was never a question about who'd take care of me. My dad had vanished when I was a little kid, and I'd never really known him except that he abused her. I'd wanted to take care of Aunt Maureen, too, but she would have none of it, except for letting me teach her a few things about technology and a couple of moves I learned from getting into scraps and fights.

Now she was gone. She'd died peacefully in her sleep. I could be grateful for that at least.

I'd known something was wrong as soon as she hadn't answered my morning text. The coroner said she hadn't felt a thing.

It still hurt that she'd lied to me all those years ago and tried to convince me I hadn't seen what I had. If she'd still been here, I'd have stolen something of hers to make my point and let her know how upset I was. Turnabouts were fair play.

The deadly blade shimmered like captured sunlight, catching my attention.

There were dark marks in the air above it, though. Scowling, I kneeled, leaned closer, and gently reached forward. Though it looked as if the blade ended in a point, I realized that it was actually longer than it looked, the tip of the blade so fine that it could barely be seen almost half an inch past where it seemed to end. The dark traces looked like dried blood.

I shuddered. Something about this dagger unnerved me. It was like...it was watching me.

I set the dagger on the ground to the left of the hole, then removed the mirror with both hands.

A wave of energy passed over me, and my head spun. I jerked back, and the mirror expanded.

"What the hell?" The dizziness intensified.

A low humming buzz came out of the mirror, and something rippled out, like an energy wave.

The mirror grew again, pulsing with eerie silver-blue light. The glass rippled like water, but its surface frosted and turned dark blue instead of reflecting the rowan branches and darkening sky.

"Stop!" I shouted as if an inanimate object would listen.

I dropped the mirror onto the grass and upturned soil near the hole, but it didn't break. Instead, it knocked against the crowbar, flipping it upward. The metal tool landed across the mirror's frame, balancing precariously on the edge as the mirror pulsed and hummed.

Another spasm of energy shot out of the mirror, and it grew again, shoving up against my knee on one side and against the dagger to my right.

Yelping, I fell forward, my right hand landing directly on the spiral dagger's blade.

"Shit!" White-hot pain seared my palm as the impossibly sharp edge sliced deep. Blood welled up immediately and spilled onto the mirror's surface where it sizzled and disappeared.

I leaned forward and tried to touch the glass, but my hand passed through it, and I tumbled forward.

The world tilted, dissolved, and vanished. My scream echoed around me as I hurtled through endless darkness. Wind rushed past my ears, my stomach lurched into my throat, and then—

THUD.

I slammed onto something hard and bitterly cold. Pain

radiated through my shoulder and hip, and frost bit into my cheek where it pressed against stone. A metallic clatter rang out beside me as the crowbar landed inches from my head.

"Fuck," I wheezed, the impact having knocked the wind from my lungs. My cut hand throbbed, burning as if I'd set it on fire.

I pushed myself up onto my elbows, blinking to clear my vision.

What the actual fuck? Where the hell was I, because this was *definitely* not Crossville, Tennessee.

I lay on frost-covered flagstones, staring up at a jet-black sky in which impossibly large light-blue stars shimmered like diamonds in velvet. My breath frosted.

Wincing, I forced myself onto my jean-covered knees and gasped. Torches hung from black metal posts, their light flickering on the flagstones. It looked like I'd landed in the courtyard of a medieval castle. What the *hell*?

"There! An intruder!"

Heavy footsteps pounded across stone. Men wearing metal armor and fur and holding swords charged at me.

Okay, now I knew why Aunt Maureen had lied to me. The box actually *had* made me crazy!

"Shit!" I scrambled backward, my hand closing around the crowbar. I swung it wildly as the first guard lunged for me, catching him in the side and sending him staggering.

My blood slicked the crowbar, but I held it tight. "Get away from me, assholes!"

"She's armed!" one of them shouted, his voice echoing strangely in the frigid air.

Another guard rushed me from the side. I pivoted and swung, but he ducked beneath my swing. A third guard circled behind me, and suddenly I was surrounded by five of them closing in with swords that gleamed in the torchlight.

I had to get out of here. Pulse racing, I swung the crowbar

again as another guard rushed me. A second guard darted out and caught my wrist in an ironlike grip.

Pain shot up my arm. A third guard backhanded me across the face with an armored glove. Stars exploded behind my eyes, and my head snapped back and smashed into the ground. The crowbar clattered from my grip.

Rough hands seized my arms and twisted them painfully behind my back. My vision swam, blood trickling from my split lip. One of the guards lifted his sword as if preparing to chop off my head.

"Halt!" a deep voice thundered over the courtyard. The voice seemed to cut straight through me, and a strange tugging pulled within my chest. "Bring the intruder here."

CHAPTER 2

Kai

Hot trepidation ran down my spine as my heavy leather boots thudded against the cool gray stones. The icy wind whipped across my face, and the smell of blood and smoke clung to my hunting leathers.

I strode through the fortified steel palace gates, my younger half-brother, Ashren, beside me, his brow furrowed and his cheeks chafed red by the wind. His bow was slung across his back, his quiver still half full. I was relieved that we'd had a successful hunt, having brought down two ice boars and a mountain goat. Servants were now dragging the carcasses to the kitchen while others tended our caribou and the hounds.

The final rays of light were fading from the indigo-black sky. My blood thrummed. In each daily cycle, my court and I used our magic to stretch dusk out as long as possible, but though it came to our court last, night always arrived. At least the stars were out, shining bright silver-blue and confirming that there was no sign of a powerful attack from the Night Court.

Yet.

But give them time. They'd attack soon, either with a

blunt display of force in which their magic blotted out the stars, or by a sneak attack, built up slowly over the nights to avoid triggering any alarms.

Something *was* happening, though, and I was unnerved. I couldn't strategize against unknowns.

Awareness prickled up and down my spine and tightened my shoulders as my stomach flipped again. It had been building inside me all day, and now I wanted to crawl out of my skin.

The air turned bitter, and another odd sensation tugged at my chest. I stopped short.

That *something* had changed.

Shouts of surprise rose from the inner courtyard. Metal clanked, and boots thudded.

I exchanged looks with Ashren and hurried toward the reinforced doors that separated the inner courtyard from the outer. A portal couldn't have opened, could it? There were only four courts and three main portals that connected the others to Dusk. We'd cut off the Night Court, the Day Court was dead, and everyone in the Aurora Court was still sleeping. If the Aurora Court had awakened, there would have been other signs.

I thrust the doors open and strode through. The guards had all clustered in the center of the courtyard, and one of my men—Folge—was holding a sword aloft as a woman with wavy blonde hair thrashed in the hold of two guards.

My legs continued moving, despite me not giving them permission to. What in the frozen barrens was this fresh hell? "Halt!"

Folge's shoulders jerked, and he lowered his sword. His brow lifted, but he nodded, then sheathed the sword.

"Bring the intruder here," I ordered. The tugging sensation intensified as the guards hauled her upright, and I got a better look at her. My stomach dropped, and my heart skipped a beat.

The woman staggered, wincing as one of her hands clamped over the other's bleeding palm. Folge motioned the guards holding her forward. The other four guards fell in behind them, ready to act if needed.

Her eyes lifted...and my world stilled. Her irises were hazel and flecked with gold, and her defiance shone through them despite the bruising on the left side of her face. My entire body drew tighter than a bowstring.

Shit.

By Fate, this could not be.

Centuries of being alone, and my mate shows up *now*? Why? And why was she dressed so peculiarly?

I hated Fate.

The last thing I needed was a distraction. The current situation demanded all my focus to protect my people from the Night Court, Bram, and his treachery.

"What are you?" I hardened my voice. It took all my strength to thrust down the urges that choked me. I tried to study her in a detached manner, but I wasn't sure I was pulling it off.

Her hair and eyes suggested her parents might be of the Aurora or Day Courts. More than a few survivors had found their way to Dusk cities and towns, though there were far fewer Aurora Fae refugees than Day because the Night King kept abducting them.

Her jaw tightened. "Cold. Bleeding. Confused. And not answering your stupid questions."

Ashren's mouth twitched. "I like her."

I shot him a silencing glare, then turned back to her. She wore an eye-burning, annoying pink shirt and blue trousers made of some coarse material. The shirt fascinated me most as it stated she was with someone. "Where is her ally?" I demanded, looking around the courtyard. "Did she enter through the portal? Did others accompany her?"

"What?" She scowled and pushed her hair out of her face. The wind picked up again, and she shivered. "I didn't come with anyone. I fell through a damn mirror."

"So who is this Stupid who accompanied you and to whom your shirt confesses?" I hated that I *had* to know the answer. Was it a suitor? No, she wouldn't refer to a suitor or lover as stupid. But still—I wanted to know. She was a striking woman, and it would be strange if she had no suitors at all. My blood burned at the mere thought, and my fists clenched. I braced my hands against my belt to keep from showing any further signs of agitation.

"Huh?" Her nose wrinkled. She looked down at her shirt, then huffed. "It's just a funny shirt. Not a confession."

I raised an eyebrow. "So you wear clothing to insult strangers, friends, and passersby? Then this is a slight. Are you implying that my men and I are stupid?"

She lifted her chin and folded her arms over her breasts. "If the shoe fits."

I stepped closer. "The way my boots fit has absolutely *nothing* to do with this conversation. Now answer me plainly, woman."

A smile curled her lips. "You're about as sharp as a bowl of mashed potatoes. Maybe this is why Aunt Maureen told me to stay away from that iron box. My mind has snapped." She frowned and looked down at her hand. The bleeding had stopped, and that seemed to surprise her.

The cut itself hadn't looked too bad, from the brief glimpse I'd gotten of it.

"Anyway, the shirt is just meant to be funny and poke fun at someone who deserves it. No one takes it seriously. If I were going to insult you, I'd call you stupid to your face."

My eyebrows arched, and Ashren bit back a chuckle.

Damn this wretched wench. She smelled like apricots and magnolias, and I wanted to smash her against me. "What is your name?"

"Hannah." She tilted her head and stared at me with unabashed defiance. "And who are you?"

My heart pulsed as if yanking at me to get closer to her, and annoyance flashed through me. Murmurs of surprise rippled among the guards behind her. Folge scowled, deep lines forming in his brow.

Ashren stepped forward, canting his head. "You don't know the Dusk King when you see him? Where exactly did you come from that you do not know King Kairos?"

"Tennessee. And no, I don't know who he is. For that matter, I don't know who any of you are. But if you open that mirror back up, I'd be more than happy to fall back through it, or however the hell it works." She huffed and muttered to herself, "That dagger must have had some drugs on it, or I'm asleep or something."

She scanned the guards, the walls, and then the sky above while pinching herself. "Ouch!" She dropped her hand back to her side, then inhaled and wrinkled her nose. "Not a dream. Got it. Aunt Maureen clearly knew how to pick some drugs then."

My stomach twisted, and my head spun as I breathed in more of her scent. The edges of my mind were fraying. Clenching my jaw, I braced myself. There were dozens of other questions I needed answered, but I could hand her over to Folge or Bren, and they would find out the basics. Yet the thought of any man other than me having any contact with her made my blood boil.

"Are you all right?" Her voice cut into me like a hot blade. Despite the sharpness of her tone, she sounded almost concerned.

Fuck.

This was bad. I needed to get myself under control. No one would keep me from my purpose. Not even my Fate-damned mate, and certainly not my ice-cursed needs. We needed to get away from each other, but I had to make sure she wasn't carrying any weapons or tools that might assist in her escape. Ashren or Folge or even Bren could search her, but that wasn't happening, and I forced myself not to acknowledge why. "Are you carrying any weapons?"

"Only my razor wit and my smart mouth." She arched a brow. "I didn't exactly come here for a fight."

"We'll see about that." I could imagine her doing more than a few things with that mouth that would be tantamount to a threat. I stepped closer—close enough to feel the heat radiating off her skin and breathe in her scent more fully. I grew dizzy.

Her cheeks brightened as well, and she took in a quick breath. Her gaze held mine and, for a moment, my lungs no longer worked.

My heart squeezed. *Fate above, damn you!* "I'm going to search you."

"The *hell* you are!" Her mouth twisted, and her voice sliced through the haze of my mind.

I grabbed her by the waist and ran my hands up and down her sides, patting her down briskly, ignoring the way my skin buzzed from touching her. "Hold still, or I'll shove you in a cell so far from the surface you won't even be able to dream of light." And even that might not be far enough away to grant me peace.

Her eyes narrowed, and her mouth set in a tight line. Some sassy response was brewing behind those gorgeous hazel eyes, but she kept it contained. She didn't seem to recognize the significance of this tugging sensation between us. Perhaps she didn't even feel it—but that was fine with me.

Fuck.

Her whole body was perfection.

I slid my hands over the rest of her swiftly, trying not to linger anywhere. Her pockets held a set of keys with a sparkling black-spotted pink pig sculpture dangling from the ring on top of a glittering ball, and a pink glittery tube labeled Strawberry Smackers. Not particularly interesting as a threat, though I'd never seen anything like it before.

Her cheeks flushed, and she glared at me. "Asshole," she muttered.

I'd have retorted something sharp and cutting if I could have rerouted the blood back to my brain. Instead, I grunted, stepped back, and jerked my thumb toward the western entrance. "Put her in the dungeon. *Not* with any of the other prisoners. No one talks to her but me. And double the guard at this portal point in case anyone else follows her example."

"Hey!" she protested as they dragged her off. Her pink and white shoes shuffled over the flagstones and squeaked as she fought for purchase. "Let go of me! I haven't done anything wrong!"

I resisted the urge to watch her go. The tugging in my chest intensified and urged me to go after her. This had to stop. I'd killed to become king, laid aside everything I'd been, and I wouldn't be distracted now.

"Well, that was interesting." Ashren sidled closer, his tone low. "Your eyes went completely violet for a bit there. Is there something you want to tell me?"

"Apparently, I should tell you that your eyes are no longer functioning." I refused to look at him as I started toward the eastern servant's entrance. My muscles tensed, though. It had been a foolish lie. There was no reason to pretend she hadn't impacted me, but I couldn't bring myself to admit it, even to Ashren. "Just stay away from her. I'll handle her myself."

"I'm sure you will," Ashren said with a sly smile.

I growled at him but didn't slow my pace. Before I'd risen

through the ranks to become king, I had entered the palace through the servant entrances. A part of me still felt more at ease with the closeness of those stone walkways because they limited the number of people who would see me, versus if I entered through the main hall. My head brushed the door jamb, and if I spread out my arms fully, my hands would press on either wall.

Ashren followed me into the narrow hall, his footsteps lighter than mine. "What do you intend to do with her?"

"None of your Fate's-damned business," I snapped. I had no clue what I was going to do with her, and I didn't need anyone pointing that out.

"Well, we have to get answers from her—" he started.

I spun to face him and pointed my finger in his face. "There is no *we* in this matter. You will not do anything to her. I will speak to her in my own time. Do you understand?"

Ashren lifted his hands while his mouth twitched like something was funny. "Indeed. If I am not to aid in this matter, what would you have me do instead?"

"Speak with the quartermaster and ensure we have sufficient supplies for the outposts bordering the Night Court. It's going to be a long, cold winter, and Bram is likely to exploit that." I didn't wait for Ashren to confirm the order. He'd do as he was told.

I turned into the next hall and took the tight staircase to the fourth floor, where my study lay. The heavy wooden door carved with constellations and dusk emblems swung open at my shove, and I slammed it shut behind me. The sound cracked through the silence like a whip.

The room was colder than usual, the hearth unlit. I didn't bother with a fire because my anger burned hot enough.

Maps and missives covered every surface of the heavy oak table in the center of the room. Smaller tables sat at intervals against the wall, and a massive desk was stationed near the window. Sideboards held unopened bottles of dark wine and frost gin. Star charts hung on the walls, their ink shimmering faintly under the lamplight. Each one showed the slow shift of constellations—the faint bleed of the Night Court's magic where it pressed against our sky. Most were enchanted, adapting and adjusting to the patterns of the stars as they shifted. But a few were hand-drawn and based on observations of what the sky should look like.

My uncle's old astrolabe sat beside a stack of ledgers, brass dulled from use, gears catching the light with each rotation. It sat just atop the map of the territories nearest the Night Court with circles drawn and redrawn around the mountain passes like wounds that wouldn't heal.

I dragged off my gloves and dropped them onto a table by a star mirror. When I glimpsed my reflection, I turned away. I had no desire to look at that man—a man with far too much blood on his hands, who was running out of time. I reached inside my coat to my tunic and removed a silver compass. My uncle's.

I placed it on the top right corner of the map, and it settled into place with a soft click.

After all that had been sacrificed, I could not falter. Not even for my mate.

A knot of grief formed in my chest alongside a hollowness that threatened to tear me apart. Memories of being cold, hungry, and afraid returned, of my father rejecting us before his death, followed by my uncle showing us compassion and allowing us to return to the safety of the city and the palace. Why were these memories returning?

Damn that woman.

This was her fault.

Her presence was already undoing me and bringing things to the surface that I had no time to deal with now. Our connection was burning through the barriers I had struggled so hard to erect. Giving in to it would weaken me, make me vulnerable. I'd be useless, both to my people and ultimately to her.

Nothing good would come of being near Hannah right now.

If I were smart, I'd kill her and be done with it.

I froze in place.

No.

That wasn't necessary. It wouldn't *be* necessary. I'd figure something else out. The situation could still be managed.

I strode to the sideboard, opened the top left drawer, and seized a bottle of lorn leaf. The dull green leaves had been ground into a fine powder. It took only a moment to mix a dose into a glass of cold, bitter frost gin, and I downed it in a single gulp. The foul taste coated my tongue. It hadn't gotten better with time, but it was the only thing that gave me peace. I poured more of the frost gin into a clean glass and tried to wash out the horrid flavor.

A burning foulness spread through me, chilling me to my core. The tumultuous feelings receded. Hannah would be dealt with soon. For now, I would let the lorn leaf do its work and get back to preparing for the next Night Court attack.

I turned my attention to the records, observations, and reports sent from the outposts and the watches. The Night Court's assaults had worsened over the years, even though King Bram himself had become uncharacteristically cowardly. Reports from the northern and northeastern ridges between the Salt Mountains and the Shadow Peaks indicated that Bram had been solidifying forces in front of our borders and that more were amassing near the Night Court's southernmost outposts.

They were going to attack the Aurora Court soon, while the court remained blanketed in sleep. If my informants were correct, Bram still didn't have the enchanted dagger needed to open the veil, though he had tried to find every single remaining Aurora Fae that lived to demand they assist him or die. But the continued massing of forces concerned me. The volcanoes had been growing in activity as well, but they had not erupted, suggesting that Bram was using his magic to keep all that power focused. But for what and when?

I made preparations for the upcoming war meeting with my brother and generals. Winter would soon be upon us. Without the presence of the Day and Aurora Courts to unveil the sun, the chill of dusk and the cold of night would make our lives all the harder. Restoring the Aurora Court would bring a little more sun, but our world would remain imbalanced.

At last, I strode to the long line of narrow windows that overlooked the inner courtyard. The torches below cast fitful halos over the stone tiles and glistened on tiny flakes of falling snow.

My thoughts returned to Hannah, and I pressed my fists into the chilled stone windowsill.

Her presence was an intolerable addition to an already tense situation. The detached feeling I sought wasn't as present as I wanted. If I wasn't back to my old self within an hour, I'd take another dose of lorn leaf. Being near my fated mate probably meant I'd be burning through the emotion-dulling herb at a much higher rate.

I dipped my head forward and closed my eyes, and numbness spread through my chest. Answers would come. They had to.

I opened my eyes and peered out into the courtyard once more, only to see a dark form moving toward the dungeon entrance. A low growl rose in my throat. I'd made it explicitly clear that he wasn't to go down there.

CHAPTER 3

Hannah

"Let go!" My voice bounced off the walls, ragged and high, as the guards yanked me to my feet like I weighed nothing.

The guard with lilac eyes had his gloved hand clamped around my right arm, and his fingers were digging into my bicep, causing a deep throb of pain. The one with a long, jagged scar on his jaw held my left wrist so tight that my fingers were tingling.

They dragged me across the stone courtyard, through a dark doorway, and down a staircase, with the one called Folge following behind.

My pulse pounded, and I tried to yank myself away, but their grips were a vise as they crowded me on both sides, putting the three of us on the same stair simultaneously.

The men and the walls seemed to close in on me as the stairwell spiraled down, becoming narrower and colder with each step. Torches burned in iron brackets, the guttering yellow-orange flames seeping smoke that stung my eyes. The shadows between the pools of light were deep and thick, clinging to the ceiling like spiderwebs made of ink.

The damp and metallic air made breathing hard, and the stone steps were slick under my sneakers. Every time I slipped, the guards jerked me up again, jolting my shoulders in their sockets. My breaths came fast and shallow, puffing white in front of my face in little panicked bursts.

I dug my heels in. "I can walk myself, thanks. You don't have to drag me like a—whoa—" My sneaker slid on something slick. "Let go of me! I didn't do anything wrong. I *fell through a mirror*." Why was I even trying to explain? A drug trip wouldn't change because of my outcries. All I knew was that I never wanted to try drugs again. Zero stars. Would not recommend. I'd put a warning on the iron box, so if anyone else found it, they'd know *why* they should avoid the strange dagger and cutting themselves...aside from the obvious, of course.

We reached the bottom of the stairs, the air even more frigid and heavy with moisture and something that smelled sour, like blood, sweat, and old fear soaked into stone. A draft slid along the floor, and icy fingers seemed to wrap around my ankles. Goosebumps raced up my legs, and I shivered.

A long corridor stretched out ahead. Torches flickered, throwing jittery light across the floor. Chains clinked softly somewhere in the dark.

My stomach dropped.

This was a real dungeon.

The kind of place people didn't come back from. And it felt as real as the fall.

My wounded hand throbbed, but it didn't feel as painful as it should. I twisted my wrist and glanced down at it. Dried blood streaked my palm and fingers, but the gash had grown smaller, despite my having gotten it just minutes ago. The edges had already knit together.

What the—

Nope. I was tripping. Of course weird shit was going to happen. Look at this *world* I literally *fell into*. It wasn't real.

But a part of me felt uncomfortable, like this might not be made up.

"Please," I tried, my voice softer and my tightening throat shoving all the sarcasm out of my tone. Even if this was just a bad trip, I didn't want to live through torture. "Just... take me back to the courtyard. Let me try the mirror. Maybe it'll—"

"There is no mirror in the courtyard now," Scar Jaw said without looking at me. "It shouldn't have worked for you when it did."

"There'll be hell to pay for it opening up at all," Lilac Eyes muttered.

My heart stuttered. "It has to work."

They ignored me, hauling me deeper underground until the corridor split like some kind of stone crucifix. The left and right passages yawned into more torchlit gloom. The guards halted, and Lilac Eyes turned to Folge. "Which way, sir? He said not to put her with the others."

"Whichever way is back to the courtyard or out of this place," I muttered.

Scar Jaw rolled his eyes and gave me a small shake.

Folge grunted and planted his fists on his belt like the world's grumpiest cowboy. Then he pointed to the left corridor. "King's in a foul mood. Put her in the farthest one. If he wishes for us to move her to another, he will tell us. Best to follow his command to the letter rather than... indulge in creativity. I'd wouldn't want to try him today."

The guards dragged me to the left, and my shoes scraped helplessly over the coarse stone, the rubber squeaking in protest. "No. Stop. *Please!*"

Instead, their grip tightened into iron bands on my arms, jerking me along.

"Let go of me!" I twisted hard enough that my hair slapped my cheek. "I can walk, assholes!"

Lilac Eyes huffed. "Don't make this harder than it has to be, woman."

"I'm not making it—ow—harder you're just manhandling me like a sack of laundry—"

"Quiet," Folge snapped.

We reached a barred iron door near the end of the corridor. Cold wrapped around me like a wet sheet, seeping through my jeans and my stupid pink shirt and knifing straight into my bones. The courtyard had been bad, all frost and bitter wind, but this dungeon was somehow worse, like a freezer carved into the guts of the palace.

Folge grabbed the door handle and yanked. The hinges screamed like something dying, making every hair on my arms stand up.

He didn't flinch. "His Majesty will be informed of your placement, and if he wishes to speak with you before you freeze, he will do so."

Folge stepped aside, and the guards shoved me forward. I stumbled into the cell, and my injured palm hit the frigid wall. I hissed as pain and needles of cold shot up my arm, tightening every muscle in my body. Shit! This was bad.

Behind me, the iron door slammed shut, and the bolt locked into place with a deep sound that thudded straight through my ribs.

I pushed off the wall and wrapped my arms around myself, rubbing my upper arms hard even though it did nothing to cut the cold. My breath trembled out in white clouds. The cell was barely bigger than a large walk-in closet, and the stone bench was rimmed in frost. A pile of old straw filled one corner, I assumed for sleeping.

Every inch of my body buzzed with adrenaline—my shoulders trembling, my stomach knotting so tight it hurt, and a strange vibration rumbling under my skin, like my nerves were trying to climb out.

My eyes burned, and I blinked until the sting faded.

"Okay. Hannah. You're fine. You've handled worse." I couldn't think of anything worse than this, but still. I didn't want to ruin the illusion.

I forced one breath, then another. I needed to snap out of this drug-induced haze. I'd wake beneath the freaky-ass tree, and I felt so cold only because of the nighttime temperature. Pinching myself hadn't worked. Neither had that cut on my hand, but it looked fully healed now, further proof I was hallucinating. At least, I wasn't bleeding out.

The guards' footsteps faded into the distance, and the silence rushed in all thick, icy, and suffocating. My chest tightened like a too-small band had been snapped around my ribs. I wrapped my arms around myself and forced slow breaths in through my nose and out through my mouth.

Okay. Think. Even if this was just a bad drug trip, I needed to get out of this place.

The cold wasn't the first threat. The panic was. If I didn't keep it on a leash, I was going to spiral into something worthless.

I moved in front of the door and crouched low enough to peer through the keyhole. It looked like an old lock with a heavy tumbler, not too complicated, if I had a strong enough lever or hook. If I'd still had my keyring, maybe I could have made something out of it. My earrings weren't going to be much good, but I pulled one out anyway, just in case. The thin silver fishhook wire didn't even budge the tumbler inside.

"Great." I shoved it into my pocket.

There had to be something I could do. I paced in the small square of the floor. In twelve steps, I reached the back, turned, and strode to the front, then back again. Movement helped keep the cold from sinking too far into my bones.

My gaze landed on the stone bench. Maybe I could break it and use it as a lever. I braced my hands on the edge and pulled upward with all the strength my shaking arms had left.

It didn't budge.

Not an inch.

Refusing to give up, I knelt beside it and felt along the underside. My fingertips brushed something metal—large screws, driven straight into the stone wall.

I wanted to yank my hair out. "You've got to be kidding me."

I moved closer to the door and examined the hinges closely. Thick metal plates bolted to the stone frame. But the bolts were exposed, with four large ones on top and three below. If I could wedge something sturdy under them, I could loosen them and attempt to take the door off the frame.

Not elegant, but desperate times called for rock-bottom creativity.

I patted myself down, just in case there was some bit of metal in my clothing that I could use. My bra didn't even have an underwire. That bastard king couldn't let me keep my keychain, could he?

"Dammit!"

My breath plumed around me like smoke. I leaned my forehead against the cold metal bars, letting the chill anchor me.

Okay. So that was a no. I needed something stronger, so I kept searching. Nothing. Nothing at all. There was no give in anything in the cell.

Time started to blur, and the cold made everything sting and burn more.

Footsteps approached, sounding less heavy than those of the guards.

I stepped back, body coiled tight with wariness. My heart thudded harder as a shadow appeared in front of the cell.

A young woman stepped into view, her movements precise, careful, as if she'd mastered the art of being unobtrusive. She appeared to be Japanese and in her mid-twenties, with soft features, porcelain skin, and shoulder-length ginger hair falling in soft layers around her face. The warm hue contrasted with the elegant sapphire-blue gown she wore. The dress looked warm, with layers to protect against the cold and embroidered cuffs and gloves to match.

As soon as she saw me, a soft smile pulled at her lips, as if she were just greeting me in a normal situation. The flash of her dark-amber eyes reminded me of Aunt Maureen.

She carried a folded navy coat lined in something gray, along with a pair of gloves.

Her gaze swept over me with professional detachment, but something softened in her eyes when she spotted the way I shook.

"Hannah of Tennessee?" Her voice was soft, melodic, but still carried the crisp enunciation of someone trained to speak formally. "I am Thea. I serve the royal household, and I saw your arrival from the window and heard your conversation."

My spine straightened, and I lifted my chin, ignoring the cold dread inside me. "If you're here to interrogate me, I really don't know anything about anything in this world, and all I want to do is go home."

Her lips twitched. "No. I am here because it would be most unfortunate if you froze to death." She pressed the coat through the bars, working it through the space with care. "Here. Take this coat and gloves. Best put them on right away. I imagine he'll be down to see you soon, but it won't do you any good to already be near death."

Oh gee. How thoughtful. Still, I wouldn't look a gift horse in the mouth. I took the coat, the thick fabric pressing over my hands. "I was under the impression he was happy to let me freeze to death." Maybe there was something metal on this coat that I could use. The silver buttons and fasteners felt sturdy.

She scoffed and tilted her head as if she'd expected that from him. "He isn't thinking clearly. Not that I recommend you try his patience any further. You're quite likely to wind up far worse off."

I shoved my arms into the coat sleeves and yanked it tight across my chest. It was heavy, smelling faintly of lavender and the same sharp tang as the torches in the hall. The lining brushed my skin, so soft it made me shiver all over again, but then the heat expanded, as if some sort of magic had made it reach me faster.

The gloves followed. Chunky wool, stitched patterns on top, leather palms, and thick around the wrists, like they'd been made specifically to suffocate cold. I flexed my fingers inside them and almost groaned. Sensation came rushing back, with pins and needles running from my knuckles to my elbows.

"Thank you," I said, a little wary but also grateful. My fingers burned as the cold receded. "Wow...I've never gotten warm this fast."

"Living in the Dusk Court during these uncertain times requires a certain skill with temperature and fabrics if one doesn't want to freeze. How did you get here, and where are you from? Are you another survivor from the Aurora Court, perhaps, who traveled to...Tennessee?" Thea folded her arms as she studied me, her expression curious.

I slid my hands down the outside of the coat. Aside from the small silver buttons and fasteners, there wasn't much. But the edges of the smaller inside buttons might just be slim enough to slide directly beneath the head of the bolts in the hinges. Maybe. "No. Really. I'm from Tennessee, and I have no idea where this place is. I've never even heard of it."

Her brows lifted. "Odd indeed. So you aren't even from this world—"

"Thea." A soft male voice cut through the cold air.

My attention snapped to the left. The younger man who'd been with the king stood there, his gloved hand pressed against the stone archway and his expression drawn.

He glanced over his shoulder down the dark hall and then looked back at her. "You heard what Kai said."

"Kai?" That didn't sound nearly as intimidating as Kairos. I bit back a smile and kept my arms folded.

Thea scoffed and mirrored his stance, folding her arms as she tilted her head to meet the man's gaze. "He can take it up with me if he has a problem, but I think it's safe to assume that he would prefer a living prisoner in a coat who was shown some compassion versus a dead captive who was kept in complete isolation in strict compliance with his orders."

"My brother's in one of his moods." He reached for her, then dropped his hand. The tension in his jaw tightened. "Just —don't make this harder than it must be."

"I make everything better, Ashren, not harder." She smiled sweetly, but the edges of her mouth pinched tightly, suggesting she was holding back something she wanted to say.

The weight of their glances zapped through the bars, quick as a current, Thea holding Ashren's gaze a second longer than needed. I felt like I should look away, or at least cough, but I just huddled deeper into the coat and considered whether the buttons would work on the lock.

Ashren cleared his throat and glanced at me. "Are you staring at something in particular, prisoner?"

A snort escaped me, though I hadn't meant it to. The harshness of his words compared with the softness of his expression when he'd looked at Thea surprised me, which probably wasn't the best reaction here. "Just wondering why the king thinks I'm going to survive down here without a coat in this temperature. I think Thea is right, and you should thank her. If it weren't for her, I'd be hypothermic by now. She's the smartest person I've met here. Granted, the bar wasn't set very high."

"A bar?" Thea's elegant brows lifted. That small smile pulled at her lips, as if she was more pleased to be praised for her intelligence than her kindness.

Of course they wouldn't understand the saying. "My expectations weren't high, but even if they had been, I'm sure you're the smartest one here."

She smiled wider.

"Thea's intelligence is not in question," Ashren said sharply. "It is a matter of what the king orders."

"And the king made his orders *very* clear," a stern voice intoned from behind Ashren.

My stomach dropped like I'd missed a step in the dark.

King Kairos stood just outside the doorway.

CHAPTER 4

Hannah

My stomach dropped as ice spread through my veins despite the enchanted coat and gloves.

Both Thea and Ashren stiffened, and the torchlight shrank back as if it wanted to be anywhere but in the sight of the bastard king himself.

Slowly, they turned toward King Kairos, and Ashren stepped in front of Thea.

The king filled the archway, his broad shoulders nearly brushing the stone on either side. His dark leathers and armor drank in the light as shadows clung to the hard lines of his body, leaving little to the imagination. His lavender eyes swept over the scene.

His jaw ticked, and every muscle in my body tensed.

I stepped closer to the bars, and my coat brushed the iron. If something was about to go down, I wasn't going to cower in the back corner like a kicked dog and would use the opportunity to my advantage if possible. My pulse thundered in my ears, but my feet planted themselves.

The king's gaze cut to Thea first. "I recall saying that no

one was to speak to the prisoner or approach her cell. Did I misspeak, Thea?" His voice was low and growly.

She dipped her head in a quick, controlled bow. "No, Your Majesty. You were clear."

"And yet, here you are." He gestured to the two of them, then his eyes flicked toward me. He took in my coat and gloves. "Equipping her with things I didn't approve of and conversing with her like she's not a hostage."

Thea and Ashren stepped back as he came to a stop in front of my cell just out of touching distance.

Hands folded tightly at her waist, Thea inhaled and straightened. "I determined it would be unwise to let her freeze. A dead person would be of little use to you, sire."

"Your *determination* is not wanted." His words sliced like a hot knife through butter. "Your *obedience* is required."

Ashren moved in front of her fully, jaw tight. "I asked Thea to bring the coat when I learned the prisoner's placement. It seemed more sensible than interrupting your other duties to inquire whether this was your preference or letting her freeze. The blame falls on me."

"Were you the one who decided to put her here in this cell?" King Kairos demanded.

Ashren's brow rose, and his head dipped, as if he didn't want to name someone.

I raised my hand. "I can answer that!" I smiled, wide and smug. I needed to get this king—I wouldn't think of him as King Kairos anymore. From now on, he was just Kai—closer, and this could be my chance.

His attention swiveled to me, that icy lavender glare as sharp as a blade.

My stomach somersaulted. It had to be from nerves. But there was something about his eyes, and I didn't know if it was because of the pale lavender or the dark violet ring that surrounded his pupils.

"Why are you lifting your hand and looking at me so fool-ishly?" King—no, *Kai's* face squinched in confusion, but then he shook his head. "Forget the question. Just tell me which of the guards it was, and *now*." He shuffled closer.

If they didn't raise their hands here, how did people ask questions? Another question for another time, without raising my hand. *Focus on the goal, Hannah.* I almost had him right where I wanted him.

"Someone's bossy." I lifted my chin, keeping my gaze on him and trying to take in his weapons with my peripheral vision. But he was too damn tall. I had to find a way to scan him without making him suspicious.

Oh! I could pretend to flirt with him. It worked on the guys back home.

I dropped my gaze in a deliberate scan of his body, biting my bottom lip. He had multiple blades attached to his belt and some attached to one thigh. Those could be easy enough to grab if I could distract him. I turned my palms upright as if weighing my options and shrugged. "In fairness, the guards thought they were following orders. You said to put me where no one else was." I spread out my arms, my hands touching either side of the cell. "Clearly, it's just me back here, so maybe you should've been more clear."

Thea's eyes widened, and the corners of her lips twitched upward. She clicked her tongue against the top of her mouth before focusing on Kai. Ashren's gaze darted between Kai and me as if he were uncertain whether to intervene or simply watch.

"What did you just say?" Kai's face twisted into anger, and he gripped the bars of the door.

Okay, I might have made him a little too mad. Every instinct screamed at me to flinch back, but I forced myself to remain in place. "That you weren't clear about what you wanted."

His nostrils flared. "I am the king and am always clear." His voice rumbled so deeply that I got goose bumps.

My stomach flipped as the tugging sensation I'd felt earlier filled my chest.

"It is my people's responsibility to do precisely as I say. The guards should have known that I wouldn't want you to freeze to death before I retrieve the information I need." He folded his arms over his chest.

Now was the time to distract him. I tilted my head, letting my hair slide over my shoulder and catch on the fur of the coat. "Hmmm, maybe the guards thought you wanted to torture me and put me on the brink of death."

His eyes flashed again, and his hand shot through the bars and seized the collar of the coat.

A startled yelp escaped me, and I grabbed his arm with one hand. I would yank off my gloves and stab him in the eyes with my fingernails if he tried to kill me. My heart raced, feeling like it was leaving my body behind.

His knuckles brushed my skin. Then, he hauled me against the bars and lifted me until I stood on my tiptoes. The place where our skin touched buzzed, like uncomfortable static.

His scent of smoke and spice with hints of blood and cypress poured into the cell. "I didn't ask for your thoughts or opinion, prisoner, so keep your mouth shut."

I definitely wouldn't be keeping my mouth closed now. "Oh, you weren't speaking to the class?" My rubber-soled shoe tips skidded a little on the stone floor, but I strained to keep myself steady. I wouldn't give the sexy villain any more of an ego boost than he'd already had. He was already too damn arrogant. As the *king*, he was definitely born with a silver spoon in his mouth.

Bastard.

With my free hand, I seized the bars near his side. I had to change my strategy if I wanted him distracted while I plucked his blade without him noticing. I smiled brightly. "To be clear, I'm not complaining about you showing off your strength. Do you do this with all the prisoners, or am I just special?"

The way his eyes bugged almost had me laughing, but somehow I managed to swallow it. His grip on my coat collar tightened. "You…" A muscle ticked in his jaw.

"Yes?" I curled my fingers along his chest with my left hand while my right edged toward the blade. "I'm listening. Are you saying I *am* special? I'm flattered." My fingers wrapped around a blade handle. "I guess I did fall out of the sky through a mirror portal."

His eyes narrowed, and the muscles in his jaw clenched so tight I thought he might break his own teeth.

My stomach twisted, and that tug in my chest made me want to press closer to him. What the hell was wrong with me? This would be easier if he didn't have a smoking hot body, sculpted features, and a glare that cut through me.

"Don't worry, sweetie. I know I'm special. It's okay to like me." I winked as I slid one of his daggers from its sheath and tucked my hand back at my side so the coat hid it from sight.

He stared at me as if he didn't know whether he wanted to kill me or kiss me. The violet ring around his pupils thickened as the pupils also dilated. How were his eyes changing color? That was weird.

Under his stare, my face heated, completely at odds with the cold gnawing at my legs. His fingers flexed in my collar, tightening enough that the fur brushed my throat. We were too close. His breath slid over my lips, warm and fresh like cider and honey. My heart hammered in my chest like it was trying to punch through the narrow space between us.

I should probably de-escalate this situation.

"Careful," I murmured, keeping my voice light even as nerves snapped inside me. "If you keep looking at me like that, people are going to talk."

One of his brows kicked up. "About what?"

I let my gaze drop to his mouth for a deliberate second before meeting his eyes again. "Oh, I don't know. Maybe about the terrifying king of whatever this frozen nightmare place is getting handsy with the strange girl from Tennessee. How you had me dragged down here, pinned me to the bars, and then couldn't keep your hands off me."

His nose wrinkled. "You mistake rage at your insolence for interest."

"Those aren't mutually exclusive." I pressed my fingers against the solid heat of his chest. Muscle shifted under my palm when he sucked in a short breath. Good. It was working. "Besides, if this is you being angry, I don't want to know what you look like when you're impressed."

His gaze trailed from my eyes to my mouth, then lower, to where the coat bunched around my chest where he held it. Heat coiled low in my belly, and I had to stop myself from crossing my legs to keep it under control.

Okay, wow. I'd never reacted to a man this way before. I had to get control over myself before I did something stupid. Although...it'd probably rattle him if I kissed that pulse point on his throat.

No. Stop. That won't de-escalate things.

But my head leaned forward as if it had a mind of its own. The damn traitor. I'd never felt this kind of draw to someone before, and there was no doubt that all he wanted to do was kill me. I had to get him to release me so I could clear my damn head. "The longer we stay like this, the harder it is to insist I'm nothing, don't you think?"

He jerked back as if burned.

The sudden loss of support made my legs buckle. My knees hit the ground, pain shooting through them, as my butt dropped onto my heels. I caught a bar with my free hand, keeping the blade hidden, and steadied myself, adrenaline pulsing through my veins.

Kai's fists uncurled, and he flexed his fingers. He exhaled slowly and closed his eyes.

I had no clue if this exchange had worked in my favor or if I'd just hammered the nail into my own coffin, but at least I'd gotten the only weapon available to me in this frigid, damp prison cell.

Opening his eyes, Kai glared icily at me. Whatever conflict he'd had before was now gone. "You think far too highly of your effect on me." He laughed a little too loudly. "Do not mistake my anger for passion, Hannah of Tennessee. You are not special. You are a problem, and one that I will resolve."

"I've got a fantastic way to solve it." I tilted my head and got to my feet. "Open up that little portal, and send me back where I came from."

Something flickered in his gaze before a muscle jumped in his jaw. He cut his attention away from me like I'd stopped existing. "Thea."

Her head snapped in his direction. "Yes, Your Majesty."

"Leave. You will not approach this cell again without my express permission." His tone was low and frigid. "Is that understood?"

Thea paled and pulled her shoulders back. "Understood, sire." She curtsied while her eyes flashed with something that looked a lot like anger. Her gaze snagged on mine, brief and defiant.

I bit the inside of my mouth. I had no clue what that was about. Maybe she blamed me for getting her into trouble.

Without hesitation, she walked away, her skirts whispering over stone as she disappeared down the corridor.

Kai shifted his weight to one leg. The leather over his shoulders creaked with the movement, his posture going even straighter, like someone had shoved a steel rod down his spine. "Ashren."

Something rebellious flashed in Ashren's eyes, but only for a moment before he recovered and squared his shoulders. "Your Majesty?"

"You will come with me." Rage bristled off Kai in waves. "There are matters we must discuss. In private."

Ashren dipped his head. "As you say."

Taking one step back, Kai swept his gaze back to me. Everything inside me tightened and twisted. Some stupid part of me wanted to tease him again, but the more rational part of my brain took over. Instead, I met his eyes without blinking.

"You're alive because your life is more useful to me than your death," he said. "But make no mistake, as soon as your usefulness ceases, so will you."

He turned sharply, cloak snapping behind him like a living shadow. Ashren fell into step at his side, posture rigid, jaw tight, hands fisted at his thighs. Neither of them looked back as they rounded the corner and vanished.

The silence that followed rang louder than their footsteps.

For a few seconds, I just stood there, hand gripping the bar so hard my knuckles ached inside the gloves. My heart pounded against my ribs, still trying to decide if it was terrified, furious, or... something worse.

"I'm getting in my own head," I muttered. There wasn't time for that. I forced my fingers to unclench and looked down at the blade I'd stolen. It was small, about the length of the space from my wrist to the middle knuckle on my middle finger, but solid and well-balanced with a leather-wrapped handle. The edge gleamed, clean and sharp, the tip wickedly narrow. It sat against my gloved palm like it belonged there.

I waited another second, making sure that I was truly alone.

"Okay," I whispered. "Let's see what you can do."

I moved to the hinges. Up close, the hinge plate was in worse shape than I'd thought. The thick steel was mounted flush against the stone, and the bolts were sunk deep. I wasn't going to *pry* a bolt out. Not with mortal strength and a baby-sized knife.

But the plate.... The plate had a faint sliver of space where cold air kissed the stone.

I angled the blade, slid the tip into that narrow seam, and eased pressure sideways, trying to lever the hinge plate away from the wall.

The metal gave a tiny groan. It barely moved, but it *had* shifted.

Yes! I breathed, pulse jumping. *Progress.*

I set my feet, braced my shoulder against the cold iron door, and rocked the blade in small, deliberate motions, careful not to let the metal scrape too loudly. Each tiny jerk widened the gap a fraction, so I kept moving. My wrist burned, and the muscles in my forearm began to shake.

Come on, you mule-brained chunk of iron! I ranted internally.

The hinge plate pulled away another hair. Then another. If I could open the gap enough, the whole door might sag off the pins. Then one hard kick could set it free.

I shifted my grip, brought my other hand up for leverage, and pushed harder. The blade strained, metal whining.

And... it slipped.

My hand slammed into the hinge, and a snap of pain shot up my arm. The knife skidded off the plate and scraped along the metal with a sharp, traitorous squeal that echoed far too loudly in the cramped cell. It slipped from my fingers and fell just outside the cell.

"Shit," I hissed, freezing in place.

I held my breath, listening.

My stomach knotted, and when the unmistakable sound of boots hitting stone moved in my direction, my mouth soured. I was going to get caught.

CHAPTER 5

Hannah

ove, Hannah, I scolded myself. Every second I didn't retrieve the dagger meant I was less likely to make it out of here of my own accord... if at all, with how the Grouch King had looked at me. I stooped against the bars and reached for it.

"Oi," a voice called from the hall. "What was that noise?"

Shit! They *had* heard me. I had to think. If they opened the door, I'd have one shot to escape, and I had to make sure it would work.

Focused once more, I gritted my teeth and stretched toward the blade lying just a short distance away. The tips of my fingers touched the knife handle, and I moved it slightly closer to the cell door before gripping it as tightly as possible.

Well, butter my biscuit. I hadn't been quite sure that would actually work on the first try.

I yanked it back through the bars and carefully shoved the knife under the heavy cuff of my coat. The cold metal pressed against my arm, the blade pricking my skin slightly, but I had no time to adjust it. Instead, I staggered to the back of the cell

43

and dropped my sore knees onto the straw, curling into a crouched position.

My heart raced as the guards' footsteps became louder. I shook my head, needing to clear it.

Those guards weren't going to open the door just because I asked. I needed a reason. Something that would ensure they didn't ignore me.

I coughed, making it as hacking and ugly as I could manage, then moaned for good measure. "H-help…" I let my voice break, thin and breathless. "Something's wrong."

Sell it, Hannah. My freedom depended on this. I dragged in a rough, ragged breath, then forced it out in a broken wheeze. Cold bit through my jeans, but I ignored it and hunched tighter, pressing a hand to my middle like I was in agony.

"The king won't like it if she dies before he can question her," the deeper voice said, followed by keys jingling. Metal clanged as someone grabbed the bars.

I glanced up and found Lilac Eyes and Scar Face glaring at me from outside the door.

"What did you do?" Scar Jaw demanded. "What are you playing at, woman?"

"N-not… playing…" I let my shoulders shake, digging my fingers into the straw. "Can't… breathe… s-stomach—" I gagged, forcing my throat to convulse. Years of watching daytime TV with Aunt Maureen finally paid off. "Please. It… burns…"

"A reaction, maybe?" Lilac Eyes pursed his lips while concern dripped in his voice. "Or portal sickness? Is that a thing?"

"How would I know?" Scar Jaw snapped. "*You*, sit up. Now."

I didn't move. I made my body go slack and whimpered,

trying to sound as whiny as one of my exes had when he'd had a cold.

"Dammit," he muttered.

There was a pause. "If she dies down here and the king didn't order it..." Lilac Eyes said, voice low.

Scar Jaw swore under his breath. "He'll have our hides."

There was a rustle of cloth and then a shifting sound, as if he'd strode forward.

"Fine. I'll check. Keep your crossbow ready in case she tries something." Scar Jaw's voice came closer.

Perfect.

The lock slid back with a heavy thunk. My heart leapt into my throat while every nerve in my body screamed in anticipation. Despite my racing heart, I kept still, leaving my eyes half-lidded and taking shallow, uneven breaths.

The hinges shrieked as the door swung open, then boot-steps crossed the threshold. The smell of leather and cold iron washed over me as Scar Jaw knelt at my side.

"Oi!" His gloved hand landed on my shoulder. He gave a rough shake and then stepped back. "Open your eyes."

I let my head roll a little as my lids fluttered. "C-can't..."

He leaned in closer with most of his body blocking me from Lilac Eyes. "Are you in pain?"

Wrong move. This was it. My chance.

My hand shot from under the coat, the knife flashing in the dim light. Drawing on past experiences when I'd been in bad fights or chased into tight situations, I twisted, ramming my shoulder into his chest to knock him off balance as I surged to my feet. Before he could react, I looped my arm around his throat from behind, hauling him back against me. The momentum carried us a step toward the door.

He choked as his hands flew to my arm.

"Don't." I pressed the blade to the exposed strip of skin above his collar. The edge pressed against his throat with enough pressure to let him feel exactly how sharp it was. My hands shook, but I held on, bracing my feet against the stone as I used his body like a human shield.

Scar Jaw froze.

Eyes widening, Lilac Eyes still held his crossbow trained on us, but he wasn't able to take the shot because Scar Jaw was shielding most of me.

"Put it down." My breath came faster in frosted puffs, and adrenaline rushed through my veins. "Or else."

The icy air went razor-thin.

"Put the weapon down. Now." I tightened my grip when Scar Jaw tried to drag in a breath. The knife pressed harder, causing a thin line of red to well under the edge.

Lilac Eyes clenched his teeth as his gaze darted from me back to Scar Jaw. "You don't want to do this."

I snorted in a way that sounded way more brittle than I wanted. "Buddy, I absolutely do. Crossbow. Floor. Now. Don't make me ask a third time."

He hesitated, fingers flexing. Sweat beaded at his temple despite the cold.

Scar Jaw tried to rasp something, but it came out as a choked wheeze against my forearm.

"Last chance." I pitched my voice low and steady. "You shoot, your friend dies before the bolt leaves the slot. And if I'm going down, I am not going alone. So. Put. It. Down."

A beat of silence. Then a second.

Blinking, Lilac Eyes lowered the crossbow. "He's going to kill us," he muttered. The crossbow creaked lightly as he eased the tension and set the weapon on the floor, then pushed it away with his boot.

"Good." My heart pounded so hard I felt it through my whole body, and a bitter taste coated my tongue. "Now, your other weapons. All of them. And the keys."

He glared but obeyed—dagger, short sword, another slim

blade tucked at his back beneath his cloak. Each one thudded onto the stone and got kicked aside. Finally, with visible reluctance, he unclipped the heavy ring of keys from his belt and let them drop beside the pile.

My chest loosened a fraction. "Back up. Hands where I can see them." I wasn't out of the woods yet, and I still had no clue how to get out of this hellhole.

He raised his hands and stepped away from the weapons. Scar Jaw shifted against me, testing my grip.

I dug my arm in tighter and pressed the knife just a little more. "A word of warning—unless you want me to slit your throat, stop wiggling."

He stilled with a low, vicious sound.

"Good," I said. "Now, you stay put. Scar Jaw, we're just going to reposition here."

I shuffled us forward, using his bulk as a shield. Every step felt like crossing a tightrope without a net. Lilac Eyes stayed where he was, muscles tensed, eyes locked on mine like he was trying to figure out the angle that ended with Scar Jaw not dead and me locked in the cell.

We reached the weapons. I nudged them farther away from Scar Jaw's boot to create space and make it a little safer for me.

"Scarves and gloves." I flicked my eyes toward the ground.

Lilac Eyes blinked. "What?"

"The blue things around your neck, keeping your throat from freezing, and the gray things on your hands," I snapped. "Take them off. Slowly. And put them on the ground. Take this guy's too."

His mouth flattened. "You won't get far. When we're found—"

"Yeah, yeah. I'll be punished, flayed, disemboweled, whatever fun thing is on today's torture special." I tipped my head. "Scarves. Now. Unless you want me to test jugular depth."

"Fuck." He tugged the thick wool scarf from around his neck and then a smaller cotton one that protected against friction.

"His too." I gripped Scar Jaw tighter, ready to cut if needed, but hoping I wouldn't have to. "Both scarves and his gloves."

Lilac Eyes glowered, but a glimmer of calculation in his eyes told me he was still weighing the odds. His jaw clenched, and then he stepped forward and uncoiled the scarf. He yanked off the gray leather gloves and stepped back.

I was a little disappointed he didn't take a theatrical bow. He could at least have some personality under pressure. Oh, well.

"Front and center in the cell." I jerked my head forward to indicate where I meant. "Lay them out on the floor with no sudden moves. I will hurt him if you make me."

Sighing, he laid the scarves and gloves down between us, fingers lingering like he was calculating whether he could lunge.

I tightened my hold on Scar Jaw and shifted the knife enough that Lilac Eyes' gaze snapped to the blood welling from the last light cut.

"Since that's done, you're going to tie your friend's wrists," I said.

His brows bunched together. "You think you can force me to do that?"

"I do—otherwise, you'll be responsible for your friend's death." I pitched my voice higher, my tone bright.

Lilac Eyes stared at me, then at Scar Jaw. Something passed between them, but all I could read was anger. Lilac Eyes set the scarves out so that I could see there was nothing else in them.

"You're dead when the king finds you," Scar Jaw ground out, voice rough against my arm. "You know that, right? He'll make it slow."

I was well aware, which was why these two needed to hurry so I could get on my way. "Then I'd better not get caught. Hands. Wrists. Tie."

Lilac Eyes knelt, movements jerky, and grabbed one scarf. "Behind him or in front?"

"Behind." I stepped back but kept the tip of the knife against his throat. I moved swiftly as I turned Scar Eyes, keeping the blade steady and my grip tight. The scratch from the blade tip had left a raised mark, and if I slipped even a little, he'd be in serious trouble. "Crisscross. Don't half-ass it. If he gets free and kills me later, I will come back from the grave and haunt you personally. I can do that because I'm not like you all. I've got powers."

Scar Jaw snarled, but he didn't resist as Lilac Eyes yanked his arms behind his back. The scarf wound around his wrists, thick and tight. Lilac Eyes cinched it with more force than necessary.

I smirked. "Wow, good to see you putting so much energy into this."

"Shut up," they muttered, almost in unison.

I chuckled. "Now step back."

Fingers flexing, Lilac Eyes' breath fogged the air. He was close enough for me to see a tiny scar by his lower lip and a fine tremor in his hands.

"One more thing." I nodded to his hands. "Your wrists."

His chin jerked up. "You want me to tie myself up? Really?"

"I don't need you to go that far." I smiled brightly despite my insides knotting. The longer this took, the more likely someone else would come. "Yet. You're going to make two nice loops for me. Big enough to slide over your wrists. Then you're going to put the loop around one hand and hold the second loop. You're going to put both your hands behind your back and slide your other hand through the second loop and then step within grabbing distance, and I'll finish the job. Or," I added when he opened his mouth, "I can open Scar Jaw's throat right now and roll the dice on whether you get me first or I get you."

His lips pressed into a hard line. "You're a menace."

"Thank you! That's the nicest thing I've heard all day." I sighed deeply. "Blue scarf. Loop. Let's go."

He yanked the second scarf off the floor, fingers working the blue wool. He tied a loose circle around one wrist, formed another loop, and held it, not pulling it tight, the knot clumsy on purpose.

I had to speed this up. He was stalling. "Higher. If you try something like that again, I'll stab Scar Jaw here out of pure irritation."

"Just do it," Scar Jaw rasped.

Adjusting the knot, Lilac Eyes made the first loop snugger but still with slack while the other hand remained free.

"Good." I nodded. "Now come here."

He stared at me for a heartbeat, the muscle in his cheek ticking, then stepped forward until he was within arm's reach. I shifted Scar Jaw enough to free one of my hands, keeping the knife at his throat with the other. "Put your other wrist in the loop. Then put your hands up," I said.

Lilac Eyes did as I demanded, then lifted his bound wrists behind him.

I shot my free hand out, grabbed the scarf, and wrenched it tight around the second wrist he'd tied and looped both wrists together.

He sucked in a breath as the wool bit into his skin. I twisted the fabric, knotting it hard, then gave the scarf a sharp jerk to test it. He couldn't pull free without dislocating something.

"Happy?" he ground out.

"Is anyone?" I flashed him a small smile. "But this is a good start."

Scar Jaw tried to jerk away again, testing my grip now that my attention had shifted. I slammed my elbow into his ribs, and he bent over, wheezing.

"You mentioned punishment." I raised my voice so it sounded carefree. "How creative are we talking here? Lava pit? Disembowelment? Do you have a brochure or reading material I can browse on my way out?"

"You'll be lucky if it's quick." Scar Jaw stood upright, though he was still breathless. "No one escapes the king's dungeon."

I patted his arm. "Good thing I'm not planning to stick around long enough to find out." Time for the finishing touches and getting the hell out of here. "Both of you, on your knees."

They both glared.

"If you think I'm—" Scar Jaw started.

The knife kissed his skin again, a fresh bead of blood sliding down its edge.

"I don't recommend you finish that thought because I'm running out of patience," I snapped. "On your knees. Both of you. Down on the ground, sides against the bench, each of you facing a wall, backs to each other."

Lilac Eyes exhaled through his nose, then knelt. Scar Jaw's shoulders heaved as he followed, grumbling.

They were pressed against the far stone wall next to the stone bench with their feet in the straw. Keeping the knife in place, I shifted behind Scar Jaw, using my shoulder to pin him while I reached for his scarf binding with my free hand.

I yanked hard, and it held. Excellent.

"Last step." I edged closer to them so I could see both their faces. "Open your mouths."

Lilac Eyes narrowed his gaze. "Well, if you—"

"Do it or else." I gave him a sweet smile, though I was quite certain it didn't reach my eyes. "I don't need either of you screaming for your murder king."

"Someone will hear you escaping." Lilac Eyes' voice was low and vicious. "Even if you gag us, there are patrols throughout the main levels and around the walls. You won't even make it to the stairs. And when you're dragged back here by your hair, you'll realize how hospitable everyone was before you spat in our faces. You'll wish you'd been left to freeze."

"Maybe." I shrugged, though his words definitely did leave a mark. I had no idea of the layout or even where I was. "Maybe not. But I'm not staying in this cell, waiting to freeze or be 'resolved.' All I want is to get home. Mouth open, please."

His nostrils flared, and he slowly opened his mouth. I shoved one glove in, then used the softer cotton scarf to tie it around his mouth in a gag. He made a muffled, furious sound as I pulled the fabric tight and knotted it at the back of his neck.

"Good job." I patted the top of his head like a dog. "Very cooperative."

Scar Jaw clenched his teeth when I turned to him.

"Look." I mashed my lips together and leaned in. "I don't *want* to kill you. I really do just want to go home. Don't give me a reason to change my mind and get violent. You both can see I don't belong here."

His eyes searched mine for a second, maybe weighing whether this was worth it. I wasn't sure, but with a guttural grunt, he opened his mouth.

I stuffed the glove in, bound and gagged him the same way, then stepped back.

Both men glared up at me, breathing hard through their noses, hands bound, mouths gagged, backs to the wall.

Guilt pricked at me, but I shoved it down. No time. No room.

"I'm sure you're lovely when you're not throwing people into dungeons." I tied their bound hands to one another and then to the legs of the bench with the tails of the blue scarves. *That should keep them for a while and keep them from banging and making too much noise.* Then I backed toward the door, keeping them in sight. My boot nudged the keyring. I scooped it up, the metal heavy and cold in my palm. Then I grabbed the other weapons.

Lilac Eyes made a muffled, furious noise and jerked at his bindings. Thankfully, the knots held.

At least one thing had gone my way today. "Yeah, I know. You're going to hunt me down. It'll be terrible. I'll regret my life choices. We can schedule that trauma later." My stomach twisted. Bold as my words were, I had to figure out how to escape this place. That portal in the sky I'd fallen through had closed, but everyone had acted as if it was common knowledge that portals like that existed, so that had to mean there was another.

I slipped out into the corridor, every hair on my arms rising at the feel of open space behind me. Heart hammering, I carried the weapons to a safe distance, set them down, then returned and closed the cell door.

The iron clanged into place, the sound echoing down the hall and making my heart jolt.

Scar Jaw lunged as far as he could with bound wrists, which resulted in a useless, furious motion. Lilac Eyes leaned forward too, eyes burning holes through me.

I found the right key and jammed it into the lock. The mechanism turned with a heavy click.

Locked.

We'd officially traded places.

I swallowed, my throat tight. "Well, that's about all for now. Don't cause any trouble, okay?" I forced a smile.

They glared. I didn't give myself time to think about it.

I shoved the keys into my pocket and sifted through the weapons. The crossbow was solid but too heavy to be a good choice to take on the run. Besides, I didn't trust myself to get off more than one shot without wasting time on figuring out how to reload. Daggers were straightforward enough. The short swords, while nice, needed belts and sheaths to be carried effectively.

I settled on one of the sturdier black metal daggers in place of the knife I'd swiped off King Grumpy Face. I cut off a strip of cloth from the coat and wrapped it around the knife blade, then slid it into my pocket and palmed the dagger. The keys rattled in my pocket against the covered blade.

"Okay, Hannah," I whispered, glancing over my shoulder at the cell. Both men glared death at me, twitching and wriggling against the bonds. "Time to not die."

I turned toward the dark corridor that the guards had dragged me down. Farther down were the stairs to the courtyard. It had been surrounded by walls with guards on top. There was little chance of making a break for safety from there. And if memory served me from a couple of Dungeons and Dragons runs I'd attempted with an ex, castles typically had one courtyard with walls around the main building and then often additional walls outside of that. Best to assume I'd have to get through multiple walls. If I could get up higher, maybe to the next floor or two, I could scope out where I was. And if these chuckleheads got free, they'd probably assume I'd head straight for the courtyard and be trapped.

I retraced my steps to the junction where the corridor split, straining my ears for any sound of concern. The torches burned lower with thinner smoke than the ones near my cell, as if even fire itself was afraid to draw attention. I paused at the corner where Kai and Ashren had turned, pressed my shoulder to the icy stone, and listened.

Nothing.

The two men I'd locked in the cell might be the only ones on patrol. I might have asked them, but I couldn't trust their answer.

I edged around the corner, scanning both directions. To the left lay a longer stretch of cells, the glow of torchlight fading into blue shadow at the far end. To the right was a short passage and then an enormous black iron door studded with silver spikes.

The torches flickered, but the flames didn't bend in one direction over another to suggest a draft of fresh air. My heart hitched. The scent of blood and sweat filled my lungs.

Chains clinked down the path to the left, and I guessed there were prisoners down there beyond what I could see. I continued forward the way I'd come in, looking around cautiously. Up ahead, maybe another hundred feet, was the start of the staircase. As I scanned the space, I noticed a small, narrow corridor that cut into the wall to my right. I'd missed it when I'd been dragged here. It looked like it might lead inside the castle.

An iron-banded door with a lock stood at the end of the narrow corridor, just a couple of yards away. Maybe it led to the kitchens or another way out. Either way, it wasn't a path they'd expect me to take.

My gut said it was the safest choice. The iron key with two flares on the blade and three grooves fit into the door's lock. It turned easily, as if it had been opened many times. The hallway beyond was warmer, the stone floor cleaner. Cautiously, I made my way into the hall. Gazing down it, I could see that other hallways intersected it, but I didn't hear anyone. On the left wall were cubbies filled with boots, gloves, rope, buckets, and so on. Thinking it might be useful, I grabbed a coil of rope and looped it up over my arm and shoulder like the world's most uncomfortable purse. The buckets were also tempting, but I didn't want to weigh myself down too much.

As I continued down the hall, bootsteps echoed faintly beyond me. I stopped and pressed myself flat against the wall. The steps were heavy. Unhurried. Two guards making rounds, if the footsteps were an indicator.

My chest squeezed.

I waited until the rhythm faded, counting breaths—four, ten, thirty—before peeling myself away and moving again.

They were probably going to check the cells holding prisoners. I had maybe minutes before they realized I was gone.

A stairwell loomed ahead like a gaping wound of stone. I hugged the inner wall and climbed carefully, wincing every time my shoes squeaked.

Still no one.

Any minute, I expected to hear shouts and alarms.

The staircase spiraled tighter and tighter to the next floor, opening onto a landing and then up to the next. The farther up I went, the more the air cooled. By the time I reached the third floor, my fingers ached with cold despite the gloves, and the air felt sharper, thinner, as if the castle was shedding warmth the higher I climbed. My lungs ached by the time I reached the top, both from fear and from the cold slicing through the air.

This cold was vicious. Worse than anything I'd weathered in Tennessee. My face and throat ached from it, but somehow the coat and gloves kept me warm. With the way the temperature had dropped, I guessed night was fully here.

That worked for me. I could use the darkness to my advantage, especially with this dark navy coat.

A narrow landing opened ahead, lit by a single torch guttering low. Another iron-banded door sat at the far end.

Please lead outside.

I slid the keyring from my pocket and worked through the keys by touch, hands shaking from exertion and nerves. One key scraped uselessly, and another stuck halfway in.

Come on.

The third key with a triangular notch slid in and turned with a dull click.

I eased the door open an inch.

Cold night air slammed into me, and the wind whistled through the gap. The chill of the hall and the stairwell was nothing compared to this.

I bit back a pained grunt and peeked out.

A stone walkway stretched before me in a long straight line, providing access to the towers that were scattered at intervals. Already, it was slick and sparkling with frost, a waist-high wall on either side. Night pressed close, heavy clouds dragging across the sky. Snow drifted down in lazy, stinging flakes. The moon appeared and vanished behind cloud cover, painting everything in shifting silver and shadow.

I crouched instinctively, heart hammering.

Two guards patrolled the walkway—one far to my left, another even farther to the right. They moved at a slow, steady pace, as if they'd been on duty for hours and nothing significant had happened, boots crunching softly, heads down against the cold.

I eased forward, staying low, keeping to the darker patches the torchlight didn't quite reach. My coat brushed the stone with each step, the fabric whispering too loudly in my ears. Then I dared a glance over the parapet.

My stomach dropped. I was so screwed.

CHAPTER 6

Hannah

I clenched my fists and peered over the edge, my knuckles burning through the leather of the gloves and the dagger heavy in my right hand. The sheer drop over the wall stole the breath from my lungs. It was the kind of height that made my stomach lurch before my mind could catch up.

The courtyard was wide and brutally exposed. Snow dusted the stone in thin, uneven patches with vague boot prints disappearing in the wind and falling snow. I could see the spot where I'd landed, but there was no shining portal above it. The door that led to the dungeon was just over there. But...no portal. No shimmer. Nothing.

Dread pooled in my stomach. It was gone.

My heart sped faster, and my throat tightened. I couldn't panic. There had to be another way home. No one had seemed shocked that a portal existed. It was clear that it was something that happened here, so I had to find the portal. It must be one of those moving portals. Which, fine, sure, that made sense. Maybe I needed to find another mirror—and a dagger like the one I'd cut myself on before. It had such a distinct blade shape and handle.

A couple dozen leather- and fur-clad guards were clustered in tight groups, some scanning the area while others talked or gestured roughly toward where I'd dropped in.

My breath caught. There were more of them than I'd expected.

At least, I'd been smart enough not to try to get out *that* way. It wouldn't have been a question of *if* I would be captured but *when*. Probably seconds.

Fortunately, my instincts were guiding me right. I hoped they'd get me home now, but with no portal and no dagger, what could I do next? Obviously, I had to get out of the castle and find a place to regroup, settle in, and make a better plan.

A wave of grief pressed over me. In the past, at times like this, I'd call Aunt Maureen and pour my heart out, and she'd click her tongue while both comforting and scolding me at once. Tears burned my eyes, and the horrible hollow of loneliness opened up once more in my chest.

If she were here right now, she'd tell me to get a grip and put one foot in front of the other because I didn't need to know the whole journey. I just had to take one step at a time.

I could grieve when I was safe.

Beyond the courtyard, the outer walls rose thick and strong, towers punching into them at measured intervals. Everything connected—walkways, raised platforms, watch-points—in what looked like a block formation. I didn't see many guards on duty up here, but the towers and boxy watch-points could have other guards out of sight.

I lifted my gaze higher.

Based on where the moon was, I was pretty sure I was looking east. The dark mountains rose sharp and unforgiving against the sky, glinting in the moonlight where the snow and ice gathered. There were no roads that I could see, just jagged rock and snow. A natural wall, crueler than the castle's. No chance of escape there.

I turned west, and my fingers clenched inside the gloves. A faint golden glow reflected off the clouds from a town or city down below. Lanternlight, fires, and movement shifted throughout.

Where there were people, there would be shelter and places to hide.

Hope flared in my chest so sharp it hurt. That was where I'd go.

BAHROOOM! A deep-toned horn sounded a single note through the night.

Shouts followed. The door the guards had dragged me through slammed open. A deep voice called, "The new prisoner has escaped!"

"Cover the gates!"

Along the walls, guards snapped to attention, their heads jerking up and their weapons flashing. The one nearest to me was still over fifty feet away, and he leaned over the wall and viewed the courtyard below.

In the courtyard, the guards broke into smaller groups of four. One set ran toward the main gates, which looked as if they led into the larger enclosed space beyond this inner courtyard. Another four ran toward the entrance to the castle and up the stairs. The rest scattered to various doors.

The heavy tramping of booted footsteps filled the air as the horn sounded again and again. On the tower roofs, more heads appeared, archers and spearmen with at least two per tower.

My throat constricted, and I took a step back. Hopefully, when I stood still, my coat helped me blend in with the dark gray stones. However, my golden hair probably stood out in the darkness.

Two of the guards on the walkway turned and trotted toward the nearest towers. The third, nearest me, straightened with his hand tight around his spear. He looked up at one of the towers to the south.

This was my chance to move. My heart jumped as I ducked behind the waist-high wall, gripping the dagger tighter and shifting the rope against my side. If I were lucky, I could reach one of the towers and then the eastern outer wall. They wouldn't expect me to be up here.

The muted sound of heavy footsteps moved away from me, but those watchmen on the towers would be looking for anything that didn't fit. Okay, not good.

I hiked the rope coil higher on my shoulder and started moving, keeping my stance low. There wasn't anything I could do about my hair. I edged along the walkway, trying to keep my movements smooth, steady, and hidden in the shadows.

My knees ached, and the stone under my sneakers squeaked with each step, but my feet never lost control. Thank goodness, they weren't as slippery as I'd feared.

Despite wanting to rush, I kept my pace slow, knowing I'd slip otherwise. The dagger rested solid and reassuring in my grip while the rope bumped against my side and hip with each careful step.

The eastern tower loomed ahead, its dark spire rising out of the wall at least another thirty feet in the air. If I could reach the connection point without being seen, I could slip around the bend and—

"Oi! Who's that?" a voice bellowed from above.

"You down there, lift your head," another called down.

Electric awareness shot through my veins as I hinged my gaze toward the voice without moving my head. In my periphery, I spotted dark shapes on the tower to my left. Shit. They'd spotted me.

The connecting junction where I'd make the turn to get to the tower was barely twenty feet away, with the eastern tower maybe fifty feet total. If I moved fast enough, none of the guards on this level were close enough to stop me. The nearest one was on a walkway junction a couple hundred feet away.

Breath locked in my chest, I bolted.

"Stop!" the first voice shouted.

"Get the ladders. Get up the stairs. Cut her off!" someone shouted from the courtyard below.

"Don't let her get away!"

An arrow screamed past my shoulder and shattered against the stone ahead, sending sparks skittering across the walkway. I veered hard, and my sneaker caught an icy patch that sent my foot skidding into the wall.

Another arrow whistled close enough to move the air by my cheek.

More shouts exploded around me while boots thundered and metal clanged.

"Don't kill her!" someone yelled. "The king wants her alive!"

Lucky me. But this luck wasn't going to hold long.

"Just shoot to injure!"

My lungs burned as I pushed harder, rushing toward the eastern tower. Pain sliced through my calf, and I cried and stumbled, catching myself on the wall before I could fully fall. Hot red blood seeped through my ripped jean leg where an arrow had clipped it. My heart dropped to my stomach. I had to move. Now.

I limped forward, gritting my teeth as each step sent shockwaves of burning pain through me. I clenched my teeth, blood soaking my sock. I had to hurry, or I could bleed out.

I glanced back. Two heavy wooden ladders had been set against the courtyard wall, and four guards had begun climbing up. The door I'd come through was now open, a guard already in the doorway with his sword lifted. The one guard who'd been closest in sight was halfway to me now, his boots thundering on the pavestones.

The tower door was ten steps away.

Nine.

Eight.

Another arrow struck the stone inches from my foot.

"If you kill her, he'll have our heads, Bren!" someone shouted from behind me. "Stop shooting! She's already wounded!"

"We've got to slow her down more. She's fast," someone— possibly Bren—responded.

I slammed into the door, my fingers scrabbling for the latch. The overhang offered some shelter in case Hotshot Archer decided I needed more injuries.

Locked.

Of course it was locked. But I had the keys.

"Surrender, woman! You can't get away!" the guard nearest me yelled as he reached the corner and charged. His voice echoed off the stones around us.

I dragged the keys free and shoved the first key into the lock. I took a deep breath and turned.

Wrong.

Fuck. I tried the next one. Wrong again.

The third with the squared teeth fit, and the heavy metal gave a satisfying click. I wrenched the door open and threw myself inside.

The guard was almost on me. I turned to look back in time to see him coming at me as he ran through the pool of torchlight, his blue eyes narrowed and his jaw clenched.

I shoved the door shut and locked it, then glanced around. A single torch burned on the wall, which I hoped meant no one was in here.

The watchtower smelled of oil, old smoke, and sweat, and was smaller than my bedroom at Aunt Maureen's. There was a door on the opposite side from me, and a ladder poked through a trapdoor in the floor. Another trapdoor was situated above me with a ladder cutting up through that square, too. I knocked the two ladders out as I heard something rustling from above, possibly a couple of floors away. They were probably coming down from the tower.

Racks lined the walls, the one closest to me on my right holding arrows. I grabbed a handful and started wedging their narrow, finely hammered metal-tipped heads into the crease where the door met the hinge and the wall to make it harder to open. Though I didn't have enough strength to shove them in deep, it would cause a bit of a problem.

A heavy fist banged on the door. "You can't hide in there forever!" Blue Eyes shouted.

"Watch me! Oh, wait. You can't!" I shouted back.

Metal scraped against the door near the lock and jangled. Did he have keys? I jammed an arrow into the lock opening.

"Hey!" Blue Eyes' outraged voice sounded on the other side, followed by another heavy thump, as if he'd struck the door.

I jammed the arrow in harder. "That's what you get for having such tiny-headed arrows!"

"You mal-malevolent harpy!" His voice cracked, as if he were genuinely shocked.

"Stupid pig," I shouted back.

"She's locked herself in the inner eastern watch tower and jammed the lock!" Blue Eyes' voice sounded farther away. Other voices responded, but I couldn't make out the words.

Let them stew. I needed to *move*. Another ragged burst of pain shot up my leg as I tried to put my weight on it.

This was getting worse faster than I'd expected.

The rack on the other side of the room held gloves, scarves, and other similar items. Nothing I could use to block the door, but I could bind my leg enough to stop the blood trail.

I yanked a scarf from the rack and wrapped it tight around

my calf. The wool scratched my skin, but the pressure dulled the pulsing sting a little. The wound wasn't too deep, but fleeing was still going to hurt like hell. I tied off the scarf, then straightened.

The tower door shook with another blow and an angry yell. The arrows I'd jammed into the seam shook as well but held for now. Dust sifted from the stones, and the lock rattled. Metal scraped like someone was testing keys, then forcing it. I jammed the arrow deeper, taking a little pleasure at the annoyed grunt.

"Wretched hellion!" Blue Eyes growled.

"Thanks for the compliment!" I rubbed my lower leg, braced myself, and then ran to the other side. No one was beating on this door, and the only footsteps I heard were the ones coming from above.

Safe or not, I had to go. I found the right key, opened the door, and peeked outside. The cold was so sharp it felt like a bite.

Snow whipped into my face, stinging my cheeks. I slipped through and pulled the door shut behind me, hands shaking. The outer wall path ran straight for another couple hundred feet before it reached another junction and split again. The warm glow of the town was just beyond that.

I locked the door behind me and started moving, faster now. No point pretending I was invisible when half the castle knew I existed. My sneakers squeaked on the snow, and each step sent a sharp jab of pain through my wounded leg. I kept my pace just short of a full sprint—fast enough to eat distance, controlled enough not to wipe out.

Shouts carried from behind me, muffled at first.

Armor clanged. Boots hammered.

Biting down hard enough to make my jaw ache, I ran.

The horn blasted again, echoing in my head with more shouts following. I was almost to the junction. Beyond it, I saw what looked like a medieval city sprawling before me, lamp posts burning with large braziers fastened to the tops of metal poles beneath small triangular caps and small fires flickering at regular intervals. People were running with torches too.

I rounded the corner and kept going in the direction of the light and the outer wall with its jagged pattern like broken teeth. Just as I skidded up to the wall's edge, the door to the tower I'd left behind slammed open. I looked back in time to see Blue Eyes and two others.

Shit. My heart skipped a beat.

I set aside the dagger, threw the rope coil off my shoulder, and looped the end around the stone post. The gloves made my hands clumsy, and the wind tugged at the rope, trying to rip it out of my hands.

"Come on." I cinched the knot, then tested it with one hard pull.

It held.

For now.

I peered through the jagged pattern of stone blocks and gaps, my heart pounding against my ribs. Down below, the city was in a panic. People ran in knots, some looking back and forth as if terrified while others peered into the sky. The wall overlooked a dark alley between the castle and a stretch of thatch-roofed buildings. It was at least forty feet from here to the ground.

My stomach somersaulted, and my body tensed as I tested the knot one more time. Heights didn't usually bother me, but the thought of free climbing down a straight drop with angry guards and a bad leg scared me.

"Stop!" one of the guards yelled.

"She's going over the wall!"

Yes, I was. Because risking becoming a splat on the stone below was better than being a prisoner. Head spinning and leg throbbing, I climbed up between one of the gaps, tightened my grip on the rope, and started down.

The rope jerked.

My stomach dropped with it.

I stopped dead, heart hammering. From here, I could still grab the edge of the stone wall if I had to. Had the knot shifted, or had the natural pressure tightened it? It scraped stone, a gritty, ominous sound, but it was holding.

More shouts filled my ears, and fear swept over me. I had to keep moving, so I lowered myself more.

The stone wall was slick with frost and rough with ice-crusted seams that tore at my gloves. I pressed my sneakers flat against the vertical surface, searching for purchase in cracks and tiny ledges. The rope burned my palms even through the leather.

My wounded leg screamed when I put weight on it, but I swallowed a cry and kept moving.

Suddenly, the knot gave...and I dropped.

CHAPTER 7

Kai

My boots struck the cold stones hard, sending loud echoes along the passage as tension radiated through my shoulders and down my spine. Worse, the damn *yank* in my chest intensified with every step I took away from that strange, infuriating woman. The way she managed to get under my skin made it even more important that I take another shot of herbs immediately. Add in the weird way she'd spoken and touched me, and how it had made things in my pants hard that had no business being erect, and she was a harbinger of disaster. Emotions and distractions would cost me everything I'd sacrificed to save my people.

Ashren's boots scuffed the floor, reminding me he was following me. For the first time in my life, I wanted to punch him and put him in a holding cell. He should've come to me when he'd realized she was freezing. *I* would've handled the situation, not *him*. Instead, he'd decided to take care of *my* prisoner.

We reached the staircase and continued up to the final landing, and the hall and stairs leading to my sanctuary. My breath frosted in the cool stairwell, but my blood roared as if I were caught in a bonfire.

Hannah of Tennessee.

The name scraped against my thoughts like grit between my teeth. What a ridiculous name! And why would Fate choose *her* to be with *me* and drop her here *now* when things were so dire?

I clenched my fists, the infernal tugging and twisting in my chest worsening. I tried not to imagine her back in that cell and tried not to remember her sparkling hazel eyes and how her soft hair smelled like apricots and magnolias.

My dick began hardening again.

That wretched woman had been cheerful and arrogant, despite being locked in an icy holding cell barely larger than a closet.

The fury vanished from my body, replaced by cold fear.

Shit.

I hadn't moved her.

She needed to be moved to a proper cell. Maybe even a room where I could keep an eye on her so none of my guards could get near her and fall victim to her oddly seductive behavior.

Folge, Bannon, and Mik had put her far away from the other prisoners, which...I didn't want her near them, but I also didn't want her freezing.

A low growl built in my chest. Why did she make it so hard for me to think straight? I needed another dose of lorn leaf.

I ground my teeth as we reached the final landing and turned into the hall that led to my study. Torches burned low, their flames guttering in the draft, casting long shadows that stretched and warped across the stone.

She could stay down there for a while longer, now that she had the enchanted gloves and coat. Yet, that thought wasn't comforting. Leaving her behind grated on me, and so did the thought of sending someone else to move her. I didn't want her spoken to, touched, assessed, or looked at by anyone else. Merely because of her strange antics, not due to actual care or a need to protect her.

My stomach churned. If I were alone, I'd be stomping and throwing things, but I couldn't do that in front of anyone else, not even my own brother.

Why did she make it so difficult to know what I wanted? I needed to focus on something else. And I knew exactly who deserved my full attention. "Do you intend to defend yourself, Ashren? Or are you hoping I'll forget what you did if you walk quietly enough?"

He exhaled slowly. "I assume you'd prefer honesty to excuses, and you already know the truth, so why should I waste my breath? You wish me to tell you what you already know?"

I shot him a look over my shoulder. "Tell me the truth, even if you think I know it."

He scoffed, then cleared his throat. "It was freezing down there. The guards followed your orders, but that woman would have frozen within a matter of hours. My actions were in line with your underlying intent that she should remain alive for questioning, which meant you didn't want her to die from the cold."

Smoldering rage blasted through me, but beneath it was something sharper, more dangerous. "That was not *your* judgment to make. You should have checked with *me*. They were given a direct order."

"They were. And you were angry when you gave it, so you weren't as clear as you usually are. I also knew what you actually intended, which is why I went down there to check on her."

I turned to face him and snarled, "You aren't telling me the full truth. What of Thea?"

Ashren halted and kept his hands loose at his sides while schooling his expression. He wasn't afraid of me. He never had been. Not since we were boys scrubbing frost from our clothes and learning what it meant to survive outside this court after my father banished our mother. No matter how angry either of us became, we always guarded one another. That meant he was one of the only people alive who would call me on my bullshit, a tedious role that I rarely appreciated in the moment, even when I recognized he was right.

Especially not when he was right.

But in *this* moment, there was something guarded in his expression. It was the look he always got when he spoke of Thea.

He dipped his head forward, then straightened. "It was my choice. I went to the dungeon of my own accord. Why do you require anything beyond that? No one forced me to act."

"Perhaps." I stepped closer, staring him down. "But I told you to speak the full truth."

"Do you swear that there will be reprisals only on me if you deem them necessary?"

The question annoyed me, and yet it took some of the heat out of me. He was loyal, Fate damn him. And so was Thea. He'd take a blade and an arrow for her.

I turned away and resumed walking, forcing myself to keep my pace even as we passed the final turn and approached the thick wooden door to my study. "You and she both disobeyed your king's order. You undermined my authority." I thrust the door open and strode through.

"I protected your prisoner and your authority." Ashren entered with his chin raised. "A frozen corpse in your dungeon would have caused far more damage than someone exercising limited compassion that honored the spirit of what you required."

I slammed the door shut with so much force that it sounded like a whip cracking through the room.

The study greeted me with its familiar chill. The hearth was unlit, the stone floor biting through the soles of my boots as I crossed to the central table. Maps and letters lay scattered where I had left them earlier, star charts lining the walls with their enchanted ink shimmering faintly beneath the lamplight. The weight of the room usually grounded me. This wasn't one of those times.

Apparently, we were dealing with multiple exceptions, starting with my *mate* falling through a fucking portal that shouldn't have even opened. Was this my punishment for killing my uncle?

I braced my hands against the edge of the table and leaned forward. "You assumed you knew what I wanted." It was hard to put into words how much it angered me that he'd had anything to do with Hannah, even while part of me recognized the wisdom in his actions. My reaction had to be due to this damnable mate bond. I'd heard it made males irrationally jealous. Damn it all to the void, the grave, and everything besides and beyond. That was the last thing I needed.

Ashren moved to stand near the window, his reflection dim in the dark glass. "No. I assumed an outcome you didn't, and I acted appropriately. I was going down there anyway. If I had disagreed with Thea's presence, I would have sent her away. She likely anticipated what I would have told her to do if she had asked, and what you wanted."

I closed my eyes and clenched my jaw. "Yes. She *anticipates* what *you* want."

"She would never go against your true wishes, Kai." He spoke in that same measured tone. "She is loyal and intelligent, and I was already on my way there for the exact same reason."

Silence as taut as a drawn bowstring stretched between us. My magic stirred beneath my skin, restless and irritated, responding to just the memory of her. The lorn leaf dulled that impulse, but not enough. How could I be this raw when the lorn leaf's influence should still be at nearly full strength? Maybe it was a weaker batch.

I straightened. "Neither you nor Thea will have anything to do with Hannah. Nor will any of the other servants unless I command it. You will take responsibility for the eastern supply inventories. Personally. Inspect the stores, confirm the numbers, and report back before the next meeting. No delegation."

Ashren grimaced and rubbed the back of his neck. "That will take days."

"So it will." I moved a small stack of notes off the map and stuffed them under a large leather book. "Consider it time to reflect on proper conduct and the chain of command. You will devote yourself to it unless we are attacked and your services are required elsewhere."

He inclined his head. "As you wish. Perhaps I'll pray for an attack. Old King Bram should be striking any night now, shouldn't he?"

There was no resentment in his voice. He would do the work and return exactly as loyal as he had left. He always did. Even now, he did not seem put out. He looked at me as if I'd been exposed, and he saw through me. Or rather...he saw how Hannah affected me.

Damn her.

Shaking my head, I looked at the map on the table. Though I desperately needed to work, I couldn't focus. My attention kept drifting back to *her*.

I hated this.

A part of me wanted to ask him what he thought of her

and admit she was my mate. But it didn't matter. We would not be together, even if Fate tried to force it. I would bury my emotions with herbs, along with decades of discipline and layers of isolation.

"So we're not going to talk about what else happened?"

My attention snapped back up.

Ashren was just standing there with his arms folded and his head canted, as if we were having a normal conversation and I hadn't scolded him and assigned him some menial task to occupy his time as a punishment.

"Talk about what?" I arched a brow.

He snorted. "I've never seen anyone get under your skin quite so much and have that effect on your eyes."

I picked up the stack of letters and coordinates and thrust them into a drawer, then slammed it shut. "It is not she alone who disrupted my mood. It is the entirety of this situation. Bram is plotting something."

Ashren's lips pressed into a tighter line as amusement sparked in his eyes. "Is that why the violet in your eyes expanded along with your pupils, Your Majesty?"

I braced my hands on the table. "Are you actually suggesting that my head was turned by some wretched little creature that fell out of an unsanctioned portal?" I barely caught myself before I asked if he thought she was my mate. Fuck, I was slipping.

"Yes." He didn't even hesitate. That hint of a smile confirmed his amusement, perhaps even approval. He suspected the truth.

I slammed my hand on the tabletop. "Perhaps you would like to add inventorying the western storehouses to your duties?"

He raised his palms in an exaggerated surrender. "Have mercy, my king."

I scowled and shot him a glare. Knowing that I was being unreasonable wasn't making this any better. "I am certain your attention would be better directed elsewhere."

"As you wish, of course." He spread his arms and bowed his head. "I will inform Thea that the prisoner is to be given nothing without your express command."

One of these days, I might have to actually punish him severely.

As he departed, I remained where I was, forcing my attention once more onto the maps, but I wasn't really seeing them, the pull in my chest tightening again as cold seeped into the room.

Hannah of Tennessee was still in the dungeons, locked behind iron and stone, and somehow the distance did nothing to loosen her hold.

If anything, it made it worse.

In the silence, there was nowhere to hide. Images of her danced within my mind. The memory of searching her returned unbidden, making it hard to think of anything else, and other parts of me harder still. Fuck. I was doomed. And I wasn't a man who would let himself be doomed.

I struck my fist against the table again, and one of the tins clattered off. The metallic ring echoed through the room, sharp and uncomfortable. Like everything else. I stooped to pick it up.

BAHROOOM!

The warning horn call tore through the night with a force that vibrated in my bones, a single deep note that set the wards humming and sent a jolt of cold awareness racing down my spine. The sound tore through the castle like a blade through cloth, deep and resonant. That wasn't the measured call for a shift change or the warning for an approaching storm. Someone had escaped.

And I knew exactly who.

I was moving before conscious thought caught up, crossing the study in long strides to the narrow windows overlooking the inner yard. I braced my hands against the cold stone sill, pushed the window open, and looked down.

Shouts erupted on the icy wind, boots pounding in frantic disarray as the courtyard exploded into motion. Guards poured from doorways and stairwells, breaking instinctively into practiced formations. One unit sprinted for the main gates, weapons flashing as they ran. Another surged toward the castle entrance and the stairs beyond it. The rest scattered outward, fanning toward every access point along the walls as the horn continued its relentless call.

Bouncing golden hair drew my eye toward the eastern parapet.

There—running along the upper wall.

Hannah moved low and fast along the walkway, her dark coat blending too well with the stone despite the wind clawing at her hair. Even at a distance, I recognized her, as if everything in me was drawn to her and demanded I be as close to her as possible.

A snarl rose in my chest.

Two guards turned toward her position, shouting as they ran, while another leaned over the wall to look down into the courtyard, shouting orders I could not fully hear. She ducked behind the waist-high parapet, then surged forward again, hugging the shadows as arrows were nocked above her.

"Hold," someone shouted from the tower.

Another voice barked, sharper. "There—on the eastern wall!"

She broke into a sprint.

The first arrow screamed past her, striking stone ahead with a shower of sparks. She veered instinctively, shoes skidding for half a breath before she caught herself and kept moving. Another arrow followed, closer this time—close enough that I felt it in my own bones.

My hands curled into fists against the stone. *How dare they harm her!*

"Don't kill her!" a voice carried up from below, high with panic. "The king wants her alive!"

Good. At least, someone was thinking.

But the archers were still firing.

She ran harder, pushing through the wind, and for a heartbeat, I thought she might make it cleanly to the eastern tower. Then an arrow struck.

Not squarely.

A glancing blow cut the back of her calf, and she stumbled with a sharp cry. Blood darkened the fabric of her trousers almost instantly, but she did not fall. She caught herself on the wall, teeth bared, then forced herself upright and kept going.

Something inside me snapped.

Rage flooded my veins, hot and blinding, magic surging beneath my skin hard enough that the air around me prickled. I wanted to tear the bow from the hands of the archer responsible and hurl him from the tower. She was wounded. She should have been down. She should have been caught.

Instead, she ran.

Pride cut through the fury like a knife and mixed within me.

Damn her stubbornness.

She slammed into the eastern watchtower door and fumbled with the lock as guards closed in behind her. Arrows struck stone at her feet, one embedding so close I felt it as if it had pierced my own flesh. She wrenched the door open at last and disappeared inside just as a guard reached the corner, sword raised. The door slammed shut.

I tore away from the window and crossed the study at a

near run, the room blurring past me. There was no chance she was escaping me. I'd track her to the ends of this realm and beyond if she thought she could escape. I burst out into the hall and down the stairs.

To the first guard I saw, I shouted, "Get the hounds!"

CHAPTER 8

Hannah

I stopped with a jerk. Panic clawed my chest. I grabbed at the wall with one hand and shoved my toes into a narrow crack.

I glanced upward, and my stomach churned. Shit! The knot wasn't seated right. The rope crept through the binding loops as the fibers twisted above me.

Snow fell in soft flakes, dusting my head, and the night sky was jet black except for a few stars and the moon itself shining above. Footsteps thundered toward where I'd tied the rope, getting closer and closer.

My heart tried to ram its way through my ribs, and I forced myself to breathe evenly. I had to calm my panicking mind, or I would be caught. I needed to climb down faster than the sliding knot was unraveling. At least, that way, the fall would be more controlled than plummeting the entire way down.

The wall tore at my gloves, coat sleeves, and jeans. As the rope bit deeper, friction-heat built in my palms until it felt like my skin might split. Snow blew into my face and melted against my lashes. With the two contrasting temperatures, I wasn't sure which was worse.

The knot slipped again, and my feet skated over an icy patch on the wall. My body dropped a full foot before I caught myself, and a raw groan ripped from my throat.

My chest slammed against the stone, and I kept one hand locked around the rope and the other gripping the rock as I scrabbled for purchase. My fingers slipped, causing my lungs to stop working, but I managed to catch on to a seam in the wall and cling as best I could. My nails dug into the stone grooves, and if not for the gloves, I'd probably have shredded my fingertips.

I glanced down to see packed earth and dark stone still a couple dozen feet below me. From this height and in this light, I couldn't tell for sure. I had no chance of coming away from a fall like that with anything less than broken bones. Maybe death. I had to get lower before I risked jumping.

The rope creaked and tensed but held.

Well, flitter. I had to get the hell away from King Grouchy Butt. I swallowed hard and made my hands move, inching them down as my toes searched for leverage. All I found were shallow seams and frost-slick stone, which didn't help much, but at least I wasn't free-falling.

Don't rush. Don't freeze. Be methodical.

I slid another foot lower, my muscles trembling as the rope shifted again. The knot above me groaned, a subtle, awful complaint that vibrated through the rope and straight into my bones. My stomach dropped as the rope gave another fraction. *Shit!*

"Get that rope before she falls!" a deep voice shouted.

"The king's calling for the hounds! Go tell them she's headed down the eastern wall. Send them out the eastern gate in case we can't drag her up," another voice called out.

My panic spiked. Hounds? Definitely *not* what I needed.

Visions of floppy-eared dogs with drooling maws and sharp teeth flashed through my mind. But who knew what they'd look like here, or what they might do?

I tried to move downward faster without putting too much stress on the rope. My shoes skidded, caught, then skidded again. The wall chewed at my gloves, front, and sleeves, fabric rasping against rough stone. The pulse in my ears pounded so loudly that I couldn't hear them above me anymore.

Slowly, I made it another foot down...then another.

The ground inched closer, but I was still too high. If I shoved outward and dropped, I could aim for the roof of the closest building in the row built near the castle wall, but it was so steep I'd probably slide off and fall just as dangerous a distance.

My arms shook with the effort to control every movement as my heart raced faster.

Above me, metal scraped stone. I looked up again. A helmeted head appeared between the stones, then another. Snow shook loose as they leaned farther out.

"There—she's on the rope there!" A dark figure jabbed a finger in my direction.

"Grab it!"

The line jerked.

My body slammed into the wall, ribs cracking against it hard enough to knock a cry out of me. Fucking bastards! The impact rattled my teeth and sent pain flaring down my side as the rope slid another inch through my grip. Heat screamed across my palms through the gloves, fierce and immediate.

"No—" The word tore free as I clawed at the stone while my fingers scrabbled uselessly for a hold.

The rope shifted again. I forced myself to descend, my hands sliding despite my rubber-soled shoes fighting for cracks to catch a grip. My breaths came fast and shallow, fogging the air in front of my face.

When I glanced up again, a gloved hand appeared above me, fingers reaching through the gap in the wall.

Then the rope snapped taut.

My feet ripped free of the stone as the guards hauled upward. My body swung out into open air for a sickening second before I smashed back into the wall. Pain exploded through my shoulders. I gasped, my vision flashing white, one hand locking around the rope while the other grabbed at the wall.

They pulled again.

I slid upward despite myself, the rope biting cruelly into my arms as my shoes couldn't find any traction. Snow spun past my face, blinding me in quick bursts. I kicked, twisted, fought to drag myself down instead of up, forcing my hands to slide farther down the rope even as my skin and muscles screamed in protest.

But the ground was closer now, and I would run out of rope fast.

Heart hammering, I risked a glance down. Ten feet. Maybe a little more. Close enough that fear shifted, sharp and focused, into calculation.

"Pull!" The command rang out in the icy air above me.

I didn't wait for them to drag me higher.

I let go.

The world dropped, and my stomach lurched into my throat. Cold air tore past me as I twisted into the fall the way experience and instinct demanded, body loose, knees bent, chin tucked. I hit the ground hard, the balls of my feet striking first and my knees bending as far as they could before my body folded, and I rolled so that my hip and shoulder slammed down hardest. Pain detonated through my side, snow and grit tearing at me, stone scraping my back.

I came to a stop, gasping, the ground brutal and real beneath me.

Holy shit. I'd made it in one piece.

Shouts exploded above the wall. "She's loose!"

"She's on the ground!"

"Is she dead?"

I sucked in a breath that felt like knives slicing my lungs and forced myself upright while pain roared inside me. I'd be sore tomorrow—if I got to see tomorrow at all. My legs trembled but held, and I pushed away from the wall before they could decide otherwise.

"Awooo—wooorrrr—awoooo!" A long series of howls rolled from beyond the castle walls.

The sound carried, low and resonant, cutting cleanly through the panic and noise, echoing off stone in a way that made my skin prickle. More howls answered, closer, the rhythm deliberate enough to turn my stomach.

Cold air burned my lungs as I pulled in a measured breath and let it out, grounding myself in the weight of my body and the scrape of snow beneath my shoes. I was upright and moving. Even better, my cut leg wasn't hurting nearly as much.

The space I'd landed in was a narrow lane that ran between the outer castle wall and the inner edge of the surrounding town. The buildings didn't press close here. They stopped short by design, leaving a clear buffer of stone and packed earth wide enough for groups of people to fit through. It was built to limit cover for anyone near the wall, but the alleys between the buildings looked to have more overhang to hide me.

Snow lay unevenly across the ground, churned by boots and wheels, darkened in places by ash and cinders. The air smelled of damp stone and old smoke, like the residue of a thousand fires burned and cleared away. Fresh prints wouldn't show for long, even as the new snowflakes dropped and clung to the dirty surfaces.

Straight ahead, through the buildings, I could see what was likely the main road, where torchlight flared and people ran in every direction, voices overlapping in fear and confusion.

"The Night King is attacking!"

"No, it's an escaped prisoner!"

"They've sent the hounds! Don't get in their way!"

Another horn blast sounded. Based on what I'd seen from the walkway, I guessed that the eastern gate lay to my right. If the hounds came through that gate, they would sweep this lane first.

I turned away from the street and ran down the alley between the nearest set of buildings.

My shoes crunched over the thin layer of snow as I scanned the ground and the structures around me. The town appeared to be set up on a rough grid. Pools of peach-orange light surrounded tall iron lampposts, and dark wood structures were set at regular intervals. From the wall, when I'd peered over, I'd seen at least four sections of buildings before the main road that led out of the castle. It opened into a large marketplace square. As I ran, I glimpsed the main road, where people milled and shouted. Several homes had single torches in the windows, as if the occupants had been roused from sleep and hadn't lit up every room.

The hounds would come out of the main gate, and then they'd track me fast.

I needed to find something to mask my scent. What might be available in a city that probably had less tech than Game of Thrones? Ash might work.

Heart hammering in my throat, I ducked into a gap between buildings and scanned for anything useful. There were stacks of firewood in iron rings, a pile of broken crates, and seven barrels sitting beneath the overhang of a broad-roofed shop. Fine gray powder and black chunks were scattered around the bases of the barrels, and a sign with an anvil hung out front. *Probably a blacksmith.* Sweet! I ran up and lifted the lid of one barrel and found it contained powdery gray ash.

Good enough for me. I glanced over my shoulder once more to make sure no one was watching, then plunged my hands in, hoping this ash didn't have anything toxic mixed with it. The ash was fine and cold as it coated my gloves. I worked it into my sleeves, my coat, my hair, grinding it in with urgency. Its scent, dark and choking, dulled any other smell, clinging to fabric and skin alike. But I couldn't put on too much. I needed to apply just enough to mask my scent and not enough to leave a grimy trail or make myself choke. Thank goodness I didn't have to bathe myself in it. Even just enough to mask my scent made my head spin and made me feel gritty.

More howls sounded, closer now, threaded with excitement as they rose in pitch.

My shoulders hitched. Shit, they were close. Part of me just wanted to run, but I forced myself to be thorough, rubbing ash over my shoes and ankles, pressing it into seams where heat lingered, and all over my hands.

More shouts echoed from beyond the walls as the howling intensified. Heavy metal groaned, and chains clanked, as if a gate was being hauled open.

I jumped to shake off the remnants of the ash so that I wouldn't leave a traceable path behind. My wounded leg barely protested at all, and my body no longer ached as if I'd been beaten. While I wasn't one to look a gift horse in the mouth, this lack of pain was not what I expected. As soon as I was safe, I needed to figure out what was going on.

I circled the blacksmith shop and crossed the lane diagonally, taking care to step in other people's footsteps, and slipped back toward the wall farther down from where I'd fallen. Ash clung to me like a second skin.

The howling intensified along with yips, and a rage-filled roar cut above the chaos.

My body tensed, and an odd tug twisted in my chest.

What the fuck was that? Heat spilled through my veins and pooled in my belly, rushing faster and hotter as a sudden urge to charge at the source of that bellow pulsed through me.

I shook my head. *No! What's wrong with me?*

I kept moving, forcing myself to focus. Ash would dull my scent, but it might not completely erase it, especially with fear and sweat clinging to my skin. I needed layers of confusion, something alive and overwhelming enough to tangle the trail beyond easy recovery.

I pushed myself into a stealthy trot, angling away from the wall and following the rear line of the buildings rather than the open street. This part of the city was quieter, built for labor instead of trade. I passed storage sheds, tack rooms, and long, low structures set back from the places of business that looked more like dwellings. A warm, familiar, earthy scent reached me.

I'd know that smell anywhere.

Horses.

A stable stood ahead, its wide doors shadowed beneath a slanted wood-shingled roof.

Relief tightened my chest as I veered toward it and shoved my way inside just as another chorus of howls rolled through the night.

Heat wrapped around me immediately, thick with the scents of hay, leather, fur, and manure. Torches burned low along the walls, casting amber light over rows of stalls. Eight shaggy horses lifted their heads, ears flicking and breath steaming in the warm air. A pair of caribou shifted restlessly a few stalls down from me, antlers brushing wood as they turned, while several elk glanced my way with mild interest before settling again, unimpressed by my arrival.

Apparently, an odd-smelling stranger bursting in in the middle of the night wasn't that alarming a prospect for them.

I ran straight through the stable, dragging my scent across as many surfaces as possible. I brushed past a horse's flank, ducked beneath hanging tack, kicked through old bedding, and shoved open the far doors. Hopefully, the scent of manure and hay now masked my path. If the hounds followed me in here, they'd stay for a while. Now I had to find a better place to lie low for a bit. Riding out of here on a stolen horse would be epic, but galloping through a strange city in a bizarre world I didn't know would also draw a lot of attention, and I had no idea where to go. It would be much easier to figure out the best path forward if I could just disappear into the shadows until the hunt died down. If it turned out I could use a horse, I could double back and grab one. For now, it made more sense to stay on foot.

Outside, the shouts grew louder.

"Did you hear that?"

"Get a torch! The hounds are coming!"

"Who escaped?"

"Should we get to the shelters just in case?"

I stopped in front of the stable doors and peeked out. Nine men and women in heavy fur and wool coats stood about twenty feet from the door, gesturing toward the castle. A woman with curly black hair leaned back to peer into the alley, her eyes white-rimmed. "Who escaped? Why are they making such a fuss?"

"Probably something to do with the Night King," a man in a thick fur hat responded.

A yip sounded from back near the blacksmith, and the hounds howled louder.

A few more doors opened. Lanterns bobbed to life and

floated like fireflies, yellow light splashing over snow and timber. People moved into the lanes, half-dressed and half-awake, some clutching tools, others weapons they clearly weren't used to holding. Most started toward the main road, calling out to one another to find out what was happening and whether they were under attack.

I inhaled shakily. *This* would help me blend in and cover my scent with those of many others. I slid out and darted forward, pretending to be one of the fleeing townspeople and matching my pace to theirs.

I spotted a building ahead, situated between two others, that looked completely dark, its roof slick with snow and icicles. No torches burned within, and the windows were sealed with slab shutters. Along the left side of the house, a window without glass was partly covered by a shutter hanging slightly askew, its hinge bent just enough to leave a narrow gap.

It had been a long time since I'd broken in somewhere, but that bent shutter was my best shot. I slid into the alley as if I belonged and tested the wood shutter. It was old, the wood swollen and splintered at the edges. I slipped my right hand out of my glove and gently slid it up to test the shutter for weaknesses. There. My fingers found the tension point. I pulled the knife out of my coat pocket and used the blade to work the shutter open.

"Awooo—wooorrrr—awoooo!"

That sounded much closer than I wanted.

Heart racing, I widened the opening carefully, then hopped up to wiggle inside, catching just a glimpse of a small room with sheets over the furniture. The opening pinched my hips and then released, and I fell into the cool darkness. With a squeak, I rolled and landed on a rug. I sprang up at once and put the shutter back into place.

Darkness closed around me.

I pressed my back to the wall and held still, every muscle coiled as I strained to listen beyond the rush of blood in my ears. Outside, the howling rose again, closer now, then scattered, the sound breaking and overlapping as the hounds continued their search. Had they reached the stable yet? It was hard to tell.

I moved slowly, one hand outstretched, feeling along the wall to orient myself. The powdery residue of the ash was making my skin itch. The darkness was near complete. I tried to count my steps and listened for any sign of movement in the house. Nothing. Just the sound of my own breathing and the distant chaos of the hounds outside.

It took a minute for my eyes to start making sense of the room. It was small, close, a weird mix of old furniture under sheets and flat stale air. I edged forward, hip-checking something low and soft—a couch, probably. The whole place smelled musty with a sweet undertone of something I couldn't place. I kept moving, sidestepping what might be an old table. My fingers found the edge, chipped and gouged. I trailed my fingers to the corner, then groped along the wall until the room widened.

Soon, I found what I guessed was a door, based on the planks. Pressing my ear to it, I listened.

No voices, no footsteps. Just the creak of wood as the building settled into the cold. Bracing, I pushed the door open inch by inch. It didn't squeak, just made a low, heavy sound like a sigh. The next room was a little brighter. A small fireplace sat against the far wall, the embers barely glowing. Two windows at the far end were shuttered with slats, hints of torchlight sliding through and casting just enough light to roughly make out the shapes of more furniture. If I had my bearings right, this side of the house faced a narrower road than the alley I'd come out of.

I edged forward, pressing close to the wall as if it were the only thing keeping me upright, and caught the edge of my shoe against a warped floorboard. The dull thud seemed to ring far louder than it should have, spreading through the house.

My pulse spiked. I froze mid-step, breath locked in my chest, muscles coiling tight as I listened for a response—shouting, a crash, the thunder of boots rushing in from outside, or the hounds howling louder.

Nothing came.

After a painful moment, I relaxed and let a tight breath loose. My heart continued to pound, loud enough that I was certain it could be heard.

It was warmer in here, at least. Not comfortable, but sheltered. The air carried the faint scent of charred wood, the lingering trace of stove and hearth that had been used earlier and allowed to die down, much like the embers in the fireplace. Whoever owned the house hadn't been here for hours.

Relief loosened something in my chest. I could stop and catch my breath for a moment. Just a moment. I needed to tend my leg, steady myself, and think. Running blindly would get me captured faster than the guards would otherwise find me.

Metal scraped at the front of the door, and I startled.

The lock clicked.

The front door scraped open with a sudden shove, torchlight pouring into the room in a harsh spill of gold and shadow. I sucked in a breath and lifted my arm too late to shield my eyes, blinking against the brightness as a tall figure filled the doorway. I noted thick red-brown hair dusted with snow and unruly from the wind.

I didn't have a chance to find cover. The man was just there and staring at me, shock flashing across his face as his gaze locked with mine. His mouth opened, already forming the shape of a shout.

CHAPTER 9

Hannah

I lifted my left hand so the palm faced the man in the doorway and kept my right hand down, the knife clenched in it tight. Every muscle within me braced for the moment he decided to shout. My heart slammed so hard against my ribs that it hurt.

"I'm not here to hurt you or anyone else." The words tumbled out of my mouth, too fast despite trying to keep my voice steady. I adjusted my stance, calculating whether it would be safer to go out the back through the window or take advantage of his surprise and charge out the front.

He snorted. "And you expect me to believe that? That's exactly what someone would say if they did want to hurt someone. Step forward."

My stomach churned. The last thing I wanted to do was step closer to him without knowing if he'd attack, but at the same time, not moving closer meant he'd most likely alert the guards, and my chance of freedom would be eliminated. I was damned if I did and damned if I didn't. Somehow, I always managed to get into situations like this. This time, I couldn't easily find a clever way out.

Taking a shaky breath, I took a step forward.

As soon as I did, he moved closer to me. He tilted his head and narrowed his eyes as he scanned me. After a few seconds, he straightened his shoulders. "Fine. I'll hear you out. Just give me a moment." With a curt nod, he stepped fully inside and closed the door with his heel.

The latch slid into place with a soft, final click that sent a cold ripple down my spine.

He deadbolted it before he looked back at me and said, "Let's get some light before we continue this conversation. You're safe here as long as your story measures up. There's no need for violence."

His abrupt shift in manner set me on edge, but he wasn't going for help or a weapon. Though, even without a weapon on him, he looked like he could land a solid punch, and from this distance, I wouldn't have the advantage of surprise as I'd had against Scar Jaw and Lilac Eyes. But I wouldn't go down without a fight.

He moved to the hearth, his boot steps loud on the wood floor. Then he knelt, his form becoming a dark bulk that blotted the mouth of the hearth into a larger darkness. I edged back toward the narrow hall as my hand clenched tighter on the knife.

"Hroooof—roo—roo—awrr." The howling had taken on a more agitated sound.

Metal clanked near the fireplace, and something stirred in the hearth. He was stirring up the embers with a poker—that could be a weapon.

I compensated by stepping back once more and preparing to make a run for it.

The embers flared, bringing a burst of soft light that faded shortly after. He grunted, set the poker aside, and then picked up a split log from a box near the hearth that I'd missed. "Sorry about the dark." His voice was as pleasant as if we were discussing going to see a movie after bumping into each other at the gym. "I was out far longer than I intended today, and nearly everything burned down to ash and embers. But this ironwood holds heat well, and the coals stay hot much longer than pine or cedar. You cold?"

A small shiver wracked me, giving me away, though I didn't want to admit to any weaknesses right now. As he set the wood on the fire grate, it thunked into place. He put on more wood and stirred the coals again, sending up myriad sparks. They circled and spun until they vanished up the chimney.

"No...." I offered a dramatic shrug, lifting one eyebrow. "It's hot as summer at noon on the lake. In fact, I'm thinking of ditching my coat and just running barefoot through the streets."

He chuckled. "Yeah, it's been ages since we've had spring or summer. These days, we have three temperatures: cold, very cold, and bone-achingly cold."

The first log caught fire, and light flared through the room, casting everything in an orange glow and lighting his profile. He kept his back to me, which worried me. I wouldn't put my back to a stranger like that. Especially not in the middle of the night when they had no business being in my home. Still, I took advantage of the light to examine my surroundings.

Two low-seated dark linen couches sat to the left of the fireplace, spaced around a squat wooden table bearing numerous ring stains, scorch marks, and scuffs. A set of cabinets lined the wall on the right, all closed with heavy wooden doors and iron latches. Two oil lamps sat in cubbies, and another two lamps sat on shelves on the wall. The only windows were on the same wall as the front door, one without glass and one with. That was odd. It had to be intentional, though I wasn't sure what the reasoning was. Both had shutters with evenly spaced latches, unlike the one in the backroom I'd crawled through. A bench sat just beneath the window to the right of the door, and beneath that bench was a pair of worn leather boots. A hook on the wall to the left of the bench was bare and waiting for one coat. I guessed he was the only person who lived here and that he didn't often receive guests.

The wall above the hearth was a mural of its own: hooks held drying bundles of herbs, coils of string, a rusted saw, a strip of beaten leather, a pair of scissors that looked ancient, a waxed cloth pouch, a long-handled ladle, and above all of it, a strange curved horn, longer than my forearm, gray and ridged, probably from some beast I'd never seen before.

He blew on the coals, then hummed when the other logs caught fire too. When he stood, I was able to really see him for the first time. He was not quite as tall as King Grouchy Pants, but he was still a few inches taller than me. Loose red-brown curls framed his face, and his dark-brown eyes scanned me with a startling level of calm and ease. When he removed his gloves and shrugged off his coat, I noted he had a runner's build. A series of burn scars marred his left forearm and hand, and he tugged down the cuff of his dark-blue tunic to cover them.

"I'm Olen." His gaze traveled from my ash-streaked golden hair to my grimy coat to my fingers, which were curled as if ready to fight. Something like understanding flickered there, then morphed into amusement as a grin split his face. "And I guess that explains why the hounds aren't already here. Found an ash pile, did you? That was clever. Then again, you'd have to be if you got out of the Dusk King's dungeon. What's even more impressive to me is you didn't put on too much. You masked your scent, but you don't look like you rolled in it, and you aren't leaving a trail of grime behind you. Nicely done."

Howls neared the house. I tensed and glanced over my

shoulder at the back room. The shutter was still closed but gaping a bit.

I lifted my chin. "You think the hounds are after me? Interesting." Why didn't he seem more worried? Did he think it wasn't possible for someone like me to cause him harm, or was this a trap? Something inside me twinged, urging me to run. But running now would put me in the direct line of the hounds.

He laughed, then raked a hand through his hair, combing out some of the dampness from the melting snow with his fingers. "Yeah, well, there's a prisoner on the loose. A clever one, too, by the looks of it. If it's not you, you're doing a great job looking like it is. That ash is going to be a beast to clean off, but it helped hide your trail. Personally, I put ash and rock salt around my home every few days. Anyway, it doesn't matter. You're here. You're safe. Just don't go near the windows or door until the hounds have gone on their way. If they don't catch your scent, they'll head to the market gate and the outer city wall."

I narrowed my eyes. "Aren't you going to question me? If I were an escaped prisoner, I'd think you'd be more worried."

He scoffed and stuck a twig in the flames until the end caught fire. Shielding the flame with one hand, he crossed to the nearest lamp and lit it. "King Kairos is a tyrant. He killed King Tobias, his own uncle, in cold blood and seized the throne." His jaw clenched. "It was nothing short of a tragedy and utterly barbaric. King Tobias took him and his bastard half-brother in after Kairos's birth father banished them. So, as far as I'm concerned, he's a traitor. And a traitor will always betray.

"I'm the castle surveyor, the inspector of works." He gave a slight twist of his hand and a dip of his head. "Or I used to be. I'm now the under-surveyor, little more than a purser these days. But it pays well enough, and as long as I stay out of trouble, it isn't so bad."

King Sour Face had murdered his own uncle? It shouldn't have surprised me, but a part of me twisted and ached. I couldn't imagine killing a family member, not even one I disliked. My dad had been a real bastard. He'd hit my mom and then stalked her until Aunt Maureen had had words with him. But as often as I'd imagined beating his face in, I couldn't imagine *killing* him.

"I love my people, my home. I am loyal to my court." Olen moved to light another lamp. "But I have no love for King Kairos. Thanks to him, we remain engaged in a violent, blood-thirsty war that will end only when either the Night Court or the Dusk Court is destroyed. All hope of peace died with King Tobias, because the Night King even has less interest in peace than Kairos does." He crossed to the cabinets and the nearest cubby with a lamp. "All anyone wants is an end to the war and bloodshed. But that goes against the crown." He turned, his face lit in profile from the lamp, showing a hardness in his eyes as if the cheer had drained. "My stance is that no good can come from a war without end. Neither the Dusk nor the Night Court can continue at this pace. Our resources are strained even without fighting and killing. The courts were meant to balance one another, and ever since—well, why am I even telling you this? You know all about it."

I scowled. "Why would I know about all that? I don't know *anything* about this place."

He drew back, then tilted his head as if genuinely confused. "You're either Day or Aurora Court, are you not? Your hair and your eyes...they aren't Dusk or Night."

I shook my head, still gripping the knife, causing some ash to sift onto my coat. "No. I'm from Tennessee. I fell here through a portal. Do you know how I can get back? I don't want to stay here if I can help it."

"A portal? Like through one of the enchanted mirrors?" His eyes widened. "I suppose that explains why he took you prisoner. And you came from another realm entirely?" He clicked his tongue against the roof of his mouth as his gaze grew softer and more distant. "That complicates things..." He looked at me expectantly. "What's your name?"

"Hannah. And, yes, I'm not from here. But what I'm getting from you is that there *are* other portals. The one I fell through appeared in the air over the courtyard and then vanished." There didn't seem to be any harm in telling him how I'd gotten here. I had to trust someone, and he hadn't thrown me to the hounds yet.

"That's pretty powerful magic. How did you conjure it?" He scratched the back of his neck as his brow furrowed.

"I didn't. It just...formed when I touched my aunt's mirror." The howling intensified, and I cast another look over my shoulder.

He chuckled. "Sounds like you've frustrated those poor hounds to the point of tantrums. You're quick on your feet. I like that." He gestured to the couch. "Have a seat. I'll get us something to drink if you like, and then we'll see about getting you back where you belong."

Suspicion flared through me, hot and immediate. I tightened my grip on the knife. Why was he being so accommodating? Why wasn't he demanding something or threatening me? People didn't help strangers for nothing, especially strangers who'd climbed through their window in the dead of night. "You're being awfully generous with your time and resources. I'd have thought you'd be more upset that I broke into your home."

"A beautiful woman broke into my home in the middle of the night after escaping someone I consider a foul and rotted soul. You haven't hurt me. Why would I be angry?" His gaze flitted past me to the hall. "It doesn't look like you broke anything either. I'm guessing you got in through the formal sitting room. That shutter has needed repairing for a while, especially with the missing glass."

"Did someone else break in?" It had looked as if I weren't the first to get in through the window.

"No." He shrugged, a wry smile on his lips. "Times have been hard, so I traded the glass for other supplies. I rarely use that room anyway, and no one here has much in the way of valuables. Besides, sometimes my brother visits and...well, he isn't always on good terms with the law. Nothing harmful, I promise. He's a good man underneath it all. Just doesn't want to be a part of any court or nation." He crossed to a cabinet and opened it. Inside were several dark, squat bottles. He removed one along with two wooden cups.

He brought them to the table and poured two glasses of what smelled like cinnamon, cloves, and nutmeg.

My mouth watered. The liquid didn't have the scent of apple cider, but it was close enough to send a pang of homesickness through me. Aunt Maureen had always loved cider.

He offered me the nicer of the two wooden cups. After I took it, he sat and propped his feet up on the table, lifted the cup as if toasting me, and took a long drink. "There. That's better."

I didn't move, holding the cup in one hand with the knife in the other. The situation felt too good to be true, and that unsettled me. Good things didn't happen to me without something equally bad or worse following. As bad as getting trapped here and threatened by His Majesty of the Perpetual Scowl and Bad Mood had been, things could always get worse. Olen could be trying to stall me. Keep me here until the guards found and recaptured me.

I glanced at the door once more, ears straining to identify where the hounds were now.

He shrugged, then took another long drink and wiped his

mouth on his sleeve. "I'm not going to hurt you, Hannah. I've got no reason to. You're clearly in a bad spot. Is it so hard to believe that someone might be willing to help you just because you're in need?"

Oddly, I'd believed that about Ashren, and especially Thea. There'd been something about the way Thea had carried herself and spoken that had made me feel like she'd have anyone's back if she thought they needed help. Ashren had seemed more cautious, as if he measured costs and decided on the best path rather than helping just anyone.

With Olen, maybe my sense of unease had grown because I wouldn't be so calm about someone breaking into my home. I found it hard to trust him. Even if he did have an incredible smile and a way about him that made me *want* to. "Yes."

He chuckled at that, then snagged the bottle and refilled his cup. "Fair enough. You've probably dealt with more than your share of problems. Beautiful women always do. But you don't have to trust me just because you're here. I'll prove that you can. If you like, I'll even take a sip of your drink so you can see it's not poisoned."

I smiled despite myself. "And what if you're immune to it?"

"Ach! You wound me!" He pressed a hand to his chest and grinned. "You really are a smart one. But no, I wouldn't drug or poison you with this. This is clovefall whiskey. To add anything, even ice, would be an insult. The one benefit of everything being so cold these days is that it's far easier to keep our alcoholic beverages at their ideal temperature. A small silver lining, but a silver lining nonetheless."

The familiar turn of phrase made me smile. Had it leaked from my world into this one? Perhaps I wasn't the first person to pass from my realm to this place. In fact, that made sense because somehow the dagger and the mirror had been in the iron chest under the rowan tree. That also meant there had to be a way back.

"My point is that you don't have to be afraid. You can stay on guard, hold that knife if you like, but you don't have to worry about me, and you can take all the time you like to determine how you feel. We're going to need time to get you to a working portal. I might know someone who can help." He wobbled his hand. "That will likely be for a price. My friend is a little more financially savvy than I am, and taking pleasure in the king's frustration and rage won't be enough for him."

"How much? And how long might it take?" I set the cup down on the table and tested my weight on my formerly injured leg. Aside from a little tightness, the pain had all but vanished. As I mentally scanned my body, I noticed that the stiffness from the fall had faded as well. It hadn't just been adrenaline masking it. If I'd drunk the clovefall whiskey, I might have credited it. Except then, there was the matter of my hand. I glanced at my palm and saw that no trace of the cut remained.

Olen tipped his head back as he drank, his throat bobbing. His gaze slid past me to the hall, then up to the ceiling, as though he were sorting through old memories hidden in the beams. "I don't know, Hannah. Maybe a favor. Maybe something rare." His mouth curved, but there was no amusement in the smile. More like concerned contemplation he was trying to hide. Something had him worried. "Let's wait until the hounds have cleared off and gone back to the castle with their tails between their legs. You can rest until tomorrow night, and then we'll find my friend. Days here are short lately, so you won't have to wait long."

Sleeping sounded like a great way to get caught. "Any chance we could move faster than that?"

"Hmmm. Well, not safely. I assume you want to keep the

king from knowing what you're doing? Most folks are loyal to him because they believe he has the Dusk Court's best interests at heart. There might be a few who would help you, but they're cautious." His jaw tightened. "Especially these days."

"Why *especially these days*?" I walked to the far wall and then back, keeping my eyes fixed on him as I examined my surroundings more.

"Well—" he started.

A heavy knock sounded like a fist to my ribs.

"Open this door. Now," a familiar, deep voice demanded.

My stomach dropped hard, as if the floor had vanished from beneath my feet.

Kai.

CHAPTER 10

Hannah

The king knocked again, harder, rattling the door in its frame and sending a puff of dust drifting down from the joist. The groaning sound went straight through me, and my breath hitched as if my lungs had forgotten how to work.

My gaze snapped to Olen, and my heart skipped a beat. I expected calculation, betrayal, or some flash of triumph. Instead, the color drained from his face, the easy warmth gone like it had never been there. His shoulders drew tight, and his eyes focused on the door.

Another blow landed, followed by the scrape of boots against stone. "Open this door. Now."

Olen caught my wrist and steered me away from the firelight and back toward the narrow hall beyond the main room. As he walked, he placed his damp boots where my shoes had been, marring the prints. His voice dropped low, just above his breath. "Go to the kitchen and take the second door. It's the larder. Don't go upstairs because the boards squeak. Don't make a sound. If his guard is with him, they'll have surrounded the house. I'll handle him."

He pressed me back, and I didn't fight. I had no clue what a fucking larder was. Guess I'd figure that out or get caught trying. I slipped down the hall, my rubber-soled shoes silent against the wood. My grip stayed tight on the knife as my pulse thundered in my ears.

"Olen! You will open this door, or it will be broken in." Grouchy Butt's shout cut through the house, followed by an even harder pounding on the wood.

The hounds howled farther away, unable to track me. The ash and stable trick had worked, so why was he here now? Could he follow me like a wolf tracking a rabbit?

Well, luck going sour was one thing I was used to.

The kitchen was dim and cold, smelling of dried herbs, old smoke, and the faint tang of iron. A solid table crouched at the center, scarred by knives and years of use, while hooks of bundled thyme and bay hung from the beams above. I crossed the space in three quick steps and slipped through the narrow wooden door that I hoped was the larder.

Thin slats and cracked plaster formed the walls, but there were tiny gaps in the inner wall between this space and the main living room. The faint glow of firelight provided enough light for me to see. The room was narrow and cramped with dry air that smelled of salt, grain, dried meat, and hanging herbs. Rough wooden shelves lined the walls from floor to ceiling, stacked with crates, sacks, and cloth bundles. The uppermost shelves held the fewest supplies, leaving enough space for me to squeeze in and hide if I could get up there.

I eased the door shut until the latch kissed wood without a sound. Darkness closed in at once, and the smell of grain and dried roots filled my lungs as I reached the thick wood shelves.

My muscles burned as I wedged a knee against a sack of grain and hauled myself up, shelf by shelf. The wood creaked softly under the strain, making my stomach twist as Kai kept pounding on the door. I worked myself stomach-down onto the highest shelf and breathed shallowly, then shifted until I had my entire body tucked into the narrow gap near the ceiling.

I turned my face toward a thin crack in the wall where the wooden frame in the plaster peeked through. Warm light bled in, painting the darkness with slashes of gold. Careful not to scrape against anything, I peered out.

Olen emerged from the hall and crossed the main room with deliberate slowness. His earlier easy manner had become rigid and strained. He reached the door and braced one hand against the wood as if steadying himself. Exhaling, he opened it with his shoulders sagging and his posture loose in a way that read as bone-deep fatigue.

"My king." He dipped his head, assuming a respectful angle that bared the back of his neck. "You honor my poor home at such a late hour. How may I be of service? Is there some matter for which the surveyor himself is unable to provide aid?"

Sour Face stood on the threshold, his dark coat dusted with frost. His presence filled the doorway as if the house itself had drawn back from him. No guards flanked him, and no armored shapes crowded the step. Just him, alone, his eyes already cutting past Olen and into the room like blades seeking flesh.

He couldn't have come alone. Maybe there were guards farther back I couldn't see. That weird tugging in my chest returned, sharper and deeper this time.

"Don't pretend you were sleeping." Smartass's gaze slid over the snow-dusted coat, the lit hearth, the lamps, the table with two cups still on it. His mouth tightened. "There's still snow on your coat that hasn't finished melting. You were awake...and entertaining."

Shit! He was observant. Had I left traces of ash behind?

Olen had walked over my footprints, but had he obscured them enough?

Olen let out a tired laugh that scraped out of his throat. He stepped aside just enough to make space, then stopped short of fully yielding the doorway. One foot stayed planted, a subtle block. "I returned from inspections far later than planned. The cold seeps into the bones these days, and it makes me slow. But the whiskey was from earlier. I was just headed to bed."

Kai's eyes flicked to the cups again. Then back to Olen's face. "You live alone."

"I do." Olen's hands flexed at his sides with his fingers curling and uncurling as if he had to remind them to stay still. He shrugged again, his gaze darting from Kai to some point outside. "Surely, if this is official business, it can wait until day."

Kai stepped inside without waiting to be invited, his hand pushing Olen back. The door thudded shut behind him, the sound echoing through the house and into my chest. He moved with unhurried confidence, steps silent on the wood as his gaze tracked around the room, keen and assessing. He stopped near the hearth, one gloved hand lifting as if to warm it over the flames, his profile hard and unreadable. "Where is the woman?"

Olen turned to face him. His throat bobbed. "What woman?"

The king fixed his gaze on Olen with an intensity that made my skin prickle. Only the popping of the wood and a settling log broke the silence.

Kai took a step forward. "You have surely heard the alarm and the hounds, so do not pretend with me. I will search the house." His tone made it clear this was not a request. "If I discover that you have been hiding her, you will be punished.

If I learn you have harmed her, you will die in agony. This is not a matter for your meddling, under-surveyor." His attention flicked toward the wall I lay behind as if he could see straight through it to me. My muscles locked, and every nerve screamed.

Olen stepped into Kai's path. He lifted his hands, palms open, then immediately lowered them as if he'd caught himself mid-mistake. "There's no need! Your Majesty, I swear I have helped no one escape. I guessed there was a prisoner loose, but I didn't know it was a woman. My home isn't a place any in need would choose. It's small, drafty, and offers little of interest. My mate was already taken from me. I would never dishonor her memory by being with another woman. Besides, your hounds are searching for the prisoner, are they not? I can think of no other reason for their presence."

Kai's eyes narrowed. The air in the room seemed to thicken, the warmth from the hearth turning sharp and stifling. "Step aside."

Olen shifted his weight instead, blocking the hall with his body as a bead of sweat broke free at his temple despite the cold. "I heard the hounds pass earlier. They moved toward Market Square. Whoever you seek is likely headed there. It's what I would do. I understand that all of us who speak with mortal tongues may be false, but hounds are not."

My heart hammered so hard I was sure the vibration would give me away. If Kai believed him, maybe—just maybe—

Kai's lips pressed tight, and his gaze narrowed. The sight made my blood chill. "You presume to advise me."

Spine straightening, Olen bowed his head deeper this time. "I presume nothing. I only wish to spare you wasted time."

"Then stop wasting it, and get out of my way." He pushed Olen aside and scanned the floor.

I closed my eyes and held my breath. Shit, King Grouch Face was way too observant. From this angle, I couldn't see our footprints. But sneaker treads were so different from boots. My shoes wouldn't have been as wet when I'd headed into the kitchen, so maybe I hadn't left any new prints. In my rush to hide, I'd forgotten to check.

Kai circled the couches, then returned, his gaze moving over the floor. He canted his head.

"Fine. Let me show you." He opened the cabinets, his gaze moving from Kai to the door to the ceiling. "No one in here. No one under the couches. See? This is so far beneath you, my king. I am honored by your presence but dismayed by this dishonor you have placed upon yourself."

Kai stepped closer—close enough that Olen had to lift his chin to meet his gaze. "You seem eager for me to leave," Kai said, his voice a soft blade. "In all our previous dealings, I have found you to be far more accommodating and eager for conversation. This manner of yours is... unlike you."

Blowing out a breath, Olen relaxed his shoulders a fraction and slumped, his stance seeming heavy with fatigue. "I am simply tired and cold, my king."

Kai stared at him for a long, painful moment, then shoved past him, knocking him into the wall as he headed for the hall. My pulse spiked. Olen's hands twitched at his sides, his fingers curling as if he might reach for something but was stopping himself.

The heavy *thud* of Kai's footsteps echoed around me. The nice parlor. The back room. The one with the sagging window shutter. But then there was also the kitchen. How fast would my sneaker prints dry? I'd probably been in here long enough that the earliest footprints would have distorted enough to mask the treads. And it didn't sound as if Olen had gone into the back room to cover mine. Or the kitchen....

I froze, my fingers curling in on my palms. The strange tugging in my chest intensified.

The kitchen door opened and struck the wall with a brittle thud. "Hannah of Tennessee, come out now."

CHAPTER 11

Kai

The moment I stepped over the threshold, my jaw locked, and my body coiled tight with restraint. She had escaped, and my instincts told me she was here. That tugging in my chest had given me no peace, nor had the image of her face in my mind. Already, the rage and need to be near Hannah again was tight beneath my ribs.

The baying of the hounds as they neared Market Square dulled in my ears. Most of the guards were searching there, which made sense if Hannah was trying to hide in plain sight. 'Most everyone was headed to Market Square to go into the shelters. I'd ordered my captains to call the people back and calm the mob, but many would stay underground because they were on edge. Their misunderstanding was reasonable.

But that pull within me was far too clear and precise to ignore.

Olen stood near a wall with his hands loose at his sides. His body angled slightly toward the hall, and he was too alert for a man insisting he was cold and tired. In all the years I'd known him, he had never behaved in this manner. I took him in without looking at him directly, my attention sliding to the floor once more.

His boot prints made little sense. The prints near the hearth had almost dried, but the ones near the hall had a pattern to them as if he had intentionally scuffed his feet. Leather boots like ours dried slowly, but even so, there was little reason for that odd shuffling pattern...unless he was covering for someone. And I knew who. I could feel the yank in my chest.

My shoulders tightened, and a muscle ticked along my jaw.

What reason did he have to cover for her? She'd barely been here more than a matter of minutes, and he knew well how I responded to slights against my authority.

My gaze drifted back to him and the angle of his stance. The way his weight favored the hall, as if ready to block it. Like he'd already debated how he would respond if I tried to pass. The idea of another male placing himself between me and her twisted violently in my chest. My gloved hands fisted at my sides, the leather creaking as my fingers tightened.

She had been here, and he had stood close to her and looked upon her beauty and her fire. Then he'd decided, as anyone would, that she was worth keeping and protecting. I wanted to burn his eyes out with the logs from his own fire.

I squared my shoulders and straightened to my full height. Then I took one step forward, sliding my gaze to the hall once more.

He flinched ever so slightly, but it was enough.

I pushed past him, and my shoulder caught him hard enough to knock him into the wall. He sucked in a breath but didn't protest as he looked from me back to the door and up. That alone told me everything.

The kitchen opened before me, dim and cold, the air sharp with dried herbs and old smoke. A scarred table hunched at the center, its surface bare. Bundles of thyme and bay hung from the beams, their shadows long and unmoving. No fire burned in the stove, but it smelled of ash, herbs, and grain. The trace of magnolia and apricots wasn't present, but...she was here. I sensed it.

"Hannah of Tennessee, come out now." My voice cut clean through the space. There was no tremor or softness in it. I wasn't surprised when she didn't answer. I'd met her only a few hours ago, but I knew she was stubborn. Stubborn...and infuriating. Pride stirred alongside the anger, unwanted but undeniable, tightening the knot in my chest.

Of course my mate was a pain in the ass. And a smart one too. Why wouldn't she be? Fate damn her! Once I got her back, I'd lock her away somewhere safe until I could sort out the best way forward, one that didn't involve either of us going insane or me murdering her for being a distraction. Fate help me, I just wanted this connection to be over. A fever burned within my veins.

The kitchen offered few sanctuaries for her to hide. My gaze swept it once, dismissing the open space immediately. A woman could not vanish into the air, and there were only so many places a body could fit.

I went to the cabinets first.

I opened them one by one, my movements focused and deliberate as I pretended to be in control. The cupboards held little of interest, and when I pressed my hand to their backs and knocked, only solid wood resounded. I closed each door with care, the soft click of wood against frame echoing loudly in the cold room.

Olen hovered near the doorway. "Your Majesty—"

"Silence." The table came next. I dropped to one knee, checked beneath the table where the shadows hid nothing from my sight.

That left one place.

The larder.

I crossed the kitchen in two silent steps and stopped with my hand on the latch as I listened. The damn yank in my chest intensified to the point that I feared my chest would rip open. She was close enough that I could feel it in my bones. Close enough that the thought of her, hidden and silent, made something fierce and territorial coil tight in my chest.

"Hannah." Her name was heavy and yet somehow sweet on my tongue. "This ends here." If Olen hadn't been here, I would have told her that I wouldn't hurt her.

Because I wouldn't. I *needed* her. Needed her back. Needed to know she was safe. I hated how much I needed this.

I opened the larder door.

Cold air spilled out, carrying scents of dust, dried meat, herbs, and grain, the darkness inside full but useless against my sight. Deep shelves climbed the walls from floor to ceiling, most packed tight with sacks and crates, the upper levels sparse enough to draw my eyes upward at once. My attention narrowed, instinct guiding it without conscious thought. She would go high and away from the floor and from marks that could betray her.

A sack of grain was compressed near the top shelf. A crate sat just slightly out of line.

My pulse slowed, and I readied to follow the pull in my chest to locate her.

The horn sounded.

BAHROOOOM! BAHROOOOM! The first blast tore through the night like a wound being ripped open, followed by a second, longer call that vibrated through the stone beneath my boots.

An attack? Now?!

I jerked back from the larder as the air itself seemed to

shift. I turned and broke into a run, shoving past Olen without apology.

He staggered and caught himself, and then I was out the front door. If we were under attack, then Hannah was in danger too. The wards might be enough to hold the attack off, but my gut clenched with caution. Something in the air tasted wrong.

Cold night air slammed into my face as I ran, my boots striking stone in long, distance-eating strides. Rage and tension radiated through me as I lifted my gaze skyward.

The sky had gone black.

Not clouded. Not storm-dark.

Pure, swallowing black, as if something vast had closed over the stars.

Fucking Bram! Now?

If I hadn't wanted to rip his spine out through his armor before this, I did now.

The wards above the city flared to life, silver light blooming outward in an immense arc. Frost-bright patterns unfolded across the invisible barrier, the sigils interlocking with flawless precision, and the magic sang as it rose. All was working as it should. Yet, the air tasted sharp, bitter.

All of a sudden, the light faltered, and lines fractured. The pattern froze mid-formation.

My blood went cold.

"No," I breathed, the word ripped from my chest.

The wards stopped forming.

The silver glow dulled and flickered uncertainly, sections incomplete, the magic straining and failing, as if something had severed its spine. Horror punched through me, followed by white-hot fury. We'd been sabotaged, and we were about to be breached.

Another horn sounded. This one announced the type of

threat, sharper and shriller. *KRAAAM! KRAAAM! BAHROOOOM!*

Night wyverns.

Screams erupted on the streets. I tilted my head back in time to see eight forms emerge from the darkness. One of the fire-eyed beasts wheeled about and barreled right at me.

CHAPTER 12

Hannah

I flattened my body against the shelf and turned my face so I could breathe without giving myself away. Wood dug into my ribs, and dust coated my tongue. My fingers locked around the knife until my knuckles burned. There was nowhere left to retreat, and if he climbed up here, I would have to strike because he'd want to kill me. Maybe if I injured his eyes, it would debilitate him enough that I could get the fuck away.

The thought of harming him horribly twisted into greasy nausea in my stomach. Shit. Now wasn't the time to get indigestion.

"Hannah." His deep voice landed low and thick. "This ends here."

For a heartbeat, the urge to answer coursed through me, but I clamped my lips together. What the hell was going on with me? The echo of my name lingered in the dark like something unfinished demanding completion.

I had to be losing my mind.

The door below me opened, and the faint tug in my chest strengthened. The space below me filled with his undeniable presence. I imagined him tilting his head back as he scanned the shelves, searching for me. My grip on the knife tightened. *Please don't make me hurt you.*

Time stretched thin, and I tracked the smallest sounds— the shift of his boots, the faint brush of leather as he moved, and the way he paused as if listening. My muscles burned from holding still, and my ribs screamed as I pressed farther back, counting breaths and waiting for the moment I would have to move.

BAHROOOOM! BAHROOOOM!

The sound ripped through the house, vibrating through the shelf and straight into my bones. My entire body went rigid. *Did another prisoner escape?*

Boots scraped against the floor, and the pressure of Kai's presence vanished. The door was still wide open, and I heard his footsteps quicken into a run.

I stayed frozen, the knife still clutched tight, and my heart hammering so hard it hurt.

His footsteps rushed back down the hall. I twisted my head toward the crack in time to see him race out the front door and into the street.

Wood scraped the floor at the bottom of the larder. I tensed and turned back toward the door, and then Olen appeared.

His blanched face and narrowed eyes made him look worse than when he'd faced King Grouchy Butt. "We have to go." He gestured for me to come down. "The Night Court breached the wards, and the city's under attack. It'll become a tomb if they can't get the defenses back up."

My thoughts scattered. I hoped I'd heard him wrong, but the screams and chaos outside backed his statement.

He extended a hand. "I know a way out of the city, but we have to go now. I'll try to help you get in contact with my friend if he survives this attack, but it won't do you any good if you're dead."

I couldn't argue with that logic. The air crackled with tension as I accepted his hand and slid forward. He helped me to the floor and pulled me into the kitchen. Then his hand wrapped tight around my wrist. "We have to hurry."

Still gripping the knife in my right hand, I adjusted my coat and followed him. But the tugging in my chest pulled me toward the open front door where Kai had gone, and a random pang of worry twisted in my chest. I half expected that if I stepped into that hall and looked down the space into the main room, I would see him standing there, framed by torchlight with his hands braced on his broad belt.

I shook my head. "Yeah, let's get out of here."

"We're going out the back window. We'll cut down the alley until we're clear of Provisioner's Row and go past Market Square to the overhang at the bridge near the Eastern Wall Gate." Olen started toward the hall.

KRAAAM! KRAAAM! BAHROOOOOM!

The first horn calls had been resonant, but the shrillness of the second horn sliced through my nerves like fingers on a chalkboard.

Olen gasped, and I jerked back to look at him and asked, "What?"

"They must have breached the wards already. Come on!" He shoved the back parlor door open and ran to the window, then shoved the shutter open and started to climb through.

"RRAAAAAAAH—"

A deep reptilian roar like a giant gator tore through the night, crushing my eardrums. My stomach dropped hard, and my breath punched out of me as the vibration shuddered through my sneakers and into my spine. The glass in the farthest back window rattled in its frame. *What the fuck was that?*

"Get to the shelters!" Kai's raw, furious voice rang out from the front, stretched tight as if he were straining to speak. "Get out of your houses now!"

CRRACK—CRRACK—CRRACK.

The whole house shook, and I stumbled back and to the side. My shoulder slammed into the wooden frame of the kitchen doorway. Pain flared along my ribs, but the doorway held, solid beneath my grip as the floor bucked again.

Air rushed through the house in a surge of vicious cold, dust, and billowing smoke. My eyes and lungs burned as another wrenching, long, and brutal scraping noise followed and the floor pitched again. Shelves burst open, dishes shattered, and wooden doors banged against the walls.

Another roar resembling the sound of an oncoming freight train ripped through the night. The sound rolled through my ribs until it hurt. I sucked in a breath and lifted my head, forcing my eyes open.

My chest locked, and I froze. The front of the house wasn't there. It was just gone. Had the sound been an actual fucking tornado?

Cold night air poured through the jagged opening, carrying smoke, ash, and the stink of burning oil. Broken stone and splintered wood lay in piles, glowing faintly where fallen lamps had shattered. Small flames licked along spilled oil, crawling fast over the debris, but not yet close enough for me to feel the heat.

But beyond the rubble, a massive black-scaled form filled the street. An honest-to-goodness dragon stood less than fifty feet away. Its chest rose and fell, slow and deep, breath huffing out in hot bursts that steamed in the cold air. Red-orange eyes burned in its skull, bright and molten, fixed on something in front of it with a focus that made my stomach twist. The tugging in my chest urged me forward. Kai was out there.

Wait. Why did I care about that?

A low growl rolled out of its throat, not loud, just deep enough to resonate through my bones. At the base of its neck, set between thick overlapping scales, something pulsed faintly, light blooming and fading in a steady rhythm that made my skin crawl. It looked like a dark gem. Silver light and oily smoke wrapped around its throat as if pulling it back. Something else circled its jaws and stretched beyond my line of sight.

"Your Majesty!" a shrill voice shouted from farther up the street as screams rang out. "The Dusk Forces are in defense positions at the towers. We—"

"Do not let the forces gather here! Get someone to bring the hood." Kai's voice cut the panicked person off, coming from somewhere up the street. "Let our Dusk Forces focus on the towers and getting the wards back up. Repel the wyverns, or the Night Forces...will take the keep while...this beast is... focused on me." His voice sounded more strained with each word he spoke.

Here was another what-the-hell question. What the *hell* did he mean by a hood and wyverns?

The person yelped. "But if you fall, then all our defenses will be weakened beyond what—"

"I said, *go*! This wyvern is a berserker." Kai's voice rumbled lower.

"Fate no! Everyone out!" The shrill voice might have shattered everyone's ears. "Out of the buildings now! There's a berserker wyvern in the streets, destroying everything. Leave the fires! Leave your belongings!"

"Hannah!" Olen gestured at me to come to the window. "Move your ass! That wyvern is set on killing the king, and if it's successful, it'll explode if someone doesn't remove that gem the right way. Every building in this city is at risk, even the castle. This place is dry as straw, and it will burn fast."

Children's cries cut through. A lump formed in my throat,

and I took a hurried step away from Olen and toward the wyvern.

The wyvern shook its head, snarling through closed jaws, though its movement was limited. Its claws gouged the stone path as more screams rippled to me. Overlapping voices called out.

"Clear Weavers' Lane, Smiths' Way, and Provisioners' Row."

"They're still in the house!"

"Halver! Where are you?"

"Has anyone seen Tebb?"

"He's trapped!"

The pull in my chest tightened with insistence that made my feet shift before I'd decided to move them. Heat from the burning rubble brushed my calves as I hurried out the wrecked opening of the house. Ash drifted past my face, stinging my eyes. My pulse thudded so loud it blurred the noise around me, but the pull didn't ease. It dragged me forward and straight down the street.

The wyvern's body heaved as it fought whatever was holding it. Its scales scraped stone with a shriek that made my jaw clench. Smoke streamed from between its teeth in thick ropes, curling and drifting away. Silver light flared again at its throat, with streaks stretching upward into the sky where more pale lines tried to stitch themselves into shapes that wouldn't hold.

Pale light flickered overhead, drawing my gaze up despite everything pulling me forward. High above the street, thin strands of silver burned against the smoke, bending and snapping as they tried to weave themselves into wide, broken arcs. The shapes shuddered and tore apart, then dragged themselves back together again, while lines stuttered into place before unraveling under another distant impact.

The castle towers loomed through the haze, their silhouettes jagged against the night. Massive bolts streaked out of their heights, and I made out feathered arrows and barbed harpoons that trailed light as they struck the attacking wyverns. The wyverns fell back, one beyond the city wall, but then they resumed their attacks, focusing on those towers.

The berserker in the street roared through clenched jaws, and the ones farther away answered. Piercing shouts tangled with their rumbles as people ran through the streets. My sight-line was partly blocked by the wyvern and the buildings, but I caught glimpses of movement through the alley, cloaks whipping and faces smeared with soot and terror. Guards and soldiers raced to what was likely their designated positions for the fight. I looked down the street, and my mouth dropped open. Entire sections of nearby houses had collapsed, beams jutting out at wrong angles, fires climbing greedily through broken roofs.

Motion dragged my focus back to the wyvern.

Dark shapes flared behind it and spread with a sound like thick fabric snapping in a storm. The shadows thickened and pulled together. The wyvern lurched as those shadows braced, held, and forced its massive body backward, inches at a time.

Kai stood beyond the wyvern, but now dark, sleek, shadowy wings spread from his shoulders and hooked into the stone street with curved wing claws, as if to help ground him.

My heart lurched, and I ran toward him.

He'd planted his feet wide in the torn street and locked his shoulders as if he were holding the world in place by force alone. Dark tendrils streamed from his hands and wrapped tightly around the wyvern's neck and jaws, straining toward the pulsing purple gem in its throat. The air around him shuddered, dust lifting and swirling as if caught in a current that centered on his body. He kept his gaze fixed on the wyvern like he believed he could intimidate it into compliance by will alone.

The pull in my chest intensified with urgency. My grip tightened on the knife I still held while my legs moved faster. My body leaned forward even as another part of me screamed to run the other way. I wasn't there for *him*. I just needed to understand what was going on. That was it.

Olen's voice cracked through the noise behind me. "Hannah! Listen to me! He's actually acting like a decent king right now. He's going to hold the wyvern until the area is cleared. We have to go *now*! There's nothing you can do to help."

He was right. Leaving would be the smart, safe thing to do. I didn't know how to help—I should go with Olen. But I didn't usually do the safe thing. Besides, I'd never even seen a wyvern before.

I took another step toward Kai.

A scream cut through the night, so raw the chaos settled. I jerked toward it on instinct, ready for a brawl.

On the far side of the wyvern, half-hidden by its bulk, a woman knelt near a collapsed wall. She looked close to my age. Soot streaked her face, and her hair hung in tangled waves around her shoulders. One sleeve was torn, and her hands were bloody, her eyes wide and frantic as she shoved at the fallen beam.

A small hand pushed out from beneath the rubble with fingers tiny and trembling as they scrabbled at the air.

"My baby!" The woman's voice broke as she strained against the beam. "Please—someone—he's trapped in the cellar."

The wyvern reared, snarling, and its claws ripped fresh grooves into the stone as it fought the shadows binding it. Fire flared along the rubble near the woman and caught spilled oil, creeping closer to where that small hand disappeared again beneath the debris.

I looked at Olen and waved him off. "Go on! I'll meet you there!" I wasn't certain where he was headed, but he'd given me enough details that I could figure it out. I didn't want to put him in any more danger than he was already facing, especially after he'd helped me.

Bolting over the broken stone, I dodged the wyvern's tail and skidded to a stop beside the young mother. The flames were only a couple of feet away from her and building fast. She tugged at the beam, and I realized it was thicker than it had looked from a distance. I moved beside her, set the knife aside, and said, "Let's lift on three."

She looked at me and nodded, her lips pressed tight.

From inside the cellar, the child cried out, "Mother, don't leave me!"

"I won't leave you, sweetheart." She grabbed the beam again.

I adjusted my grip. "One. Two. Three!" Together, we lifted. Pain shot up my arms as I shoved. My muscles locked, and my teeth ground together as the wood scraped against stone. The woman cried and shoved with me, her hands slick with blood and soot and her shoulders shaking as she leaned her weight into it.

The street shuddered, and stone cracked somewhere close by, followed by a heavy crash that rocked the ground. The wyvern's tail whipped past in a blur of black scales and slammed into a pile of rubble hard enough to send chunks of stone skittering across the street. One struck my shin, and I hissed, nearly losing my grip.

Gritting my teeth, I pushed harder, breath tearing out of me in ragged bursts. The beam lifted a fraction, enough for the stones beneath it to shift.

The child's hands clawed at the gap, pushing aside bits of rubble.

"Climb up!" his mother cried out.

"I can't! It's too high." His voice broke as he started sobbing again.

The sound twisted my heart, and tears pricked my eyes. I tried to adjust my grip on the beam and brace it against my shoulder, but it was too heavy. We had to wedge it against something, or it was going to fall and crush all of us. The fires spread across the rubble, the heat making the snow and ice melt and sizzle as it evaporated.

"Let's wedge the beam against the wall. I'll try to hold it up while you get him." My shoulder already ached, but I braced myself. I refused to let this child die.

Together, we shoved the beam until we'd narrowly wedged it onto another broken beam on the wall. I staggered, bracing my shoulder against the wood to keep it from dropping. The heat spiked as fire crept closer, sparks snapping against my coat. "Hurry!"

She dropped to her knees and started clearing away the rubble as she reached for the child. "I'm coming, sweetheart. Stay calm."

The beam shuddered against my shoulder as the wall behind it groaned. Stone ground on stone with a low, sickening rumble while dust sifted into my hair and collar. Hot grit stuck to my skin as the fire crept closer, and the heat and smoke stung my eyes.

Another roar tore through the street, setting my teeth on edge. The wyvern thrashed harder and wrenched its body sideways, as if it were trying to tear free by force alone. Dark smoke rose outward in billowing coils, the silver and black cords around the wyvern's snout tightening and flaring in response, pulling taut.

The very air shuddered. The silver light brightened, with lines doubling back on themselves and knotting tighter as if drawn by unseen hands. The shadows around the wyvern's neck thickened, dragging it down one inch, then another. More stones cracked, and the purple light pulsed out of the wyvern's chest.

Kai staggered and dug his feet harder into the ground, his wings pulsing and the hooks of his wing claws grinding down deeper. The darkness around him rippled as if struck by a gust. The tendrils at the wyvern's throat brightened and darkened together, pulsing faster and squeezing around the gem. The wyvern screamed through clenched jaws and slammed its tail again.

Stone exploded to my left.

The tail clipped the wall hard enough to send a cascade of rubble crashing beside us. Chunks of stone bounced across the ground. One struck the beam with a dull thud that jolted my shoulder. The wall I'd braced it against shifted, and the angle changed enough to make my stomach drop.

"No—no, no," I gritted out, digging my rubber-soled sneakers into the rubble as the beam sagged.

The mother gasped and lunged for her child, her shaking hands clawing at loose stone. Flames surged closer, licking the base of the wall, and smoke poured upward in thick, choking waves.

"Hurry!" The word ripped from me as I shoved upward with everything I had left. My arms screamed, and my muscles burned as I kept the beam in place by sheer will. "You have to hurry! I can't—"

The wall shifted again. I groaned and kept hold despite my vision blurring as heat rolled over us in suffocating waves. A pained cry rose in my chest. Then the plaster crumbled.

CHAPTER 13
Hannah

A hand slammed against the remnants of the wall beside me, causing me to startle. I lifted my head in time to see Olen crowding in behind me, his face streaked with blood and ash.

"Took me a moment to get free of the window." He set his jaw and pressed his shoulder under the beam. The wood groaned, lifting another inch as his strength joined mine. My arms screamed, and my vision darkened at the edges, but I held strong. I could have kissed Olen, considering how happy I was to see him.

The child's hands reappeared, grasping wildly at the edge of the hole. His mother leaned farther in, one knee sliding on ash, fingers locking around his arm.

She hauled hard, straining as the child's shoulder cleared the edge. "I've got you," she sobbed. "I've got you."

The beam dipped another inch, and pain exploded through my shoulder as I fought to keep it from dropping. Olen grunted and shoved up harder, grinding his boot into the ground to keep it from sliding.

Another impact rocked the street, and the beam jolted as

the wall shifted again. Stones cracked loose beneath my shoes, and fire surged up the rubble pile, sparks snapping against my coat and hair. One burned my cheek. "We've got to move!"

The woman dragged the child free, clutching his small, soot-smeared body tight to her chest. The boy coughed, then cried as he buried his face in her shoulder. Limping, she carried him out of the wyvern's path.

The wyvern roared again, thrashing as the silver and dark threads cinched tighter around its throat.

"We need to shift this beam. But you've got to get out from under it before I let go because the whole wall may go with it." Olen grunted, and his face reddened with strain.

"Okay. On the count of three." I adjusted my aching hands. "One, two...three." We both pushed, and then he lifted while I ran out.

The beam scraped cracked stone and crumbling plaster as Olen shoved it aside. The grating sound ripped through my skull, and I stumbled away on legs that didn't feel like mine. My shoulder throbbed with each step, hot pain pulsing in time with my heartbeat. Smoke poured over us in thick waves, making my eyes sting until tears ran down my face.

Behind us, the wall sagged.

A low groan rolled through the rubble while loose stones shifted, slid, and dropped in a clattering rush as the fire climbed higher through the broken timbers. Orange light flickered across the street, reflecting off the wyvern's black scales and the wet street in a shimmering, feverish haze.

The wyvern wrenched its body sideways, and the street shifted as the house collapsed. The wyvern's tail snapped out in a brutal arc and clipped the ruined facade of the next house, sending a fresh spill of stone and splintered wood crashing into the street. Heat rushed out with the debris and a blast of air that smelled like burning tar and old dust.

Kai's wings pulsed wider and then dug down deeper, the

darkness around them rippling as if it had been struck. He curled his fingers and clenched his muscles harder, his jaw so tight it looked like he might crack his teeth. The black cords and silver light shooting from his hands to the wyvern thickened, dragging the wyvern's head down more as it fought, while the pulsing purple light from its chest lit then dimmed.

I'd never seen anyone face anything that big before, and I'd been to plenty of rodeos. An odd feeling knotted within me, and my heart twisted. Who was this guy? He'd murdered his own uncle, but he stood here now, facing down this huge beast and restraining it to keep his people from dying.

Kai's stance shifted, and his knees bent deeper, as if the ground were trying to shove him backward. The shadows at his hands thickened further, twisting and climbing up the wyvern's throat toward that gem, tightening until the wyvern's snarls turned ragged and strained.

I looked beyond him to scan the street. No one was coming our way carrying a hood or any sort of fabric as he'd asked for, and it seemed like his strength was waning.

Olen's hand clamped around my arm hard enough to bruise, and he yanked me back. "Come on." His eyes were bloodshot, tears running down his cheeks and leaving trails in the soot on his face. "He can't hold it much longer, and I don't think his guards are going to get here with the hood in time before it reaches him or breaks free."

I looked at Kai. "Why does he need a hood? Explain." The smoke burned my throat and made my voice raspy. I hadn't realized how much closer it was to him now. Was it getting closer to him, or was he moving in closer to strengthen whatever it was he was doing?

Olen tugged once more. "They've got to cover its eyes with a special heavy cloth. It disrupts the magic." His fingers tightened on my arm as the street shook again. "It has to be woven with the right enchantments, or you have to force the beast's outer lids shut. Wyverns can see through most things, and once a berserker wyvern locks onto a target, it doesn't let up until it or the target is dead or the enchantment's gone. It will explode into night fire if it dies while the enchantment is active, and it'll also blow if anyone tries to yank the gem free without severing the bond properly. The only way to stop it is to break eye contact consistently and completely for at least a minute so the gem can be removed safely. After that, regular magic will work on the wyvern, and it can be handled. But we don't have that cloth, so we need to move."

Another alarm shrieked through the city, cutting down my spine like ice. Olen went still beside me, his head snapping up and eyes wide as he searched the smoke-choked street.

"That means a gate was breached." His voice had gone thin. "Enemy forces are inside the walls now. Come with me if you want to live."

I blinked hard. Did he just quote the Terminator at me?

The mother was stumbling away, clutching her child tight but dragging one leg behind her as if her ankle had twisted under the rubble. The child's sobs rose and fell against her shoulder, his little hands fisted in her hair.

I pointed at the mother and her son. "Get them to safety. I'll be right behind you. I just need to take care of this."

His eyes held mine for a beat, then he pivoted toward the mother and caught her elbow before she could stumble again. "This way." He put an arm around her waist and helped her take her weight off her injured leg.

Olen steered them down the street, away from the wyvern's lashing tail and the spreading fire.

He glanced back over his shoulder. "Bridge overhang near the Eastern Wall Gate. Head straight down this path, then around the fountain with the elk." His arm tightened around the mother as he pulled her forward. "There are shelters in the brown wall under the black pines. If you aren't there by the time I get her to safety, I'm coming back for you."

I nodded and forced a smile.

Olen turned away and moved faster, guiding mother and child through the smoke and down the path. He led them to the opposite side of the road and gestured to another woman with three small children, saying something I couldn't hear.

It didn't matter. It was about time for me to ride this world's version of a bull. I focused on the wyvern as heat from the fire hit my face and ash landed on my lips.

Kai grimaced as the wyvern jerked its head again. He brought it back down steadily, his muscles straining and the veins in his neck bulging. "Move, Hannah!" he gritted out. "Go back to the castle." He didn't look like he'd last much longer before he snapped like a piece of dried cheddar. Part of me was surprised he'd even noticed me while he was trying to keep that thing contained.

Another snarl rumbled out of the wyvern, and its tail lashed back and forth. The scaled tip caught the edge of another wall and punched through the plaster as its wings flared out. The clawed tips dragged through the rubble and the fire, sending up showers of sparks as it fought to get free and move forward.

This was a stupid plan. But I couldn't let all these innocent people die because King Grouchy Pants couldn't hold a wyvern in place all by himself. I mean, I couldn't hold one in place at all—I hadn't even known wyverns existed—but I had to help.

Smoke scraped my throat with every breath, and my eyes watered. The ground quaked as the wyvern jerked hard, and the silver and dark cords around its throat snapped tight, pulling it back with a sound like strained wire.

I took a deep breath and ran toward the wall jutting up over the wyvern's back and climbed. The plaster crumbled under my sneakers, flaking and breaking with each step. But the wood underneath provided enough support for me to brace myself and move higher. One of the planks from what had once been a second floor cracked and fell past my head, sending up a spray of ash. The fire had reached the base of the wall and started crackling up, making the plaster spark.

I coughed hard but kept going, checking each handhold and pushing upward. Another groan rolled through the rubble around me as the wall creaked even louder. My eyes wanted to shift down to see how far up I was.

Nope. Stop that, Hannah. Nothing good will come of that. Sweat rolled down the back of my neck.

I reached the top of the jagged wall and hooked an elbow over it, dragged my body up, and swung a leg across, straddling the broken edge. The street dropped away on the other side in a smear of smoke and firelight. The wyvern filled the gap between buildings, its powerful muscles bunching and straining as it fought Kai's bindings. A series of dark ridges lined its spine, and the scales on its body were bumpy like a crocodile's. Plenty of handholds, as long as I was able to hold tight enough.

The wyvern whipped its tail around again, and one of the remaining walls cracked and split into two pieces, falling into the next wall like a domino chain. I didn't wait to see if it would strike the wall I'd perched on. I leaped.

For a breathless instant, there was nothing under me besides heat and smoke. Then my sneakers hit the beast's back with a skidding thud. My feet slid, and my hands shot down as I caught one of the ridges. My fingers curled around it as my body pitched forward. With a frightened grunt, I stopped myself before my body slammed into more ridges. Shit, that was close.

The ridge bit into my palms through my gloves. I gripped it tighter, my breath quickening.

The wyvern froze, its neck arching and its back dipping like a cat realizing someone was trying to pet it when it didn't want to be touched. Then it convulsed, a furious roar blasting through its sealed jaws. It thrashed and bucked as much as it could, and I tightened my grip, glimpsing Kai over its head.

Shock flashed across Kai's face, and his lavender eyes widened. "Hannah!" He lurched forward as if losing his grip on the magical strands, his dark wings flaring.

The wyvern started to jerk its body back. Kai's expression darkened, returning once more to that intense focus. The shadows around his wings flared and tightened, the silver threads glowing brighter around the wyvern's throat. His jaw locked as he dug in even more.

"Get off!" he shouted. "And get back to the castle! I might not be able to hold it, and you don't need to be here if I can't."

I coughed and dragged myself forward along the wyvern's spine. Each movement felt like climbing a moving roof in a storm. The scales shifted under my hands as the muzzled wyvern bucked, trying to throw me backward. I jammed a knee against a ridge and pulled myself forward anyway.

"Oh, screw yourself on a rusty crowbar, King Grouchy Britches." I scrunched my nose at him as I peered around the wyvern's neck from about ten feet in the air. My feet gripped the rough scales and broad neck, and my hands wrapped tight around the ridges. "Whoever is coming with the hood isn't here yet, and I don't believe in letting innocent people burn, so here I am. Don't get it twisted—I'm not here for you. Just try to keep this beast steady, and I'll handle the eyes, okay?"

The wyvern twisted again, muscles rolling beneath me in a massive ripple. My grip slipped for a breathless second, and my stomach dropped. I tightened my arms and hauled myself forward again, despite my palms burning through the gloves as the hot ridges scraped skin. The wyvern shook itself, and my head jolted back so hard that my teeth snapped and I nearly bit my tongue.

Kai shot out more tendrils of shadow and restrained it to keep it from moving closer or back, though, now that it was only perhaps thirteen feet away from him. "What did you call me?" Sweat beaded his forehead, and he knotted his fist and tucked his elbow down as if to secure it. His wings dug deeper into the stone as he braced his feet.

"Just focus on the wyvern, King Sour Face." I crawled along its neck, getting closer to its heated breath and the burning eyes I'd seen through the smoke. The gem at its throat pulsed beneath me, the throb of light rippling through the scales like a heartbeat. Dark smoke drifted from its mouth in slick coils, darkening the air beside my shoulder.

"What exactly is your plan, *woman*?" Kai demanded through gritted teeth. "If you don't get off that beast this moment, I will bind you next!"

If I survived this ride, he wouldn't be calling me *woman* much longer. I didn't care if he was a king or a drug lord. They all died in the end. I grimaced at the thought of killing someone, but I kept moving. "Yeah, well, if you're going to tie me to your bed, you have to buy me dinner first."

He grumbled something that sounded like a combination of exasperation and shock, then shot out three more silver tendrils and two more shadow cords, all wrapping around the wyvern so it couldn't thrash as much.

The wyvern tried to rear, and the world tilted backward. My stomach flipped, and my arms locked, my thighs clenching until they shook. I pressed my chest to the ridges and crawled higher, one hand at a time, until the top of its skull came into reach.

My eyes focused a little higher, at the base of the horns where they flared out from the skull and curled back like two perfect, thick handles. I glanced up and noticed the silver marks in the sky had joined together in intricate patterns. I couldn't tell where the enemy soldiers were, or even if there were any.

Hot breath blasted from the wyvern's nostrils in hard bursts, dampening my face and hair. It smelled like smoke and iron with something rancid beneath it.

The wyvern shook its head, trying to fling me off. My arms snapped straight, and pain shot through my shoulders. I grabbed the horns and swung my body forward, forcing myself into place over its head. It had a big head, but I was pretty sure I could make this work. It'd just be awkward as hell.

"Hannah of Tennessee, if you die—" Kai growled. His wings dug deeper as the rock around them cracked. The muscles in his forearms tightened even more.

"If I die, you can say, *I told you so*. Now let's just be glad I'm not wearing a dress!" I plopped myself down in the center of the wyvern's head between the horns and adjusted my grip. My pulse raced as I scooted my butt down between its eyes.

The wyvern stiffened as if shocked. Firelight flashed off wet, burning eyes that cut sideways toward me, the pupils narrowing with a fury so intense my skin prickled.

Fear choked me. Well, damn. Here went nothing.

CHAPTER 14

Hannah

Before it could paralyze me, I pushed through the fear and widened my thighs. I shoved my feet down so that I had a sneaker on top of each of the wyvern's eyelids, then pushed, lifting my butt as I clenched my glutes and core, dropping my body down with all my might.

The wyvern's thick and heavy outer lids resisted, trembling with the strain as it tried to wrench its eyes open.

Fuck! This was an awkward position.

The burn that ran through my thighs and butt hurt worse than the advanced Pilates course I'd taken after I'd been drinking the night before.

An almost indignant grumbling snarl rose from the wyvern, and it tried to jolt back. Kai made some sort of strangled gasping growl.

"Shut your eyes, wyvern!" I shouted, hoping it obeyed commands when someone was on top of it. Most guys did, so why not him too? I clenched my hands around the horns until my fingers cramped and tried bouncing to push them down more.

The lids gave a fraction, then another, grinding shut under force.

The wyvern screamed through its teeth, a furious, muffled sound. Its body thrashed beneath me, but its eyes remained closed despite the lids trembling under my sneakers. Its head snapped side to side as it tried to jar me loose. I clung to the horns and pressed harder, my calves burning and my thighs shaking as I forced the lids down again each time they twitched.

Then they finally shut, or at least it seemed like they had. I couldn't exactly see from this wide-stance reverse tabletop.

"Keep its eyes shut. I'll hold it steady," Kai bit out.

"Sounds better than dying," I snapped back as smoke clawed at my lungs.

The wyvern bucked again, violently enough that my teeth clacked and my stomach lurched. Still, the lids stayed sealed under my weight, the wyvern trembling with rage that had nowhere to go except into its thrashing body. The burn through my hamstrings and glutes intensified, and my shoulders screamed at me.

Smoke curled past my face in greasy strands until everything blurred at the edges. I locked my knees, leaned back deeper, and dug my heels down when the head trembled and the beast tried to shake me off once more. The rage-filled, muted growls rumbled through my whole body.

I couldn't see Kai anymore. The curve of my own body meant I was looking over the back of the wyvern's head and into the sky. The town was engulfed in flames, and the silver patterns continued to form in the sky. I expected to see enemy soldiers charging down the street at any minute, especially from the shouts and clashes of metal that rang from farther ahead near what I assumed was the Market Square and perhaps in the streets beyond it. The battle wasn't far away.

More silver and shadowy cords crawled over the wyvern's

neck and jaw, brightening and dimming in uneven pulses that matched the way its body shuddered beneath me.

"You're welcome," I yelled down into the chaos, breath tearing out of me as my muscles burned like the buildings beside us. I tried not to think of the fact that I was completely on display in this pose. Oh, fuck, it hurt! "In case I didn't hear your thank you and all."

A rough sound came back like half a laugh and half a snarl. "You are the most ill-timed, infuriating complication I've ever had, Hannah of Tennessee."

"Had? You never truly had me, King Kairos of Grouch Land. I escaped," I bit back. This was the longest minute of my life, and I realized I had no idea how long it would take for him to remove the gem. Talking had to help distract from the agony, right? And bonus, it made him angrier, since I clearly brought out his best side.

Another grunt followed.

The wyvern jerked hard enough that my left foot almost slipped. Agony lanced through my tensed lower back, and I tightened my grip on the horns and forced my weight down again. My sneakers ground against the lids as they twitched, trying to open.

Fast and uneven footsteps pounded over stone and debris, coming toward Kai from the direction of the castle.

"What in all the cursed hells is going on?" Ashren's breathless voice shouted. "Is she—what's she doing to its head?"

"Hey, Ashren." I forced cheer I didn't feel into my voice. "I'm just being a hood. What took you so long?"

Another set of footsteps skidded to a stop closer to the wyvern's head, and someone sucked in a sharp breath.

"Do I get up there and put the hood on now...or leave her there?" It sounded like Ashren was near Kai.

"Leave her there. Steady the wyvern. I've almost got the

gem," Kai bit out. "Don't let it slip or open its eyes, or the enchantment will backfire, and we'll all be dead."

What the fuck? I was literally sitting on a giant bomb? Olen hadn't mentioned that, if the wyvern opened its eyes, we'd all go up in flames! I'd thought, once the eyes were shut, the bomb risk went away.

"You can't be serious..." Another familiar voice rose in disbelief.

My attention jerked in that direction, and I forced a grin when I saw Blue Eyes looking up at me.

His mouth opened, and then he closed it as he stared. "You can't stay like that forever."

A defiant laugh clawed its way out of my chest despite the burn. "Watch me."

My legs trembled harder, and my muscles screeched in protest. Sweat slicked my palms in the gloves on the horns, and it was like the wyvern sensed my distress. It surged and arched its neck as it tried again to wrench its head free.

The world lurched, and so did my body.

I slid an inch, maybe two, and hot panic blazed through me. I slammed my heels down again and leaned on them with everything I had, forcing its eyelids to stay shut.

"Hold." Kai's urgent voice turned to a rasp. "Ashren, add more restraints to the head and neck. The gem is nearly freed. Gavriel, prepare the sleeping draught for it. Hannah, I will signal as soon as it's free."

"Well, don't hurry on my account." I tried to ignore the hate mail my muscles were sending directly to me. "I could do this all day."

"I don't think you should." Gavriel's blue eyes were wide and white-rimmed as he stared at me. "Isn't your leg injured? I thought you got shot."

"Gavriel!" Kai barked. "Eyes off her, and prepare the sleeping draught. Keep watch for attackers instead of her leg."

Silver light flared along the side of the wyvern, and the beast stilled even more.

The resistance beneath my feet spiked with a brutal push that made my thighs tremble so violently my vision flashed white. *Bend me over and fuck me.* I couldn't hold this position for even another minute at this rate.

"Good," Kai growled. "Almost there. That's my good—" He paused for a moment. "That's...effective. Keep your thighs steady and your feet planted, Hannah."

I hated how my stomach flipped at his words. Had he been about to call me his good girl? Fucking arrogant bastard. I pressed my heels harder and stared up at the night sky. My muscles burned like they were tearing apart, every second stretching thin.

The tremor in my thighs turned into a full-body shake. The kind that started in the muscles and climbed into the teeth. My heels dug into the wyvern's lids until my arches cramped and my body became drenched in sweat. Heat pulsed up through the soles, slick and angry, and my grip on the wyvern's horns slipped a fraction as sweat pooled in my gloves.

A metallic snap rang out beneath me.

The pressure under my feet changed like a cord had been cut inside the beast. The lids still fought to open, but the fight in them stuttered.

Kai grunted again, and something clicked. "It's free. Get clear, Hannah!"

Relief and fear slammed into me. I let my weight shift forward and off the lids, then dragged my feet backward toward the ridge of its snout, keeping my hands clenched on the horns. The wyvern's head jerked.

The band of shadow and silver around its jaw tightened again. The angry grunt that rose from its chest made it sound like the beast was now more confused than rabid. I steadied myself and looked down. Kai and Ashren stood in front of the wyvern like anchored storms, shoulders rigid and hands lifted. The shadows and silver cords wrapped tight around the beast's jaws, throat, shoulders, and the base of its wings held it steady while it trembled and snarled through clenched teeth. The purple gem was nowhere to be seen, thank goodness.

"Gavriel." Kai's words came through his teeth. "Draught. Hannah. Off!"

My legs were jelly, and my calves twitched uncontrollably. I shoved my weight backward, rolled off the crown of its skull, and slid down the ridges of its neck with my chest pressed to its scales as I dismounted in an undignified fashion. The world tilted as the wyvern shuddered, and my stomach lurched into my throat.

I hit the curve of its shoulder and lost purchase. Air ripped from my lungs. My palms slapped down, caught on a ridge, and I clung there, knuckles white. My feet scraped for traction, finally finding a shallow groove between plates of scale.

Stone, smoke, and firelight swam together below. I forced my hands to release, slid, and struck the ground hard.

The street still vibrated with the wyvern's restrained fury, but it did not seem so powerful now, even if the air did taste like burning oil and charred wood. My lungs burned with every inhale.

Kai's gaze cut to me like a command. "Go wait by the castle gates, and we will talk."

The order set my temper on fire. My legs wobbled, but I turned anyway, forcing myself into motion toward the alley that I believed led to Market Square, where Olen had told me to go. Each step felt disconnected, as if my feet belonged to someone else. The bruise in my shoulder pulsed with my heartbeat, but I was gaining momentum.

"Hannah!" Kai's voice snapped at me, closer than it should have been. "Don't be obstinate. Our physician will care for you."

I threw a look over my shoulder and kept moving. Smoke curled between us in gray ribbons. He was still holding the wyvern down with Ashren, jaw clenched, eyes hard, as if my choice of direction offended him as much as the beast had.

Gavriel ran to the front of the wyvern, holding up a large dark cloth soaked with something that I could smell even from here, like vinegar and bleach. It made my nose sting. He swung the cloth up and dropped it over the wyvern's head in one neat motion, then grabbed the edges of the cloth and sealed it around the dragon's snout.

I lifted my chin. "Just because I helped save your people, it doesn't give you the right to order me around. My previous suggestion that you fuck yourself on a rusty crowbar still stands." Apparently, my survival instincts had taken the night off. I tapped a hand to my forehead. "You take care now. It's been...something, but I'll let you get back to it. Take it easy."

Kai's wings flared wide, and the claws dug deeper into the stone. His shadows rippled, and his eyes sparked with rage. "You are in *my* kingdom, and I—"

"I've done worse for less." I winked at him and then took off in a shaky run. My legs hated me as much as he did, but they'd carry me out of there.

Kai barked, "Gavriel, stop her."

I glanced back. The cloth on the wyvern's head shifted as the beast wavered, and Gavriel hesitated, hands still wrapped around the damp fabric as if he didn't want to remove even an ounce of pressure too soon.

Kai's voice sharpened. "Now."

I quickened my pace, not checking to see if Gavriel obeyed or not. Stone slapped under my shoes, and cold air knifed into my throat. I veered hard into the next alley, moving in the direction Olen had mentioned.

Not as many people were running down the street. Hopefully, they'd gotten to the shelters.

I cut left around a toppled barrel and nearly went down when my foot caught on a broken cobblestone. I caught myself on a wall and pushed off again, teeth grinding as I forced my leg to obey.

"Stop running!" Gavriel shouted. "You can't get away."

He was wearing a heavy fur coat and armor, and it sounded like his steps were far slower than mine. As long as I didn't slow my pace, I'd be fine.

"Yeah, watch me!" I threw myself forward, forcing my stiff muscles to move faster. Olen had told me to go straight down this path until I spotted the elk fountain.

The alley opened into a wider street, and noise slammed into me—metal striking metal, shouts tearing through smoke, the deep bellow of horns, and a rolling thunder of boots and bodies. Firelight flickered against stone, casting everything in jerking orange pulses.

The fight was close, which meant I had to be careful. The last thing I wanted—other than being caught—was getting stuck in the middle of an actual battle. I cut across the alley while mentally noting Olen's instructions so I could get back on course. I had to lose Gavriel. I kept close to the buildings as I neared the main road and what I guessed was Market Square, based on its openness and a number of shattered booths that lay in pieces around a large fountain.

Now I could see the shine of armor through the haze. Soldiers clashed together in clusters, black-armored warriors pressed against gray-armored ones with blades flashing. A line of gray warriors had formed near the marble fountain, enough to block the majority of black warriors from advancing as the gray warriors pushed forward. Bodies moved in tight patterns—practiced, brutal, efficient. But it didn't seem like the gray warriors, who I assumed were the Dusk Forces, had much of an advantage.

My skin prickled, and instinct had me focusing on the

towers in the wall beyond me and then the shadows overhead, on any shape that might drop on me from above. The air vibrated with distant roars, but the battle in front of me was close and hungry. They were all focused on each other, and there was a gap in the fighting to the left that I could take advantage of.

Gavriel's footsteps had fallen away, but I was certain he wasn't far behind me. I slid along the fountain's curve and tried to pick a path that kept me out of the main crush, aiming for the Eastern Wall Gate Olen had described.

Three black-armored soldiers emerged from another alley and stepped into the square. One saw me and pointed.

I tensed as my hand went back to my pocket. Then I remembered I'd dropped the knife. Well, obviously, I hadn't planned well.

I angled away and broke into a run, but strong hands seized me from behind. The hard grip bruised, and something that felt like metal clamped over my wrists, so tight that I thought my bones might break even through my coat. My captor adjusted his grip to hold my wrists in one hand. I sucked in a sharp breath and kicked one leg back. Rage flashed through me, so hot my vision narrowed. Pain shot up my foot as I stomped down on metal. I hissed, teeth bared, and tried to wrench free anyway.

I turned, half expecting to see Gavriel, but a black-armored soldier had caught me.

A sour taste filled my mouth, and adrenaline coursed through me.

"Don't make this harder than it has to be," he growled in my ear. His other hand fisted in my hair and wrenched my head back.

The other three approached, scanning me up and down.

"Let go of me, or I'll bite your face off," I snarled. My

pulse kicked hard, and I yanked against the grip on my arm again.

He jerked my head back harder as he continued to grip my arms with his other hand, forcing me to bend unnaturally. As I twisted, I glimpsed him holding both my wrists with his metal glove. There didn't seem to be any exploitable weaknesses from this angle. Shit!

"Unhand her!" Gavriel's voice rang through the air behind us. "She's not a part of this war!"

Two of the black-armored soldiers unsheathed their swords and started toward him. "Then come take her back."

"Take her behind that building. Let's see if she's worth the trouble." One of the soldiers in front of me grabbed me by the chin, his metal gloves digging into my cheek so hard I was sure he cut me.

I spat at him, the spray of saliva spattering over his helmet. "Hands off!"

They laughed harshly, and my vision blurred as pain ripped through my mouth. I didn't even see which one had hit me. I sagged back, ears ringing. I blinked, trying to shake off the disorientation and get coordination back into my limbs. Blood filled my mouth, and I spat it on the ground.

"She'll be fun," one said, his voice echoing and distant. "Everyone will want a turn with this one even if she does have some ash and soot on her. That fire must have been worse than we thought. Don't ruin her mouth yet."

"Soldiers," a deep voice barked in front of me. When I opened my eyes, I saw that a fourth black-armored warrior had arrived. His armor was sleeker, and his helmet had a spike and horns, all black. A carved black crest of a full moon was situated on the brow, surrounded by branches. "You should know better than to conduct yourself in this fashion."

"The king will want this one, Night General," the guard who held me said with a dark laugh. He shook me like a doll to prove his point. "Look at her! That hair is gold, even if it does have ash in it. She's obviously Aurora Court. And he won't care if we have fun with her first. He hasn't cared about anything except conquest for decades. He said we're supposed to bring any possible Aurora Fae in."

"On the battlefield, you are under my command," the Night General growled, his hand on his sword. "We will take her with us, but you will not touch her. None of you will. Now take her to the steeds. She rides with me."

My body lurched forward, and as I tried to yank myself free, I stumbled and lost my footing. Holy crap. Maybe I should've listened to Kai after all.

CHAPTER 15

Kai

Heat poured off the wyvern in punishing waves, rolling over my face and making the skin of my cheekbones sting. Having to restrain this wyvern on such a narrow street and prevent it from doing more damage had nearly drained me, especially when I couldn't move much myself to maneuver when it kept pushing back and forth.

It didn't help that *she* had been reckless and become the hood herself. Damn woman. It'd worked, but I still wasn't convinced she hadn't knocked her head on something when she dropped through the portal.

Smoke coated my tongue, oily and bitter, and every inhale scraped my lungs as if the air had turned to grit. But that wasn't as debilitating as knowing Hannah was running toward the Night Court battle. They would spot her and probably jump to the conclusion that she was Aurora Fae since her golden hair was still obvious despite the light dusting of ash. And if they spotted her, they'd probably want to take her to the Night King for testing. I had to get to her.

Seven houses had caught fire, and the flames continued to

spread. I held my stance, boots planted wide on the uneven stone, knees bent deep enough that my thighs ached with a strain I tried not to show. With the wyvern blocking my view, I couldn't see how far Hannah had gotten. All I could do was get this beast unconscious so I could follow Hannah and not have to rely on Gavriel to catch her.

Fuck.

I'd sent him after her, and they weren't back. I could barely stomach the thought, even though I had made the right call. Gavriel was fast, disciplined, and...well, available, but that knowledge did nothing to ease my concern. Nausea twisted in my gut as if I'd eaten bad venison and pickled eggs, and the damn urge to run after her had me distracted from the task at hand.

Hannah had been swallowed by the chaos of the city, but her presence still grated along my nerves. The memory of her on the wyvern's head flashed unbidden—legs shaking, strange pink and white shoes grinding down on its eyelids, and manner bristling with defiance, as if fear were an inconvenience she could shrug off. And that mouth of hers... Oh, that fucking mouth.

As soon as this wyvern was settled, I'd go after her myself, catch her, and then... Well, putting her back in a cell wasn't going to work. I didn't know whether to punish her, reward her, or both.

My wing-claws remained buried in the cobblestones behind me and hooked through cracks between stones, anchoring me like iron spikes. The wyvern wasn't struggling as much as before, but a line of fissures had spiderwebbed outward from where its claws had punched into the street, and each time the wyvern surged, those cracks shivered wider under the pressure.

Every twitch of its joints sent showers of sparks into the air, many landing where flames already crawled greedily through spilled oil. The cloth Gavriel had dropped over the beast's head bulged and shifted with each huff of its breath, darkening the cloth at the snout, where foam and spit soaked through. Even blind and bound, it kept trying to lunge forward.

Ashren stood at my left, his shoulder brushing mine as the beast thrashed. His mouth was set in that familiar way that meant he'd already determined his next three steps. "We're keeping it from sleeping?" He pursed his lips. "We brought a strong enough sedative to put it out for at least twelve hours. There's room for it to recover in the lower stable near the western gate."

"Good," I rasped and cast my gaze to the sky. The wards had almost reformed. The battle sounded as if the Night Forces hadn't gotten beyond the Market Square, and it appeared as if the towers had repelled the wyvern attack. There were no stirrings of additional attacks to be seen from this vantage point. Surely they weren't leaving when they'd already breached the eastern gate?

Why wasn't Hannah back? Gavriel should've already returned with her.

Ashren kept his hands raised and his shadows braided seamlessly into mine along the creature's neck and shoulders, reinforcing the points under the most strain. He didn't need instruction. We'd known each other's fighting styles before we'd even been brought back to the kingdom after our banishment.

"So...she rode the wyvern into submission. That seems promising. I'm guessing that was her idea, not yours." His voice pitched low enough to carry only to me. "I don't imagine you objected to the view."

I shot him a glare, but before I could say anything, the wyvern surged again. Its claws gouged deeper into the stone, and its wings shuddered against broken walls. Firelight rippled across its scales in harsh flashes, and the cloth over its eyes rubbed the cobblestones as its head dipped under the force of the bindings.

I tightened my fingers, keeping the cords at its jaw cinched. "Sleep."

Anger surged through me as the massive beast lowered its head to the ground and then fell asleep. Overriding the will of a living creature and forcing it to become a berserker, then sending it to its death in such a senseless fashion, was abominable. Had I been inside the castle when it attacked, a sizable chunk of the castle would have been blown apart, possibly killing me and dozens—perhaps hundreds—of others, crippling our court. The Night King had managed to break down the wards long enough to get this beast and several others through them, and nearly driven it mad.

Bram was nothing like he'd once been. My uncle's face flashed back into my mind, and I remembered him saying, *This isn't Bram. Bram would never act this way. Something must have happened.* He was right. This kind of magic was reprehensible and cruel. My former friend was nothing like he had once been.

The cloth over the wyvern's head rose and fell slowly, its breathing deep and slow.

The fire sent waves of heat against my back. Sweat pooled under my armor, then evaporated as another gust of hot air rolled through. Smoke snagged on the edges of my wings and curled around my shoulders. I recalled my wings, allowing them to dissipate. I pressed a hand to my coat pocket to check the gem. The enchantment had been successfully detached from it and the wyvern, but it could be used again. When I fished it out, my fingertips brushed the ridiculous little pig charm on a sparkling ball that Hannah had kept on a ring.

Now that I was no longer restraining the wyvern, my magic began to restore itself. I thrust the gem into Ashren's hands. "Take this somewhere safe. Make sure the wyvern is brought indoors. The fire attendants are on their way?"

Ashren tucked the gem in his coat's inner pocket. "They are. Folge is leading the Dusk Forces. Response teams have moved out already, and based on the sounds, they still control the towers and have fought off the other wyverns. We're fortunate this wyvern didn't attack while you were in your study."

The wind cut sideways through the street, strong enough that my eyes watered. It came fast and hard and shoved at the bones instead of sliding past them with the biting ache of the wild north winds. Hard pellets of snow stung where they struck exposed skin and hissed when they hit hot stone.

My chest tightened as my tug toward Hannah grew into something hot and insistent. It pulled forward in the direction she had run, toward Market Square, where the noise thickened and thinned in uneven pulses. Then it yanked at me so hard, I could barely stand there anymore.

Ashren was still speaking, but the words slid past me as the air pressure dropped, sudden and deep. My ears rang, and the wind howled between the buildings and screamed down the lanes in gusts that rattled shutters and sent loose embers spiraling upward in angry bursts.

VROOOHM.

The sound punched through my chest and lodged there. I tensed, and something inside me shifted recklessly.

Retreat? The Night Forces were retreating?

That made no sense. Not now. Not when they'd breached the eastern wall and their forces were already inside the city. They should have pressed harder. They should have committed. This kind of withdrawal meant strategy, not defeat.

I turned toward Ashren, jarring my aching spine. "Don't trust it."

His gaze was already on the rooftops, scanning the smoke and falling snow. His jaw set as the same conclusion landed.

"They're pulling back too early. Why would they not at least try to reach the keep or hinder our defenses in some meaningful way? What did they accomplish? Their berserker didn't succeed."

Another horn echoed, farther off, answering the first from the outer eastern towers to confirm. The wind carried the call strangely, warping the sound. Snow thickened, flakes turning into blinding white streaks that slashed across my vision. Was it possible they were retreating because of the storm itself?

It was a full night's ride back to the Night Court, and through driving snow, that ride swiftly became dangerous. There were few safe havens in the wildernesses between the cities of any court. But their abrupt departure didn't settle within me. Something was off.

The tug in my chest flared again, urgent enough that my breath caught. My feet shifted without permission, angling toward the street that led to Market Square. Heat drained out of my hands, replaced by a crawling unease.

Hannah.

Her name struck like pressure tightening beneath my ribs, making it hard to draw a full breath.

I took off.

Ashren matched my pace instantly, our boots crunching over ice-dusted stone as we ran past the slumped bulk of the wyvern and down the street. The firelight dimmed behind us, replaced by an orange glow diffused by smoke and snow. Wind tore at my coat, snapping the edges hard enough to sting my wrists.

The city sounded different now. Less chaos and more quiet. Shouts were spread thin, and metal rang less often. The absence set my teeth on edge. Where was Hannah?

Something was wrong, and that knowledge ached through my bones and soul.

A shape broke from the haze ahead, running toward us

instead of away. My focus locked on the movement before my mind caught up, and we slowed to a stop in front of one of the courier stables.

Gavriel stumbled into clearer view, snow clinging to his hair and shoulders and face drained of color. He skidded to a halt before me.

The tug in my chest snapped tight enough to hurt. "Where is she?" The words came out low and rough, my throat dry.

His ash-gray expression told me before his mouth moved. A thin line of blood seeped at his temple where snow melted pink. "She's gone."

The world tilted. My mind exploded as I braced my hands against my belt, trying to hide my anger and fear. "*Explain.*"

Ashren stepped closer, his body angled between us. "She escaped?"

Gavriel swallowed and curled his hands into fists. "The Night General took her, and they left."

The air punched from my lungs. My vision narrowed, the edges darkening as heat surged hard and fast through my chest. The tug there flared into something painful, like a hook driven deep, and yanked.

"I almost caught up to her near the square." Gavriel's words tumbled faster now. "The soldiers grabbed and struck her. They wouldn't listen. I was almost there—" His jaw clenched, and his shoulders slumped as if replaying the memory cost him physically.

My temper flared. I wanted to demand why he hadn't been able to stop them, but my recriminations against him were equally against myself. I should have been there, and *I* should have stopped them. "Did they hurt her?"

Gavriel nodded stiffly. "She spat on one, and he struck her. She didn't fall, but she was hurt. The Night General intervened before they could do more, and he gave the order to take her. He had her restrained before I could reach her." His gaze didn't leave mine. "Then they left."

A low, tearing sensation ran through my chest like a rib had cracked inward. Heat flared behind my eyes, sudden and blinding. My wings wanted to burst free again, the phantom pressure building along my spine even though they were folded away. I tasted iron, smoke, and cold all at once. "Which one struck her? Could you identify him?"

"No. They were all fully covered in armor, including helmets, and I wasn't able to hear their voices well. They weren't officers or leaders, but they didn't act like they were enlisted." Gavriel lifted his hands.

Fine. I'd kill them all then. It would reduce their count, which was a win for my people. "I'm going after her." My boots hit the packed snow hard enough to jar my knees, and I cut toward the stables. "Gavriel, with me. Ashren, make sure the city is prepared for the storm and that repairs begin. Block the broken points in the wall and gate with a binding ward if the storm looks like it will be too severe for work to begin."

Gavriel fell into step beside me.

Ashren followed reluctantly and pinched the bridge of his nose. "Kai, there are about two hundred soldiers from the Night Court fleeing to the border to get beyond the elder tree barrier before this monstrous storm hits. We don't know if they have reserves—"

"This is my kingdom, and I know its terrain and the traps, including the beast paths and yeti dens. Gather a group of fifteen warriors and send them after us. And take Olen into custody as soon as you find him. He helped her hide." The stable doors banged open under my hand, and the scent of hay and leather rushed out to meet the cold. Lanterns shook on their hooks as the wind shoved inside. There weren't any horses kept in the courier stable during the winter, only elk and caribou that were kept saddled and prepped at all times in case messages had to go out or a rescue was needed. Though the elk were faster, given how bad the storm was likely to be, tonight called for caribou.

The urge to get to Hannah had me hurrying for the grey and black courier caribou nearest the door. It was saddled with packs strapped tight along its flanks and ready for travel. The saddle bags included one bag of emergency rations, limited medical supplies, blankets, liquor, a cloak, tether lines, and enchanted flares. I feared one emergency bag might not be enough, so I snagged another and attached it. Hannah wasn't prepared for this weather. "Make sure those who come are properly outfitted. This storm will bring at least another foot of snow, and there's about a foot and a half already."

Moving alongside another caribou, Gavriel pressed a hand to its hazel-brown muzzle and then climbed into the broad saddle.

Ashren set his hands on his belt and released a slow breath through his teeth. I knew he wanted to go with me, but one of us had to remain behind to see to the castle and ensure this hadn't been a diversionary attack. The Night General's presence suggested it wasn't only a diversion, but that wasn't a risk we could take. I had to get to Hannah, and Ashren was the best option to handle things here.

He went to one of the large bins in the back of the stable and returned with a pair of boots and a small bundle of clothing. "She's wearing those strange shoes and trousers with holes in them. There's little chance any of that is properly insulated, even with the coat and gloves. She'll need these, or she'll lose her toes. There's a hood and scarf in there, too. They're not pretty, and they smell like caribou, but they'll do."

Annoyance flared because I should've thought of that. I buried it since Ashren had helped. I clapped my hand on his shoulder, then took the boots and nodded, grateful he understood. I strapped them to the back of the caribou with the additional bag, grabbed a spare scarf for myself as well as one of the thick wool hoods, while Gavriel did the same.

Time to move.

Ashren continued to hover as we made final preparations. "All the way points and restoration huts have been fully stocked. Don't risk coming back in the storm after you get her if it becomes as bad as it looks. We'll have search parties ready. If they're heading west, watch for the yetis. The cubs are just now learning to hunt. If they're heading south, the howlers have been gathering en masse near the river."

Grunting in acknowledgement, I checked my gear once more. This land was wild and dangerous with numerous predators, even in stormy weather. Ice imps, rime weasels, and frost adders were all opportunistic hunters, drawn to heat and immune to storms like this. Ice imps in particular loved metal. They were more than happy to attack a large group if they felt they had the advantage.

My mind rapidly sifted through all the things that Hannah might need once she was free from those wretched bastards. My gut told me she'd get free somehow. She was infuriatingly resourceful and unwaveringly independent. But that put her in even more danger. She wasn't prepared for the cold, the storm, or the wilds. I knew the Night General wouldn't be cruel to her. He'd appeared more than once in battles and attacks over the past decades, though neither my spies nor my court's magic had been able to unmask him. He was a holdover from when the Night Court had been honorable, but that didn't make me trust him with Hannah.

I unfastened the tether binding the caribou to the wall and then swung into the saddle.

Ashren's voice carried after me. "If you lose the trail—"

"I won't." I took the reins and directed the caribou out the double doors and into the storm.

My mount surged forward, its muscles bunching beneath

me and its breath steaming in thick bursts. Gavriel appeared mounted beside me a heartbeat later. We tore out of the yard, around the broken booths, and straight toward the Eastern Wall Gate, hooves striking sparks from ice-glazed stone.

The wards recognized us, and silver light unwound in spirals ahead. They parted without resistance, the sensation of passing through them cold and sharp against my skin. The wall fell away, and the empty, dark land opened before us. The winds were blowing snow so hard that the attackers would at least have a hard time navigating it.

Wind slammed into my chest, stole the breath from my lungs, and tore at my coat until the fabric snapped and strained. Snow drove sideways, needling into every bit of exposed skin and stinging my eyes until they burned. The caribou didn't falter, its legs eating up ground with relentless precision.

Very little sentient life lived out here, especially this close to the city. Only scrub, frozen earth, and the vast, white-dark stretch beyond.

I scanned the area around us, and my heart skipped a beat.

Fresh tracks, cut deep.

The Night Forces weren't even trying to mask their departure, all of their magic likely focused on getting them out and safely back to their own lands. I leaned forward and urged the caribou on faster.

Already the storm was worsening, the winds picking up. I leaned low over the caribou's neck, every muscle locked and every thought stripped down to one brutal line.

Hannah.

The caribou stretched into a longer stride, its hooves striking against packed snow and racking through my bones. Cold slid through the seams of my coat and settled along my spine, numbing everything except the tight, burning focus pulling me forward.

I was used to the cold, but Hannah wasn't. She had to be freezing, and I had to get her before the cold took her life.

The snow thickened as the terrain turned rougher. Rocks jutted through the white in dark, broken lines. The wind shifted direction without warning, hammering down the slope and forcing the caribou to lean into it with its shoulders angled and legs driving harder. My thighs screamed with the effort of staying balanced, but I welcomed the pain. It anchored me and kept my mind from splintering.

Gavriel kept pace alongside me, his head down and his focus on what lay ahead. If we were separated, his caribou would take him home.

I pushed my magic outward, allowing my vision to focus as the storm resisted me. It took effort to separate shadow from snow and to force shape out of chaos. Pressure built behind my eyes, and a dull throb developed in my temple, increasing as the mountains loomed closer.

There.

Movement shifted along the mountainside like a wound cut into the snow. Nine dark columns carried spurts of light from enchanted torches to guide them and protect against the storm. Normally, they'd carry a little light for the recruits who weren't fully Night Fae or whose skills were not as developed as the elite and highborn, but this storm made even fae with excellent night vision need extra help to see.

They climbed steadily through the worsening conditions, their spacing tightening as the slope steepened and forced them into narrower lines. I tracked them instinctively, my gaze snagging on the biggest group, clustered near the center where the mounts moved more slowly.

Fuck! I should have known. It was the path Bram had preferred whenever he'd traveled here and speed was of the essence, but the weather made it exceptionally dangerous.

They were angling toward Spire Pass, a narrow space that

cut between two of the broadest mountains in this range. Even yetis avoided it while hunting because of how dangerous it was. The Night General was gambling on speed and on the storm burying his trail. If they got through the pass and reached the other side beyond the barrier, the terrain became much safer.

But they wouldn't.

Not with the snow buildup on the left snowcap. It already had the dull slab look of a snowy cliff about to collapse. The avalanche would barrel down into the pass like it was a funnel. They should have taken the side on the right. They probably couldn't see it—even my own men couldn't see as well in the dark as I could. I'd be sending them into a trap as well because that avalanche wasn't an if—it was a when.

I jerked my head toward Gavriel and used my magic to project my voice to him. "Turn back and warn the other group that was to follow us that there'll be an avalanche at Spire Pass on the northern side. Do *not* enter the pass without preparation."

Gavriel nodded, his face flushed beneath the scarf. He reined the caribou around and doubled back.

Panic damn near choked me, and I gripped my reins tighter, urging the caribou faster. The animal surged forward, breath tearing from its lungs in harsh, steaming bursts. The gap shrank enough that individual figures resolved through the storm, cloaks snapping violently, heads down against the wind. The vibrations from their ascent hummed faintly through the ground, a low, ominous tremor that set my nerves on edge.

Snow hissed as it slid in small sheets from higher up the slope.

My fingers ached from the reins biting into my palms. Every instinct screamed at me to take to the air and close the distance, but the storm would shred my wings. I'd used too much strength and magic on the wyvern, and I wasn't replenished yet.

Silver flashed through the storm ahead, and the troops halted.

Terror knotted in my stomach. *Please don't let that be ice imps.*

A change rippled through the lines like a snag in fabric, with mounts skidding and bunching and riders shouting over one another as they tried to re-form in the deepening snowdrifts. Then, I heard it. The thin, keening sound of malicious cackles cutting through the air.

Each time an ice imp attacked, bright silver light punched through the air like the burst of a white flame. The storm carried their cries to me in broken pieces, raising the hair along my arms even through fur, wool, and leather.

They darted at the edges of the columns, too fast to follow, leaving brief streaks of pale silver that winked in and out as if the snow itself had grown teeth. Some dove low near the caribous' legs, the mounts screaming a panicked, raw sound that punched straight through my chest even from this distance.

The lines buckled. Riders yanked reins, and the caribou tried to keep their footing on the slick incline, but the slope was already failing them. Every movement sent tremors into the snowpack above, and I felt the subtle shift in the mountain's weight in my bones.

Hannah. Where is she?

That golden hair of hers should be easy to spot even with its luster dulled from the pale ash, so I urged my caribou forward, scanning the columns for her. When I reached the base of the mountain, I rode to the far side of the path so I avoided entering the pass but kept moving in the same general direction.

A crack ran through the top edge of the snowpack, barely visible through the storm, but my magic sensed it like a bruise under my skin. A shout carried downwind, then another, higher and panicked. The columns began to move again, but not with disciplined intent—with fear pressing at their backs.

Riders swung weapons at the imps, their blades ringing uselessly against air. An ice imp skimmed past a helm and left a bright frost-burn line that smoked in the cold.

My caribou ate up the distance. The cold tore at my lungs, but the heat in my chest grew hotter and tighter as the tug of the bond strengthened into a pull that threatened to yank my heart from my chest.

A body shifted near the head of the line farthest south.

A flash of gold broke through the storm as if a cloth had fallen away. My heart slammed so hard my vision blurred. The bond flared, a white-hot surge that stole my breath.

It happened fast. She tumbled off the side of a caribou, her arms flailing. Then she hit the snow and rolled. Powder burst up around her, swallowing her for a heartbeat, and then she fought her way up, staggering like her legs had forgotten how to work.

A sound tore out of me that I did not recognize. It scraped my throat raw. My hands clenched so hard on the reins that my fingers went numb. Rage flashed, hot enough to drown the cold, followed by terror that seemed to split my ribs wide open.

The wind roared, and underneath it, the imps' laughter rose, frantic now, as if the chaos delighted them.

The bond yanked, and my chest tightened until it felt like it might collapse. I drove the caribou straight toward her, my heart hammering so hard that my hands shook. The only thought that remained was brutal and simple.

Get to Hannah.

CHAPTER 16

Hannah

Fur and leather scratched my cheek with every jolt of the Clydesdale-sized caribou. My body was draped awkwardly across the caribou's broad neck, with the center of my stomach pressed against the horn of the saddle and my side pressed to the Night General, who was resting his forearms on my back while holding the reins.

He pressed down on me iron-solid, keeping me pinned there like an inconvenient sack of potatoes. The thick rope around my wrists was awkward but not painful, leaving my fingers numb and aching but more from the cold than tightness.

The Night General didn't seem worried about me escaping. He'd even wrapped a wool scarf around my head and face to protect me from the cold. Probably because we both knew this wasn't a situation I could run away from. Even if I got free, I'd have to get something to ride and figure out where to go. But I wasn't going to give up. I'd been working to free myself from the rope. A metal clasp on the caribou's neck harness had a jagged edge that I'd been rubbing the rope against, working through the fibers discreetly and tugging at the knot. This was the only advantage of having my torso hanging over the caribou's shoulder, since the headache I was getting was no picnic.

It was a slow process, but it wasn't like I had anything better to do. I'd made good progress, but time was working against me. I could count the seconds by the pulses of pain through my face. Blood had dried on my lips and down my chin, my face split and aching, not only from the blow but also from the sheer cold. My cheeks stung where the first soldier had grabbed my face, wearing metal gloves. The raw skin was cut, and every brush of the scarf reminded me of the wounds. The scarf had dulled the roar of the storm, but it dragged roughly against those wounds, scraping with each breath. Cold pressed in from all sides, but the enchanted coat held the worst of it back with a muted warmth clinging stubbornly to my core. My gloves helped, too, keeping my fingers from freezing solid.

My feet were another story. I tried kicking them to keep the blood moving, but it wasn't doing much. These pink and white sneakers were a cruel joke out here. The deepening snow had already covered the caribou's fetlocks when we'd left, and it was deeper now.

As we traveled, cold seeped through soaked fabric and bit straight into bone. My toes burned, then went numb, then burned with a deep, vicious pain that made my calves tense and shake. Hypothermia was probably setting in, and I had maybe another hour before it turned severe.

Torchlight bobbed and smeared through the darkness, the flames of the soldiers' torches bending sideways in the wind. They cast broken pools of orange across the snow, stretching out shadows that twisted and vanished as the caribou pushed forward, heads bowed against the storm.

The rope was stiff with ice, the fibers rough against skin already rubbed raw where it had slid past the glove and rubbed my wrists. I pressed my thumbs together and rolled my wrists in small, careful movements, letting the caribou's long stride mask the motion. Pain flared bright and sharp, shooting up my arms. I leaned into it, jaw locking as my breath hitched.

The final knot shifted.

My pulse jumped in a rush that made my vision swim. I went slack, letting my weight sag, then twisted again, harder. The rope scraped and burned, then went slack.

I twisted my head up to see if the Night General had noticed. He wasn't even looking at me. Though his horned helmet masked his features, his head was tilted up as if searching for something. We seemed to be in a snowy pass, near a jagged mountain wall. The terrain ahead of us slanted upward at an alarmingly sharp angle.

Twisting my wrists against the metal buckle, I caught the rope and tugged. My hands slid free in a rush of pain, and the heat returning to my fingers made them curl reflexively. Needles prickled under my skin as circulation returned.

I held my hands still against the caribou's neck for a painful breath, shaking. Free hands changed nothing. I still couldn't see past the torchlight and blowing snow, and I couldn't get my feet under me. I was surrounded, and I'd never been so cold in my life.

The caribou stiffened, its muscles bunching under me. Somewhere in the wind, several voices cackled—high, thin, metallic, and wrong enough to hollow my chest.

Silver light exploded in the storm.

"Ice imps!" the Night General yelled as he unsheathed his sword. "Take off their heads. Keep moving forward."

For a heartbeat, everything snapped into violent clarity.

Dozens of small, strange creatures with burning silver eyes burst from the snow, each about three feet tall and all sharp angles. Their bodies flared silver-white and exploded in bursts of silver light as they leapt at the troops. Soldiers shouted as silver claws struck and skidded off armor, glinting in the firelight. They drew their swords and swiped at the imps as the caribou pressed on. Torches spun and fell, the flames hissing as they hit the snow and kept burning.

"Steady!" the Night General shouted as he brought his sword down on one of the ice imps and severed its head from its spine. Silver blood shot into the snow.

Something struck his caribou's flank, and we veered hard. The impact jolted straight through its frame and into mine, knocking my teeth together. Another hit landed, and the animal lurched sideways, hooves scrambling for footing in the churned snow as it made a bellowing call.

The Night General shifted behind me, his knees tightening to steady us, but the caribou twisted again, forced out of line by another blow. The sudden lateral movement wrenched me loose.

My throat dried as I slid, and the scarf pulled away.

I hit the snow, the breath knocked clean out of my lungs. Cold swallowed me as I plunged deep into the drift. The snow pressed against my face and chest and went down my collar and into my mouth. I gagged and rolled, clawing with my hands to dig myself out as the ground shifted beneath me.

Silver flared again.

I raised my head. The fight fractured into frozen pieces— soldiers struggling to keep formation, caribou pushing through the chaos with heads low and shoulders driving, and ice imps darting and striking wherever the line thinned. The Night General continued to fight as several ice imps attacked him again. Then the light vanished, and the storm swallowed it all.

I staggered to my feet and stumbled away.

Each step was a fight. Snow mid-thigh dragged at my legs while my sneakers soaked through instantly. Cold bit at my feet with relentless agony. My mouth tasted of blood and ice, and my hands shook as I held them out for balance with numb and clumsy fingers.

Several of the riders had fallen.

Ahead of me, a caribou broke free of the line, forcing its way laterally through the snow. It had no saddle, and I assumed it was one of the pack animals. Empty holders slapped its sides, the straps torn, and whatever it had been carrying gone. It was moving in my direction.

I'd only ever ridden horses, and I'd only gone bareback once. But if I was going to get out of this place, I had to move fast. How much harder could it be to ride a caribou bareback?

The snow fought me for every inch, and the wind tore at my breath. Another silver flash burned the scene into my eyes, and I clambered onto a rock and lunged for the caribou. My hands caught thick fur, and my chest struck its side. For half a breath, I was on, but then it pulled me off the stone, and I slid, my feet and legs plunging back into the snow. Shaking with the cold and struggling to catch my breath, I knotted my fists deeper in the fur and hauled myself up.

It glanced back at me as if this was the most normal thing I could be doing, and then powered on.

Shit! This was nothing like riding a horse. The caribou was at least six feet tall at the shoulder, its movement low and rolling, with fur so thick and slick it was hard to get a grip. My legs flailed and caught on the torn straps before I clamped them as tight as I could on the slick fur and locked my arms around its neck. "Okay—okay. Thank you. Don't leave me."

Silver flashed at the edge of my vision, and an ice imp launched toward us, its body flaring white. I screamed and kicked out, my sneaker connecting with something hard and unyielding. Pain shot up my leg.

The cackling imp sprang again at the back of the caribou. The animal kicked it squarely in the chest and continued upward, moving onto a jagged ledge of rock as the snow beat down on us harder, and the wind howled.

KRRACK.

A sound like a gunshot rang out overhead, and my head snapped up. The caribou didn't slow, but it angled sharper uphill, its hooves biting into the packed snow and stone along the mountainside as it moved steadily upward. I flattened myself against its back and held on for dear life.

The crack sounded again, deeper and close enough that it seemed to sear through my chest. The stone beneath us shuddered as the caribou shifted its weight and continued upward as if it knew exactly where we were going and that we had to get out of this pass. I glanced over my shoulder, straining to take in the scene as the ice imps bolted and the soldiers tried to keep moving forward. The ground shook like an earthquake, and a deep rushing thunder filled the air.

Acid burned my throat. Shit. An avalanche?

My hands fisted deeper into the caribou's fur as a sense of helplessness swept over me. Memories from my time skiing in Colorado shot through my mind. I'd learned that, if you were caught in an avalanche, you needed to move to the side, swim to the top, create an air pocket, conserve energy, and keep your feet downhill. But that was what to do if you were caught in it, not what to do before it hit you while you were bareback on a caribou.

This caribou seemed to know what it was doing, and I had no chance if I got off, so I held on tighter.

Another crack split the air above me and to my left. Sound tangled in the narrow space, echoing strangely between rock walls I could sense more than see. The noise grew, swelling from the left, then rushed lower, downward through the pass like a river raging below.

Were we clear?

The caribou angled upward again, still climbing and moving laterally along the wall.

Its stride steadied. The scraping and testing of its hooves smoothed into a faster rhythm. My body bounced with the change, and agony exploded in my stomach where the horn had bruised me. I tightened my grip without meaning to, the pain in my fingers burning and then fading into a dull, distant ache.

The vibrations lessened.

Pressure in my ears eased a fraction despite the roar still moving fast below us. The caribou kept up its hard, ground-eating pace. There was no rise and fall like a horse, and no moment of weightlessness to steal a breath. Every stride shoved forward through its shoulders and into my chest, rattling my ribs and clacking my teeth together.

The edges of the agony blurred together until I couldn't tell what hurt most. The cold was no longer sharp, just wrong and distant. I tried to flex my toes and couldn't feel them move as the wind tore at my face.

My heart pounded.

Without the scarf, the wind cut straight across my mouth and cheeks, burning my skin raw. My lips split again, and I tasted copper as warm liquid ran down my chin. My breath came fast and shallow, little clouds torn away before they could warm my face. I tried to slow and deepen my breathing and couldn't make my chest obey.

The caribou shifted direction slightly and quickened its pace.

"Hrrrooooh—rrruuuh!" A deep rolling call sounded through the storm to my left.

My caribou lifted its head and tilted its antlers back to the point they brushed the top of my head. "Rrrroohh—hrrruuh!"

The change threw me off balance, and my stomach

lurched hard. Panic flared, hot and bright, cutting through the fog in my head. I locked my arms tighter around the caribou's neck and squeezed my thighs until they burned.

A little farther away to my right, a third responded with a similar call. Additional responses cut through the wind, as if the herd was signaling to one another that they had survived.

We'd survived the avalanche, but I probably had only minutes before I lost all dexterity. My brain was slowing, and thinking was hard.

My head dipped forward and bumped the caribou's neck. The dull impact barely stirred anything but a vague sense that I should lift it again if I didn't want to fall asleep and slide off. If I fell, I'd probably be dead within minutes.

"Hrrr'KAH—rruuk! Hrrr'KAH!" The call came from a little to the left, a harsh bark.

The caribou stopped beneath me so abruptly that my chin hit its neck. Its spine went rigid, breath blasting out in a sharp burst that steamed against my cheek. The calls fractured, the rolling contact calls breaking into harsh, clipped notes that cut through the wind as the caribou barked back and forth, the sounds driving straight into my skull.

My caribou answered with a shorter, deeper bark that vibrated through its chest and into mine. Its weight shifted back as its hindquarters braced and forelegs stamped against the deep snow as if it were trying to solve a problem. The herd called in staggered echoes, the sounds passing fast and clipped through the dark as the wind whipped harder against us.

"RRAAAAAAOOOHHH!" A roar filled the air, and a massive form rose up, blue light flaring in the darkness.

Shit! What *was* that?

My eyes burned, my eyelids slamming shut too late. Pain stabbed behind them, white and blinding, and tears spilled and froze at the corners of my eyes. I tried to crack them open again. Everything blurred, the light far too bright. My head jerked down, and my breath tore out of me.

My caribou lowered its head and spun to the right, charging away from the noises. My arms locked around its neck again on instinct.

The run was relentless—pounding with no lift between strides. Each strike jarred my teeth and sprayed snow against my legs.

The roar came again, closer.

"RRRRAAAOOOHHH—HHRRUUUM!"

The caribou snorted and lengthened its stride, its hooves striking faster and closer together.

Something slammed into the snow behind us. The impact rumbled through the slope and into my spine, and the caribou drove harder. Its shoulders lifted in a shallow bound over broken ground, its stride hitching for a breath before slamming back to earth and into that crushing run. The shift wrenched my balance loose. My palms slid, and my fingers scraped flattened hair slick with melting snow.

Another roar thundered right behind us.

"RRAAOOOHH—KRRUUM!"

The caribou cut sideways, its hooves skidding before regaining traction. The jarring impact tore my grip away. I tried to grasp its neck again and failed.

I hit the snow chest-first, knocking the breath out of me. Cold flooded my face and collar as I rolled, powdery snow packing into my mouth and nose. My shoulder struck hard, and my head bounced, causing my ears to ring.

Terror strangled me. I had to move because, if I didn't, I was toast. The really dark, burnt toast that got thrown out to decompose on its own.

I tried to rise, my hands plunging into the snow, but my elbows folded, and my knees slid out from under me. Glaring blue light stabbed through my closed eyelids before they cracked open. I fought once more to get up, then slipped and rolled over and over in the icy snow. The entire world submerged in darkness.

I no longer knew which way was up, and my legs weren't responding.

Snow burst up around me as something hit the ground close enough to jar my bones. Arms hooked under my shoulders and back, then wrenched me up and crushed me tight against a solid wall. Panic flared through me, and I tried to twist free. But then the darkness claimed me again, and everything faded.

CHAPTER 17

Kai

My heart raced from the strain of lifting Hannah from the snowy ledge she had fallen against and getting us back onto my caribou. As we rode, snow lashed sideways into my face and scoured my skin even with my enchanted hood and scarf. I couldn't imagine how Hannah felt right now.

Her body sagged against my chest, and her head lolled against my shoulder.

Fuck. She was losing coordination.

The pressure in my chest had eased once she was in my arms, but something worse than fear took hold. I *needed* to find a way to warm her fast and protect her from the wind. As her head bobbed, I guided her farther down against my chest so that I could better shield her from the wind's vicious bite.

Her breathing was shallow, and her body trembled. I pulled her closer and locked my arms around her waist. There was no time to waste. She had to get warm, and fast.

Even if I couldn't be with her, I didn't want to lose her.

The caribou surged beneath us, its hooves grinding forward through the drifts. I looked at her face, noting her lips were split and the cuts were raw. If those guards survived the avalanche, they would die for what they'd done to her. I didn't care about the cost.

I removed my scarf and wrapped it gently around her face. The cold was making her injuries worse. "Please keep being a pain in my ass, and don't die." I pressed my cheek against her temple, hoping that any kind of heat would help her.

She was fighting for her life, and all I could do was urge this caribou on faster. My body heat had to reach her with her body crumpled against mine.

"Stay with me," I murmured near her ear. We were close to one of the safe shelters intended for survival during bad storms and hidden through a series of enchantments and wards so that our enemies couldn't find them. There was one half a mile from here, over Broken Spine Ridge.

As if Fate were mocking me, the storm howled louder, but my caribou didn't slow down or lose its footing. There was over two feet of snow, and it was still coming down.

The wind battered my back, sliding through every seam of my cloak. Thick snow drove sideways across the ridge, stinging any exposed skin, while ice formed on my lashes. The caribou lowered its head and grunted, shoulders heaving as it forced its way forward, its hooves striking packed layers of snow that cracked under our weight.

Time ceased to exist as Hannah began to move even less. My magic, more than my sight, guided us to the last ridge where the safe house was. Fate, we had to get there in time. The thought of Hannah not surviving had me pushing the caribou harder and clutching her even closer to my chest.

Something snapped and tightened around us, changing the pressure, and then the small cabin appeared. Its dark stone and treated timber form crouched low against the slope, sheltered by ragged rocks. The slanted roof was heavy with snow that hadn't fully drifted over to block the entrance, thanks to ancient magic woven into the protective foundation of this structure.

My lungs filled fully for the first time since before Hannah had dropped into my world. Thank Fate. There was a chance I could save her.

As the wind died, the stinging eased. The caribou angled toward the cabin door, and its hooves struck packed ground instead of loose powder. It slowed to a controlled stop.

Keeping my hold on Hannah, I swung down and bent my knees to absorb the impact. When my boots were planted, I adjusted her in my grip.

She didn't stir. The joints of her fingers were stiff and curled tight against her chest.

My entire body stilled. I had to get her inside. I gritted my teeth, and my legs burned as I charged to the door.

The thick wooden door opened on iron hinges that groaned. Inside, the sound of the storm reduced to a low, distant roar. The air inside was still and cold, smelling of old ash, animal, and dried resin. I needed to warm the place as soon as possible.

The caribou entered too, its hooves striking the packed earth floor with a familiar hollow thud. As soon as it was in, I shoved the door closed. Darkness engulfed us, but my eyes quickly adjusted. It was much easier to see without the snow obscuring my vision, and I would've breathed a sigh of relief if not for Hannah barely hanging on to life.

I glanced around. Eight narrow beds lined each of two walls. I lay Hannah on the nearest one, its white linen sheets nearly the color of her skin. After making sure her head didn't hit the wooden frame, I removed the wet scarf and brushed my fingers over her reddened cheeks.

I hissed under my breath. Her skin felt like ice, but she was breathing and shivering. There was still hope. Heat was the next priority.

I strode past benches arranged by a wide firepit circled by gray stone. The last occupants had followed proper procedure when they'd left and stocked the firepit with kindling and wood on the central grate. Of all the woods available to us, they had used ironwood, which was some of the best for heat. I owed a favor to whoever had followed protocol. Maybe Fate was showing us some mercy tonight, though part of me feared that mercy would serve only to make it hurt more when Hannah was taken from me. My chest clenched.

No.

Nothing would take my mate from me. Certainly not the cold.

I seized the flint from the metal caddy that held the hearth tools and struck it against the steel. Bright sparks snapped, and soon, smoke curled up from the wood, reaching the peaked ceiling where special vents had been placed. The fire caught, and heat crept outward in slow waves, pushing back the chill. But it wasn't enough.

Looking over my shoulder, I confirmed there was plenty of wood stacked along the wall nearest the door. Racks above the wood pile held tack and blankets meant for the animals since the space had been designed for caribou to also stay in and settle without panic. A trough stocked with hay and winter grass occupied the corner by the tack wall and the wall with the door. Of course, the caribou had headed straight there, its reins dangling down its side.

I hurried back to Hannah's bed and pulled it as close to the firepit as possible, making sure to angle it so that her entire side was exposed to the heat and not just her feet.

Then I went to the caribou and removed the packs. I brought one of the medical supply bags to the bed and knelt beside her. Her lips were pale beneath the cracks and blood, and cuts along her cheek looked as if they'd been made by metal and worsened by the cold. I took her pulse as I watched her uneven breaths. The enchantments in the coat and gloves weren't intended for temperatures this low or in garments that were wet from melting snow. Before I gave her any medicine, I had to get her stabilized and assess her injuries.

"Hannah." I leaned closer, one hand resting on her shoulder, and softened my voice. "Wake up. I need to take these wet clothes off you, and I'd rather do that with your permission than surprise you." My heart ached, watching her. This was my mate. I'd do anything to protect her, but she didn't know that, or that we were mates crafted from Fate's own design.

If she knew, I doubted she'd have acted as she had. She'd dropped into this realm without knowing anything about it. That much was clear.

A dark huff escaped. We hadn't even been aware of one another's existence yesterday, and here I was, determined not to let her die. I knew so little about her, except that she was a fighter. And that, as my mate, she would be treated with respect even if we couldn't be together. "Wake now. You'll have an opinion, I'm sure."

I moved to her feet and pulled off her strange pink and white shoes. They were soaked through but with some faint stains from the pale ash, and her strange white stockings were dripping wet. Her toes and heels were gray-blue and frigid to my touch. "These half boots of yours are entirely foolish. The color suits you, but they're impractical. There is no structural support or insulation. I'll get you better footwear when we're back at the castle."

Holding my hand toward the fire, I felt the heat rising. Good. It was steadily warming, but it wasn't so hot as to be dangerous. Most of the smoke spiraled up through the vent, but a haze was settling through the room. The warm smoky scent filled my lungs with a soft aroma of magnolia and apricot.

Hannah's body jerked, and a rattling inhale tore through

her. Her eyes fluttered open and stared, unfocused, and her hands twitched against the furs. Her fingers were still curled, and she shivered hard. Her teeth started chattering.

I would've felt relief, but she wasn't safe yet. I needed to try to get her talking. "There you are. Good to see you awake. Don't sit up. You need to rest." I stripped her gloves off and placed her arms at her sides. Then I started to undo her coat, unlatching each of the fasteners with care.

"S-so cold. It burns," she gasped. Her hands balled into clumsy fists. "Where—" Her voice broke off as she trembled.

"Easy. You have hypothermia. We need to get the wet clothes off you so we can get you warm. Once your temperature rises, I have clean and dry clothes for you to wear." I opened her coat, revealing the pale shirt that announced she was with Stupid. The irony hit me. It felt fitting, as she made me feel foolish and undone simply by existing. Which I hated!

The soaked shirt outlined her body with perfect clarity. A traitorous surge of interest pulsed through me, and shame poured after it. I focused on the task.

I lowered my gaze to her strange, light-blue trousers. They were drenched, with the fabric torn at her knees and several other places. Her chafed knees were blue, as were the other areas where her skin was directly exposed.

Fire churned within me. Who the hell left her this poor? Even poor fae dressed better than this. In fact, I'd never seen clothes like hers before. No mate of mine would be permitted to dress in such ragged attire.

I found the salve in the medical bag and applied a thin layer of the pale cream to her wrists and the tops of her hands, appreciating the scents of tallow and lavender. "This will help with the pain and help you regain your body heat more easily."

Her skin was waxy and pale, and her lips blue.

A knot formed in my throat as I lifted my gaze from her

body to her face. "Forgive me. I don't intend to impugn your modesty, but I need to take your clothes off to warm—"

"I d-don't give a f-fuck about modesty." Her teeth chattered. Though there was a thickness to her voice and a bleariness in her eyes, her spirit shone through. "I j-just want to get warm. D-do whatever it takes. T-take them all off. I'm f-freezing!"

A lump lodged in my throat. She wasn't warming up fast enough. I needed to do more. I ripped off my own coat and tore away my tunic and the undertunic beneath. Next came my boots and my trousers until I stood before her in nothing but my underclothes. I started peeling off her damp clothes, trying not to notice her nakedness, but my eyes devoured her body.

My dick rose to attention, impossible to hide in the thin clothing I now wore. Disgust flared through me at my own desires and primal urges. I should be focused solely on her health—she deserved better than this uninvited reaction.

Gritting my teeth, I continued to work with steady hands. Her shirt released from her skin with a soft, sucking sound. The wet, pale fabric of her strange undergarment outlined the soft curves of her breasts and revealed the hard peaks of her nipples, pebbled tight from the cold. I forced my gaze to remain clinical, but my blood heated despite the chill still lingering in the air. Then I saw her stomach and ribs, and my anger surged.

Dark bruises spread in thick bands across her torso, climbed her sides, and encompassed her shoulders. My breath left me in a sharp rush, and my chest tightened until my ribs ached. The firelight caught every uneven color and edge as I took in the depths of my inability to protect her. Every mark was a testament to my failure.

"C-cold!" she gasped as the air hit her bare skin. Her body curled up instinctively.

Dammit. Here I was, making her discomfort worse. Shaking off my anger enough to focus, I started working on the peculiar metal fastenings on her trousers. The stiff and heavy fabric resisted as I tugged it down over her hips and thighs. They, too, were darkly bruised, especially her left hip, as if it had been thrown against something multiple times. Even the bruise-free skin beneath was mottled, the flesh cold and clammy under my fingertips as I worked the ruined garment free of her legs.

The burn of the cold and the pain of her circulation being restored would likely keep these bruises from speaking their full pain. One small mercy, perhaps. She didn't appear to have any large open wounds, but there were smaller scrapes that bled a little. The slash across the back of her leg from the arrow had healed completely, leaving only a faint scar.

If she was what I thought she was, her bruises would heal far more slowly until her body heat had been restored. Cold temperatures inhibited healing for Aurora and Day Fae. Her ears might be rounded, but given her appearance, I couldn't imagine she was anything but one of them.

The fire snapped and crackled beside her, its heat warming my face. I moved closer so my body blocked any stray draft from the far side of the bed. I set the medical bag at the top of the bed. "I'm going to help with your body heat. That's it." Then I climbed into the bed, intending to put her back to my chest and layer the blankets over us, then give her the medicine. But as the mattress dipped, the wicked little creature twisted and thrust herself against my body as if she could burrow into my chest and envelop herself in my heat.

I stiffened, and a startled hiss escaped my lips. My arms clamped around her involuntarily.

"Oh! You're so warm!" She shivered and shoved harder against me.

Fuck, she was strong. And still too cold. It was like holding the most beautiful ice sculpture that had ever existed. Her chest touched mine, and she whimpered, the soft sound slicing through me like lightning. I couldn't breathe.

Whatever she wanted—anything she wanted—she would have, as long as she didn't leave me. Nothing would take her from me.

Her head rested against my chest, and her breath shuddered against my bare skin.

My throat bobbed as I fished out one of the more pungent of the tonics from the medical bag. "I have medicine for you." I uncorked the top and pressed the bottle to her lips. "Just sip. Try to stay awake for a few minutes, then you can sleep. It will help restore your blood flow and heal you, though you'll probably be stiff for a day or two. You may have some scabbing, but those will fall off soon."

"Thank you. The snow and ice felt like it was trying to scrub the skin off my face." She parted her lips, wincing slightly, as if she felt the sting of the cuts. I tilted the flask to let the amber liquid flow. A little spilled down her chin and onto her neck and breasts, but most went where it needed to. She grimaced. "It tastes like blue cheese and licorice."

A startled laugh escaped me. "I wouldn't know. I've never tasted blue cheese or licorice." The medicines did taste foul, though. I knew that from experience.

"Lucky you." Her fingers curled against my ribs, still clumsy, still cold, but seeking warmth with a desperation that made my chest ache. "Where are we?"

I smoothed her hair back from her face and wiped away the melted snow. Her magnolia and apricot scent strengthened over the smell of smoke and sweat. "A way point. It's an enchanted place of safety and protection, stocked with basic resources and simple spells."

Her eyelids cracked open, and she looked around, her gaze drifting to the caribou, the dirt floor, the firepit, and the northeastern corner that held a half-moon-shaped well with a lid for easy access to water. "This place is enchanted?" she asked softly.

A smile tugged at my own mouth. "It doesn't look like it, I grant you. But its simplicity is part of what makes it easy to hide. These way points were built long before my time. The magic is strong but of a simple variety that lasts a long time and has few ways to go wrong. It's also easier for us to hide its presence."

The caribou huffed and then lowered its head once again to the food trough, and she wrinkled her nose.

I couldn't hold back my smile because I was confident that I understood her concern. "The wards protect us, but the magic will also absorb whatever waste is left and eliminate odors. Including that in the spell was a wise choice as, at times, there have been as many as twenty hunters and almost as many beasts of burden jammed into this place. The stench alone would have perhaps made some prefer the cold."

She snorted. "Thank goodness. The last thing I want is to freeze, drink blue cheese mixed with licorice, and smell caribou feces. Especially all at once. Do you use spells to keep it warm here? Seems like the fire might be redundant?"

The urge to kiss the top of her head and nuzzle closer rose within me, but I pressed it down. Our position was intimate as it was, and she didn't need to be thinking about that...even if I couldn't stop. "There are spells that help with the warmth. It will never freeze in here, but given your state, even that was too cold. The spells help the fire heat faster and last longer. You're safe here. Now, another sip."

She grimaced, and her nose wrinkled. "Ugh."

"It could be worse. If the yeti had bitten you, we'd be following far more unpleasant healing methods." I studied her face, noting that the skin no longer looked as waxy. The cuts and scrapes were showing signs of healing, though that wind-burn needed time.

"Yeti?" She swallowed again, shaking her head. Her tongue darted to her lips. "You have yetis?" Her eyelids lowered as exhaustion warred with confusion.

I forgot she wasn't from here. "Before you fell off, a large creature spooked your caribou. You remember it?"

"That random glowing blue thing?" Her eyebrow cocked.

"Yes. That was a mother yeti defending her cubs. Their fur glows blue when they want to become more threatening. The bright light can blind and stun some beasts, especially when they're used to the dark."

"It certainly gave me a headache," she grumbled. Her eyelids closed, and her cheek pressed against my chest.

I set the back of my hand on her neck and tested her pulse. It was steadier. "Are you in pain?"

"It's better." She yawned. "Thank you."

"You'll be all healed very soon." I lifted the medicine flask away, corked it, and set it aside, then wiped her mouth and neck with a corner of the blanket. "You can sleep now."

No matter what type of fae she was, the tonic should work fast, warming her from within and stabilizing her body's core temperature while restoring blood flow as she slept.

I pulled the furs folded at the foot of the bed up and over us both, layering the heavy pelts until we were cocooned in warmth and shadow. The firelight flickered against the ceiling, casting dancing shapes across the rough-hewn beams. Her shivering continued, but it did not seem so severe. The medicine was starting to do its work, and she wasn't showing signs of complications. "You're safe now, Hannah. Just rest."

I tucked my chin over the crown of her head and savored the warmth, willing it to soothe and comfort her. My mate was sleeping, and the fire burned as the storm howled outside this safe place. I kept my body wrapped around her, gently rubbing her arms and soothing her blood into circulation.

It was impossible not to notice how beautiful she was. Every line and curve of her. She was a pain in the ass, but her gorgeous breasts could make a paladin or a monk weep. I had to keep myself under control because we would remain in this place until the storm and the danger passed. But perhaps it was fitting that here, in a place stripped down to the essentials, she and I would get to know one another as we were. Or at least as much of ourselves as we could reveal for now.

Yes, that was enough. Enough that, as angry as I was to have found my mate at such a dreadful time, part of me was also glad to have found her at all. She existed, and...terrifying as that was to recognize, I wouldn't trade her for anything.

I stroked her damp hair back from her face. I just had to figure out a way to transition—

Fuck. Fuck!

Something was very wrong.

CHAPTER 18

Kai

I t was me. *I* was wrong.

I was the king, for Fate's sake! I should be able to control my emotions...

I tensed, despite Hannah being in my arms. I'd burned through the lorn leaf I'd taken mere hours ago. How was that even possible?

It had to be because of *her*.

Now, here I was, full of emotions that weren't numbed and a raging dick with a mind of its own. My decisions would be compromised until I could take more of the vital herb.

Guilt weighed on me. I tried to think about blood, guts, and strategy, but I couldn't focus because I was enjoying holding her. And that was the problem. My kingdom had just been attacked. I needed to be planning, anticipating threats, and forming solutions. Innocents died when their leaders became emotional, even if it was for a good reason. And I was holding one of the best reasons ever.

With the heat of her skin against mine, the softness of her curves pressed to my chest, and her scent threading through the smoke, I couldn't focus on anything but *her*. My dick hardened to the point I feared it might explode.

I gritted my teeth and shifted my hips back to put distance between the evidence of my arousal and her body. The last thing I wanted her to do was wake up with it poking her bruised stomach.

She murmured something unintelligible and pressed closer. Her fingers curled against my ribs as if she were anchoring herself to me, and a low groan escaped my throat before I could stop it.

This was torture. Exquisite, maddening torture. And all I wanted to do was break, but she deserved better than that after everything she'd endured.

I was a king, damn it! A war king. A leader whose people looked up to him. And she was undoing me just by lying here.

I forced myself to remember the bruises I'd seen, the raw skin, all the damage done to her in such a short time. Rage flared, hot and welcome, burning away some of the lust.

Those soldiers who had struck her—I would find them. I would make them suffer in ways that would make the Night Court's darkest dungeons seem merciful. Assuming they had survived the avalanche, of course. Yes, good. I could focus on that.

But even that fury couldn't suppress the bond's demands. It sang through my blood, a constant thrum that grew louder with every breath she took against my skin. *My mate.* She was my mate, and she was naked in my arms, and I was supposed to be protecting her, not fighting the urge to—

No. Absolutely not.

I was *not* some rutting beast. I was the *king*. I had control. Discipline! I would not dishonor her or myself.

Once I was certain she was deeply asleep, I eased myself from the bed, dressed, and walked back to the supplies. I removed one of the enchanted flares, notched three lines into its side to indicate our location, and stepped outside in my bare feet to help cool my blood and stop thinking with my dick.

The enchantment kept the worst of the storm at bay, but the ground was still cold as frozen iron. The storm still raged, snow driving sideways in sheets that obscured everything beyond a few feet. The flare would work regardless of the storm, and I didn't want Ashren risking himself and our forces, searching for us in this weather. Gavriel should have gotten back in time and warned the other force not to follow me directly to the avalanche, but Ashren would send out rescue parties to search for us soon after, taking into account the risk. At least the threat of a full-on battle was no longer present.

I activated the flare and hurled it skyward, watching as it burst into brilliant silver light that shot toward the castle. Only certain individuals would be able to see it, and the mark of our location would be revealed only to them.

From the looks of this storm, we had at least another several hours before travel would be safe.

I stayed in the cold until my problem receded. It felt like eternity, but finally, I was able to return, stomping my snowy feet on the packed earthen floor. The caribou huffed as if it somehow understood what I was doing and found me pathetic. I couldn't disagree. I *was* pathetic.

I couldn't stand there, staring at Hannah like some lovesick fool, so I turned my focus to the back of the house, where a hearth held iron hooks and a blackened pot. Above it, shelves were stacked with salt and wrapped bundles. The supplies called to me, and I answered, pulling down bundles of dried meat, hard biscuits, a small pot of preserved berries, and a sealed container of seed cakes soaked in honey. I worked without conscious thought, unwrapping, arranging, preparing portions despite my own belly screaming in protest. When

Hannah woke, she would need food. This was the best I could offer, and that grated on me. Mead and liquor would offer more bite and flavor, but it was probably best if she didn't have alcohol until she was fully recovered.

The fire crackled and popped, sending shadows dancing across the walls. I added another log, then a second, building the heat high. The caribou watched me with dark, knowing eyes as I moved past it to check the trough was full.

I came back to the food and set a plate aside for Hannah, covering it with a cloth. My stomach knotted tight with tension and something I refused to name.

The caribou's tack needed attention, so I worked on the leather straps, checking for damage, oiling the worn spots, adjusting buckles that didn't need adjusting. My fingers moved with mechanical precision while my mind circled back to Hannah with maddening regularity.

She shifted beneath the furs, and I froze. But she only sighed and settled again, her features slack with exhaustion.

Snow hissed against the wards outside. My city had been damaged, my people wounded, time was running out, the Night King would return...and still my thoughts circled back to Hannah like a moth to flame, burning each time they drew too close.

I paced the length of the cabin with my hands clasped behind my back to keep them from reaching for her. The furs rose and fell with her breathing in a rhythm I found myself matching without meaning to. Every few minutes, I stopped to check that her color remained improved and that the medicine was doing its work.

Each time I drew close, her scent wrapped around me like a snare.

This was pure, undiluted madness.

I had faced down armies and held my kingdom together through betrayal and war and the slow erosion of everything

I'd once believed in. I had killed my own uncle with my bare hands and lived with the weight of that necessity every day since.

And yet, this strange, stubborn, infuriating woman from a world I didn't understand had reduced me to pacing like a caged animal in a way point.

I pressed the heels of my hands against my eyes until stars burst behind them. The warm bond pulsed as a constant reminder that she was there, that she was mine, that I had nearly lost her, and that we had yet to solidify all that the bond demanded.

The caribou snorted, and I dropped my hands and glared at it. I didn't need a beast's commentary on this matter.

"Ugh..." Hannah's voice came out raspy from sleep and cold damage.

I spun to face the bed. The furs shifted, and she lifted her head with her tangled hair wild against the dark pelts. Her eyes blinked open, unfocused at first, and then she took in the unfamiliar surroundings. "I was..." She pushed herself up on one elbow, wincing.

I was at her side before I'd decided to move. My hand hovered near her shoulder without quite touching. "You're safe. We're in the way point. Do you remember what happened?"

Her gaze found mine, and something in her expression softened. "Thank you." The firelight caught the amber flecks in her eyes, turning them to molten gold. She was still pale, marked with cuts and windburn on her cheeks, but the waxy quality had left her skin, and her lips had regained their kissable pink color. At least, the splits had fully healed. The bruises on her torso were the ones that worried me most because of their depth.

I startled, and my throat tightened. "You—" I shook my head, struggling to process her kind response. "You did not deserve to die in the cold. And you helped me protect my people. Even if you did refuse to return to the castle as you were ordered."

She wrinkled her nose and looked up with half-lidded eyes. "Then you should have thanked me there and not barked at me like you owned me, King Grouchy Pants." She stretched and yawned. The faint bruises on her forearms were still visible, but the darker ones on her shoulders had lessened.

My chest tightened, and my heart skipped a beat. Though I was scowling at her, she beamed that wry little smile of hers at me, pulling her lips up ever so slightly to the left in a way that cut straight through my heart. This woman was dangerous. She didn't even know how much power she had over me.

The urge to tell her she was my mate rose within me again. She had no idea what we were to each other. Perhaps that was for the best. She had fallen into a new world where nothing was familiar to her, and now she was trapped with me. Explaining mate bonds and all they involved would be a difficult business under these less-than-ideal circumstances. Throwing her in an icy holding cell in my dungeon had not been the best of ways to make our introduction.

That didn't mean I couldn't bargain with her, though.

I grunted and strode to the shelf. The cloth-covered plate sat waiting, and I carried it and a waterskin to her bedside, keeping my expression stern despite the warmth that threatened to crack through my facade.

"Here." I thrust the plate at her, pulling the cloth away to reveal the dried meat, hard biscuits, and preserved berries. "It isn't much. The way points aren't stocked for fine dining, and I..." I cleared my throat, irritated at my own hesitation. "I apologize that it isn't better. But you need to eat. Your body requires fuel to finish healing. Eat all of it, or you will see how grouchy I can be."

She blinked at the offering, then at me. Something unreadable flickered across her features, and she cocked an eyebrow. "What? You'd throw me out into the cold after you rescued me? Seems like a waste." She pulled herself into a sitting position, keeping the furs tucked around her chest with one arm while she took the plate with the other. Her movements were still stiff, careful, but steadier than before. The medicine had done its work well. "Fortunately for you, I don't like being hungry. I love food, and I'm not picky. I don't want to die either, so you won't get a peep outta me."

A peep? What was that? I wanted to ask, but I was afraid of where the conversation would go. She used such odd sayings.

Still, I relaxed. For once, she wasn't going to fight me on something.

She lifted a piece of dried meat between her fingertips and studied me. "Did you already eat?"

"You care?" My brows rose.

"Well, I don't know my way out of here, and I don't have the right stuff to survive." She scowled, but it didn't reach her eyes. "So, I kinda need you alive. It's rather unfortunate."

I'd never struggled so hard to keep the corners of my mouth from lifting. "Ah, well, don't worry. I could skip a few meals and be fine."

"You aren't answering my question." She lifted her chin. "And don't lie to me. I can tell if someone's lying." She tilted her head and popped the dried meat into her mouth. The spark had returned to her hazel eyes, and they danced, even though I knew she had to be uncomfortable. Muscle soreness wouldn't vanish that swiftly, and the worst of the bruises would take at least two more days to heal.

"I would not disgrace myself with a lie, and I have tended to all my needs that could be satisfied." I raised an eyebrow back at her, mirroring her expression.

She studied me, chewing the dried meat slowly. "That's not an answer."

"It's the answer you're getting." I picked up the flask of whiskey and took a shot. Not as good as lorn leaf by a long shot, but I needed something to quiet this storm inside me and chill the heat raging through my veins. I wiped my mouth on the back of my hand. "And we need to talk. You cannot try to escape again while we are out here. We are in the middle of the wilderness, and even if you took the caribou, you would have no chance of getting to safety before you froze to death or were torn apart by predators." I paused, then lessened the gruffness in my voice. "Though you would certainly make matters difficult for them, and I have no doubt that you would prove resourceful. You have done so at every turn thus far. You have a warrior's spirit."

She stared at me, her brow still creased. With a dip of her head, she lifted the waterskin as if in a toast. "Go on."

I took another drink of the whiskey, focusing on the burn and trying not to imagine what thoughts might be sliding through her mind or what it would be like to hold her again and test our spirits against one another as mates did. True mates challenged one another to be better, smarter, and fiercer. And she did all of that as easily as breathing. "I have no desire to harm you. We started on the wrong foot, and your arrival was a...great surprise to me. But I don't wish for it to remain this way. So...I think it is time we made a bargain, Hannah of Tennessee."

CHAPTER 19

Hannah

Let's make a deal.

My mouth dried to the point that I couldn't swallow. I paused, knowing I couldn't take a bite of the hard, flaky biscuit I'd raised halfway to my mouth.

The heat from the firepit brushed my cheek, and the fire popped hard enough to make me flinch. For some reason, his words sounded like an ominous version of *We need to talk.* Still, I couldn't let him know he'd unnerved me. Men liked having that power, and maybe that was why he wasn't currently as grouchy. Softening me up to try to get me to agree to sell my soul and live in an icy, cold prison cell. He might be sexy, and I enjoyed looking at his body, but I was going to pass.

With my free hand, I took a large swig of water, then bit the biscuit. Not wanting to rush an answer, I chewed and swallowed. "What kind of bargain, Kairos of Hypothermia Land?"

The corners of his mouth twitched, and then he dipped his head forward and set his hands on his belt. "To start, you need to understand something about yourself." His gaze moved over me in a way that made my skin prickle. It wasn't leering, just thorough. He took a step closer to the bed, stopping a finger's-width from touching distance.

That strange yank in my chest had strengthened overnight, and a traitorous part of me wanted to inch closer so we could touch. The memory of his warmth and the comfort of his arms around me made me ache.

No, this could always be part of the ruse. Plenty of guys had used me and then gone cold right before they went psycho. *Come on, Hannah. Focus. What is wrong with you? He's trying to lead you into his trap.*

I straightened my shoulders, causing aches to flare all through my stiff body. To hide the pain, I huffed. "And what is this *thing* I need to understand? Other than a delightful pain in the ass." My stomach still ached from being carried bent over the caribou saddle and all the falls I'd taken.

"You are at least part Day or Aurora Fae. Perhaps both," he said flatly.

A bark of laughter escaped me, and the caribou exhaled before shifting its position and resuming its breakfast.

Me too, friend. Me too. I pulled back on the bed and squared my shoulders. Of all the things I'd expected Kai to say, that wasn't even in the top ten. "That's ridiculous. Nice try, but I'm gonna call that shit."

"Shit? How would that be shit?" He stared at me without blinking. "It's neither shit nor ridiculous."

I reached for another biscuit, more for something to do with my hands than because I wanted another. Also, to keep myself from punching him. He thought I was an idiot? "My mother and Aunt Maureen would have told me. They told me everything. Sometimes too much." Between their horror stories about men and intimate positions I never wanted to think of them in, I'd begged them to keep information like that to themselves.

He set his jaw and kept his eyes locked on mine. "I know the signs, Hannah. You're fae."

And the sky wasn't blue. Did he expect me to blindly believe him? For being so smart, he underestimated me. "I'm human. I've always been human, and I always will be." I folded my arms, then winced at how the change in position pulled at my bruised muscles. Dropping my arms, I lifted the furs around myself and pushed my hair back so he could see my ears. "My ears are round, dumbass." Dropping my hair, I rolled my eyes, but an unsettling feeling spread through me, as if I were trying to understand how this might actually be true.

He shook his head. "I know you aren't human. Perhaps your family simply did not tell you."

"So, you have some fae-sensing magic that alerts you to one another? Because where I come from, people don't just forget to mention they aren't human. You don't even know my mother, my aunt, or my absent, deadbeat sperm donor." My sperm donor was one of the worst humanity had to offer, at that, although things might have been better if he had been a literal sperm donor whom she had never met.

"Sperm donor?" His brows furrowed. "How is that even possible? You have to have sex to bear a child, so a penis isn't optional."

We might understand each other's words, but we didn't speak the same language... clearly. "They had sex, but he didn't stay." Still, I liked how confused Kai looked right now. How far did their medical science go here since everything looked roughly medieval? We humans didn't really know about eggs until the 1700s. "But where I come from, there are sperm banks and donors, and sperm can be medically placed with a woman's eggs to fertilize them."

"Humans lay eggs?" He ran a hand through his hair. "I've heard enough for now. My point is, I may know your family. And you do not have to be full fae to carry the powers of your bloodline, especially if you are from a powerful lineage." He spoke these words as evenly as if he were telling me that I had qualified for a great deal on car insurance or debt consolidation.

One of the logs in the firepit shifted and sparked flames, and I startled.

My tongue thickened in my mouth as my brain struggled to wrap itself around all this. An uncomfortable little whisper in the back of my mind and the twinge in my gut said it could be true. There had always been odd things about my family. But maybe I was just trying to make sense of them and imagining connections where there weren't any. "What proof do you have?" For once, I couldn't come up with a sassy response.

He turned back to the fire and put more logs on it. The burned wood shifted, and the fresh wood crunched against the charred logs and the metal grate. "Your appearance, for one. You share all the features of the fae of both courts. The gold in your hair is especially lustrous, which is a feature shared by both the Day and the Aurora Fae, though the Aurora are best known for that trait. And your eyes are the right color as well. There is also the strikingness of your beauty. It is exceptional, a trait shared by the royal and noble houses."

I stiffened a little, trying to smile and play it off. "You're laying it on too thick now." I couldn't hide the dark amusement that colored my voice. The joke didn't land, though, not even with me.

He narrowed his eyes. "I would presume you have received a great deal of male attention from the humans in your realm." As he said that, one of his fists curled at his side. He straightened, a muscle ticking in his jaw.

My eyebrow lifted. "Well...some. Yes." I pressed my lips into a tight line, not wanting to say more than that. It never went well. Not for me, Mom, or Aunt Maureen. Our lot was heartbreak and disappointment if we were lucky. Bruises, beatings, and obsessive stalkers if we weren't. And I was rarely lucky.

His upper lip curled for just a breath. He then snatched up the poker and stirred the coals. Smoke spiraled into the ceiling vent, and the thick woody scent permeated the air.

Exhaling, he focused on me once again. "You always smell of magnolia and apricots, even when you've been sweating and bleeding. Fae scent presents above all other scents of their bodies. And I have not known you long enough to determine this, but I would presume you are one who rises with the sun and who feels loss and sorrow in the dead of winter and at night. True sunlight does not bother your eyes nearly so much as it does other people, even when it is blinding."

"It's called SAD—seasonal affective disorder." My scowl deepened, and my fingers curled into the deep, soft fur blanket. "Lots of people have that!" And he was right about the smell, though it was never overpowering. I never needed perfume or deodorant, which was nice. "And I—I don't always smell like that. It's just...I don't smell bad."

The violet in his eyes deepened, and the ring thickened. "And then there's your healing. The Day and Aurora Fae do not heal as swiftly in the cold and dark as they do in the light and heat." He gestured to our surroundings. "The difference in the way that your leg and hand healed before you were exposed for a long period to the cold. The physical cold slows your healing as well, which was why you were in such bad shape last night."

I refused to admit it, but the speed at which my first few injuries had healed had taken even me by surprise. But that didn't mean he was telling the truth.

"And beyond that, there's the way in which you arrived. You could not have entered a portal, nor used a magical dagger to open a portal with your blood, if you were not fae. And for your blood to work at all, either the blade and the mirror had to be enchanted to respond to you, or you had to be of a line for whom the blade and mirror work automatically. The only thing that keeps me from saying you are from a royal line is that you lack the ring around your pupil."

I blinked, trying to slow my racing thoughts. "Ring? Oh... like yours?" He did have a band of violet that was always changing size. "That means you're royalty?"

"Royal blood, and a powerful fae." He nodded, as if he still could not fully accept that I might not be royalty. "But it is possible that your absence from our realm has muted your abilities and powers. You need time to rest, recover, and draw upon your abilities."

"I don't have any abilities," I snapped.

"You do." He stared at me, unrelenting as the stones around the firepit. "And you *are* fae."

His confidence grated on my nerves like sandpaper. I wanted to throw something at his infuriatingly composed face and continue arguing with him, but the words caught in my throat. Because deep down, in a place I didn't want to examine too closely, something stirred. A recognition I couldn't name. He was making me even more confused and unsettled.

The biggest problem I had with accepting what he'd said was that it would mean Mom and Aunt Maureen had hidden something vital from me. We'd always been so open with each other, and if this was true, they—and especially Aunt Maureen—had betrayed me. They'd been my rocks for my entire life... well, until a while ago.

My heart fractured.

"Even if that were true," I said slowly, each word dragged out of me like pulling teeth, "what does any of this have to do with your bargain?"

The orange light of the fire carved shadows along his left side as he faced me, the haze from the smoke giving him an almost mystical appearance. "I give you my word that, if you agree not to run, and you remain under my care during your time in this realm, I will see to it that you end up where you belong. In exchange, all your needs will be provided for, and I will allow you access to my library and archives so that you may search for the precise mirror and blade that you used to create the portal, learn all you wish of your people, and determine the extent of your abilities. We will solve the mystery of who you are."

My head jerked back. He couldn't be serious. Did he really expect me to accept that? "The library part sounds nice, but I'm not interested in staying in a freezing cell. Thanks, but I'm going to pass." I'm sure his sorry ass would love for me to remain his prisoner, but I would *not* be going back to that.

His entire being tightened, and his nose wrinkled, returning his demeanor to the Grouch Potato he'd been before. He took a step toward me, and I prepared to fight.

The furs moved as I threw the plate to the side and prepared to defend myself. My body screamed in protest, but I refused to be taken prisoner again.

"Here I am, trying to be cordial, and you assume I'll throw you into the same prison cell." He grimaced and glanced at the floor. "My intention is for you to be a guest and stay in one of the guest rooms near mine."

My stomach lurched, and for a second, guilt weighed on me. I quickly pushed it away, because what else was I to suspect, given how he'd treated me when I arrived? "It would've been nice if you'd included *that* in the proposal. What did you expect me to assume?"

"After saving you and bringing you here to heal, I thought I'd earned some goodwill." He crossed his arms.

The caribou huffed loudly and shook its head while looking at him.

I held back my giggle, barely. "See, even he agrees with me." I pointed to the beast.

He glared at the animal. "You do like to eat, right?"

The caribou grunted and then turned his head toward the wall.

In that moment, I realized how smart these creatures truly were. "Okay, so you're offering me a bedroom at the palace and to have all my needs met, along with access to your library. What do you get out of it? You aren't just offering this out of the goodness of your heart."

"I'm not." He stared at me with those gorgeous lilac eyes. "The Day Court was destroyed decades ago in an attack by the Night Court. All but those few Day Fae who were visiting or living in the other courts or who lived in the Wilds were killed. Some refugees, like Thea, live in my court. The Aurora Court, however, was plunged into an enchanted sleep spell that covers their whole land. A barrier stands between us and the entirety of their kingdom, preventing us from even entering that land. But it *must* be reached and the kingdom restored, because our realm cannot survive if things continue in this way. Our environments are out of balance. The days are short, the light limited compared to what it was. While the seasons continue, the winter is colder and longer and bleaker."

I nibbled on my lip. "How did the Aurora Court go...to sleep like that?" It sounded similar to the story of Sleeping Beauty, but not exactly, and he probably wouldn't get the joke.

"The Night Court began this war decades ago, after the Night King's betrothed from the Day Court rejected him. In the attacks, the Aurora Court came to the aid of their Day Court ally, intending to cast a spell upon them that would put the Day Court in a protective slumber to protect them from the Night King's wrath until the matter could be resolved, and to protect them from the Night King's wrath. But the Night Court had already moved, and the attack was in progress, obliterating the entire Day Court and turning it to ash and cinder. The spell was reflected back on the Aurora Court, and all within that kingdom were put into a sleep. Only a member of the Aurora Court with strong magic can undo the spell. Which is why I require your help, and why the Night King will be desperate to test you and determine your value. If you can be of assistance to him, he will keep you. Otherwise, he will kill you as he has done all others he deemed useless, including other Aurora Fae."

A shiver ran down my spine. After what those Night Guards had said, I'd rather be locked in Kai's prison than taken to that court. At least, with Kai's guards, I wouldn't constantly be afraid of being assaulted or taken advantage of.

I ran a hand over the fur blanket. "He wants to wake the Aurora Court? Why? So he can kill them?" I adjusted my position, wincing at the ache in my stomach and core. I tucked my legs under myself, and the furs slid down a little, baring my still bruised shoulders.

His gaze fell to the curve of my shoulder, and his tongue darted over his lips. "No, he wants to bring balance, and if he rescues them, the Aurora Court will be in his debt. He could use that to force them to become his ally and work with him to destroy the Dusk Court—my court."

"And you...do you want the Night Court destroyed?" I forced the words out, even though I knew it was dangerous to ask. But when had I ever cared about what was safe when it was this important? Kai had already proven himself a complicated man, but I wasn't on board for genocide, no matter who it was against. If he'd killed his own uncle, he was capable of murdering others.

"No." He spoke the word with such finality that it felt like a physical blow. "I do not. If I must kill them to save my people, I will. But that is not what I plan. This land needs all four of the courts alive and thriving for balance, but now..." His eyes shuttered, and his throat bobbed. "Now, at best, we can hope for some healing and warmth to return with the

Aurora Court when its people are awakened. I hold no animosity toward the Night Court as a whole. King Bram was..." His gaze dropped to the fire, and the lines of his brow deepened. He shook his head, as if he'd thought better of what he was going to say. "He has changed from who he was. Heartbreak may have been the cause, but regardless, he is responsible for the death of one court in its entirety and countless lives in the other courts from the war that has followed. It cannot be permitted to continue. If I have to sacrifice his people to save mine and the Aurora Court, then I will."

The weight of his words settled over me. I stared at him, trying to reconcile this man with his vow.

I wrapped my arms around myself. The furs pooled around my waist, except for the one I was hugging to my chest. "So...what happens if I'm not related to the Aurora Court or strong enough to help?"

Something flickered across his face. "I will see to it you get to where you belong, regardless of where that is," he said firmly. "But I also give you my word that I will not harm you, Hannah. You are under my protection. Unlike the Night King, I won't kill you."

I wanted to believe him, which was dangerous. Some stupid, naive piece of me that should have died years ago actually wanted to trust this brooding king. "And if I say no?" I lifted my chin, meeting his gaze head-on. "If I tell you to shove your bargain and take your chances without me?"

His jaw tightened, and for a moment, the shadows in the corners of the cabin deepened. Then he released a slow breath through his nose. "Then you would still be under my protection until the storm passes and we return to the castle. After that..." He paused, and something like pain crossed his features. "I would not force you to stay. But I would ask you to reconsider. Many lives hang in the balance. Not just mine. Not just *my* court. The Aurora Fae have been sleeping for decades, their cities full of children and families trapped in slumber. An entire court of people, frozen in time while the world around them crumbles. And if all others fall before they wake, then eventually, they too will die, and this whole world will be a wasteland."

Damn him for making this about innocent people instead of politics and power. I could have said no to a king demanding my obedience. I couldn't say no to helping children trapped in magical sleep, or to helping the ones in his kingdom, either. The face of that little boy whose mother had been desperately trying to reach him through the rubble flashed through my mind. "And you promise you won't ask anything else of me?"

"I won't ask anything else of you in exchange for this bargain. Within the week, we should be able to determine whether you are Day or Aurora Fae. It may take longer to reveal the mirror and the dagger that brought you here. I would ask, though, that you would allow me to examine your injuries again." He gestured to my body. "The salves and tonics should have done a great deal of work in restoring you, but some of the injuries—especially to your torso—concern me."

"Yeah, well, it's no picnic for me either, but I'm open to anything that could help me out." I exhaled and lowered the furs. The cool air hit my skin, raising goosebumps despite the fire's warmth. I looked down at myself, taking stock of the damage for the first time since waking. My arms showed faint yellow-green shadows where some bruising had faded, though it didn't hurt even where my bra straps cut in a little. My legs looked better, too, the mottled patches softened to something almost normal. But my shoulders still had a number of dark marks, and my torso, hips, and thighs...

Dark purple and deep blue spread across my ribs and stomach in ugly blooms, the colors vivid against my pale skin.

The bruises wrapped around my sides where the saddle horn had dug in during that hellish ride and on my left where the caribou's straps must have pinched me more than once. More clustered along my hips where I'd been grabbed and thrown. I could see a few of the darkest ones through my light turquoise panties. It looked like I'd ridden a bull and been squashed by it. Still, it all looked far worse than it felt, which was something at least. Whatever he'd given me must have dulled the deeper aches. Aside from stiffness, I really didn't feel that bad at all.

Kai's breath caught, and he tried to cover it by clearing his throat. He moved closer and stopped at the edge of the bed, then lowered himself to his knees on the packed earth floor. The position put his face eye-level with my stomach and close enough that I could see the firelight dancing in his eyes. "May I touch you here?"

CHAPTER 20

Hannah

Heat pooled in my belly, and I suddenly wanted to rub my body against his. If he didn't touch me, I might combust. I nodded, not trusting my voice. Something about seeing this powerful king kneeling before me and asking permission sent a flutter through my chest that had nothing to do with bruised ribs.

His hands hovered over my skin for a heartbeat before making contact. When he touched my skin, a faint buzz vibrated and moved with his hands along my body. His touch was clinical at first, with careful fingertips pressing gently along my ribcage, testing each bone. His palms were warm, almost hot, and I found myself leaning into that heat despite myself. He had large, strong hands, and I wanted to press against them and feel them more.

"Tell me if anything hurts beyond being bruised," he murmured, his attention focused on his examination. His pulse jumped in his throat, and his breathing turned shallow.

I really looked at him for the first time without the haze of cold, panic, or fury clouding my vision. He was definitely easy on the eyes, and I couldn't tear mine away. Everything about him, from the sharp line of his jaw to the sleek dark indigo hair to the breadth of his shoulders, was just...perfect. And those arms of his were ideal for snuggling and holding, especially with his shirt sleeves rolled up to the elbows and tight around his shoulders. His taut muscles moved with practiced care, and I traced the lines of his forearms and biceps down to his chest and abdominals with my eyes before I could stop myself.

He was beautiful. Infuriatingly, impossibly beautiful in a way that made my heart ache.

His fingers pressed along my lower ribs, and I sucked in a breath. He shuddered in response.

"Did I hurt you?" His voice was a low rumble that made my core throb. Concern flashed in his eyes, then faded as he studied me. His pupils blew wide, and the lavender of his irises turned violet.

"No." I swallowed hard. His touch sent sparks skittering through my body, lighting up places that had no business lighting up right now.

His hands stilled. "You seem to be healing well. I don't think there's any internal bleeding, but the pain may return. I have a salve that will help with the stiffness and bruising, if you'll allow me. I put a stronger warming one on you last night, but this one is more restorative and will focus on the bruising specifically, as well as preventing additional pain."

"Okay." The word came out breathier than I'd intended, and I cleared my throat. "Sure. Whatever helps."

He leaned forward and removed a small tin from a bag on the bed. When he opened it, the contents smelled like lavender, eucalyptus, and vanilla.

"Lie back," he commanded, causing inappropriate fluttering in my stomach.

I complied, settling against the furs and focusing on the beams of the ceiling. The logs shifted again in the firepit, the flames casting dancing shadows overhead. My heart hammered against my ribs in a rhythm that had nothing to do with injury. *Just keep breathing.* It wasn't the first time I'd been around a handsome man.

His fingers dipped into the salve, and then his hands were on me again.

The first touch made me suck in a breath. The salve was cool at first, but his palms warmed it. Wherever he pressed, heat bloomed and spread. He started at my ribs, working the ointment into the deepest bruises with slow, circular motions. His thumbs traced the spaces between my bones, pressing just hard enough to ease the tension without causing pain.

My entire body felt light, and my eyes drifted shut as his hands moved across my stomach. The broad sweep of his palms covered so much skin at once. I bit the inside of my cheek to keep from making any embarrassing sounds, but a small sigh escaped anyway.

His hands faltered for a heartbeat before resuming their work.

I cracked one eyelid open and caught him staring at my face. His expression was tense with something that looked almost like hunger. His chest rose and fell faster than before, and that muscle in his jaw was working overtime.

A small, satisfied smile tugged at my lips. Good. At least, I wasn't the only one affected by this.

He moved to my hips, and I had to fight to keep my breathing even. His fingers traced the curve of my hipbone, spreading the salve along the ugly purple marks there, and every nerve in my body seemed to light up at once. Heat pooled low in my belly, entirely separate from the warmth of the salve.

Oof, calm down. He was just treating my injuries, and I didn't need to make this more complicated. I had to be misreading him due to my own foolish fantasies. There was nothing sensual about medical care. Nothing at all.

Except...his thumb was making slow circles on the sensitive skin just above my hip, and his other hand had splayed possessively across my stomach, and I was pretty sure neither of those things was strictly necessary for healing purposes.

I shifted, and his hands stilled.

"Am I hurting you?" His voice had dropped to something rough and low that shuddered along my consciousness and made my insides flutter.

"No." I swallowed again, forcing myself to look at him. "Definitely not hurting."

Something flickered in his eyes, dark and heated. He held my gaze for a long moment before resuming, his movements slower now, more deliberate. His hands traveled up my sides, thumbs brushing the undersides of my breasts with a touch that made my breath catch even through my bra. He was watching my face, cataloging every reaction, every hitch in my breathing.

"The bruising extends higher than I realized." His voice was almost hoarse. "I should—"

"Yes." The word came out before I could think better of it. "You should."

His jaw clenched, and for a moment, I thought he might pull away. Instead, his hands moved higher, spreading the cool salve across my collarbone, down over the swell of my breasts where smaller bruises had formed. His touch was featherlight there, almost reverent, and I had to close my eyes against the intensity of it.

This was a terrible idea. I knew it was a terrible idea. I'd known this man for barely a day, and most of that time had been spent being imprisoned by him, running from him, or nearly dying. None of those things should have led to me lying almost naked under his hands while my body responded like it had never been touched before.

But damned if I could make myself care right now.

His hands moved to my shoulders, the salve warming under his palms as he worked the tension from muscles I hadn't even realized were knotted. I let out a long breath, my body melting deeper into the mattress beneath me. His thumbs pressed into the hollow at the base of my neck, and a sound escaped me—something between a sigh and a moan that I couldn't have stopped if I'd tried.

His fingers traveled up the column of my throat, slow and deliberate, spreading warmth as they went. The touch could still be argued as medicinal, but the way his breath had gone ragged told a different story. His fingertips traced my jaw, a slight tremor in them that felt like barely leashed restraint.

He stopped with his palm cupping my cheek, thumb resting just below my cheekbone.

I froze, my mouth dry and my gaze fixed on his. He stared down at me, his eyes searching my face with an intensity that made my pulse stutter.

Everything slowed, and neither of us moved. My head spun from not being able to breathe.

"Hannah..." My name escaped his lips, broken, almost pained.

I moistened my lips, still staring up at him. "Kai?"

He leaned closer then, his thumb pressing my lips apart where my tongue had just been. "Am I hurting you?" he asked again, his face mere inches from mine.

"No," I whispered. But if he had been, I'd've asked him to hurt me more if it felt like this.

His lips brushed mine, featherlight at first, questioning. A shiver ran through my entire body, and the buzz jolted throughout. Then his hand slid into my hair, cradling the back of my head...and he devoured me.

The world dissolved.

His mouth was warm and tasted faintly of the whiskey he'd drunk earlier and something wild and sweet that I couldn't name. He kissed me like I was something precious... like he'd been waiting for me. His lips moved against mine with a tenderness that made my chest ache.

My fingers found the hard planes of his chest beneath his gray tunic. His heart thundered beneath my palm. He made a sound low in his throat—half groan, half growl—and the kiss deepened. His tongue swept against my lower lip, and I opened for him without hesitation.

This. This was what kissing was supposed to feel like. Fuck! He knew what he was doing.

Every kiss I'd ever had before this moment paled in comparison. This was fire and safety wrapped together, desire and comfort intertwined so tightly I couldn't tell where one ended and the other began. His hand tightened in my hair, tilting my head back to give him better access, and I arched up into him, not caring about the bruising.

His other hand found my waist and urged me closer until there was no space between us. The furs slipped away entirely, and I didn't care. All I cared about was the heat of his body against mine, the way his muscles tensed beneath my fingertips, the desperate sound he made when I scraped my nails lightly down his chest.

He broke the kiss only to trail his lips along my jaw, down the column of my throat, finding that sensitive spot where my pulse hammered wildly. His teeth grazed the skin there, and I gasped, my back arching off the furs.

"Hannah," he breathed against my neck. The way he said my name was like a prayer, like a curse, and it cracked something inside me wide open.

I pulled him back to my mouth, kissing him harder and hungrier. My fingers tangled in his dark hair, and he groaned into my mouth as I tugged. His hand slid down my side, over the curve of my hip, pulling my leg up around his waist. The movement pressed us together in a way that left no doubt about how much he wanted me, with the hard ridge of his dick pushing against my core.

I needed him badly.

A sharp knock struck the cabin door.

We froze, his mouth still pressed to my throat, my leg still wrapped around him. The knock came again, three hard raps that echoed through the small space.

"Your Majesty?" a muffled voice called from outside. "We tracked the flare. Is everything well?"

CHAPTER 21

Hannah

My heart pounded, and Kai's entire body went rigid against mine. For a moment, neither of us moved. Then he pulled back, his eyes still dark with want but rapidly cooling into something harder—much like his dick, which was still pressed hard against me.

"Fuck," he breathed, the word barely audible.

I couldn't have agreed more. This was catastrophically bad timing. Apparently, my bad luck was returning.

He was off me in an instant, moving with a speed that left me blinking at the ceiling. The loss of his warmth hit me like a physical blow, and I scrambled to pull the furs back up around myself in case whoever it was barged in.

"A moment," Kai called steadily toward the door. He grabbed one of the bags on the far side of the room and ripped a blue cloth bundle out of it. Then he tossed the bundle at me and started rummaging through the bag.

It landed in my lap. I blinked, looking at the pile in front of me until reality caught up. Clothes.

Yeah, I didn't need anyone else seeing me this way. I unfolded the bundle with fumbling fingers, still trying to get my heart rate under control. The soft, muted blue fabric reminded me of a winter sky just before dusk. Not surprisingly, it looked like the sort of thing I'd seen folks wear to the Renaissance Fair, but of a much higher quality. I tugged what I assumed was an undershirt over my head first, grateful at how soft it was against my skin. Even if it was tight around my breasts and hips in a way that left little to the imagination and wasn't especially flattering. Next, I tugged on a long-sleeved shirt with a rounded neck. It was looser but still a bit snug at my breasts, with sleeves that had to be shoved up to keep them from covering my hands.

The pants were another story. They were loose through the legs, which was comfortable enough, but when I tugged them over my hips and backside, I realized they were decidedly tight across my ass. The kind of tight that made me very aware of exactly how much fabric was stretched across exactly which curves and whose hands I wouldn't mind having on me. The garment had ties instead of a zipper, though, so it was easy enough to fasten at my waist.

As I twisted and tried to find some give, I caught Kai checking out my butt.

"Take a picture. It'll last longer." I pulled the pants up a little higher and adjusted the ties as I fixed him with a coy look.

He pressed his lips in a tight line and dropped his gaze back to the caribou, which was still near the trough. "That won't be necessary. You'll need these." He tossed a pair of soft leather boots to me. While the soles were rigid, the legs were floppy. The insides were lined with soft gray fur, and a pair of gray wool socks had been stuffed inside one.

He avoided looking in my direction again. "They'll be big for you. We can stuff rags into the toes to make them fit better."

I smirked as I sat on the bed and pulled on socks. "Oh, I'm sure you know all about stuffing things."

His spine went ramrod straight. Probably not the only thing that did. I bit back my own smile, knowing I probably shouldn't be poking him like this. Instead, he should've been poking me, but humor was all I had left.

My socks from yesterday were now dry, thanks to the firepit, so I balled them up and shoved them into the toes.

Kai moved around the cabin, stuffing supplies into bags, checking straps, saddling the caribou, doing everything in his power to avoid looking at me or speaking to me.

I startled. Wait. Was he going to avoid me? When I acted cold like that, the guy I was with was toast, and I wanted to get away from him, pronto.

What an asswipe.

But then I caught him sneaking another glance as I stood to test the boots, his gaze dropping to where those pants clung before snapping away. I gritted my teeth. Nope, I didn't play games unless I was the one in charge.

As I finished, he guided the caribou toward the door.

When he opened it, a rush of cold wind sliced through, and I sucked in a breath. Harsh white light spilled across the floor. Bulky, dark shapes crowded the doorway, wearing fur hats rimed with frost, scarves pulled high, and coats thick enough to blunt the wind that shoved in behind them. The smell of cold iron and wet wool rolled in with their boots.

Kai brought the caribou forward and stepped through the doorway without acknowledging me again. As he went outside, he spoke to someone, but I couldn't make out the words. Two soldiers entered and started shifting the wood and spreading out the coals in the firepit. I adjusted my boots once more and wiggled my toes against the balled-up socks. They weren't the most comfortable of shoes, but I was already grateful for the warmth.

Kai returned to the doorway and gestured for me to come out. Though I wasn't particularly fond of obeying anyone's orders, I did want to leave this place. The cold set my teeth on edge even from here, but I forced myself forward.

As soon as I stepped out, I was engulfed in bright white light. Though the sun above was watery and pale yellow, it reflected off the miles and miles of snowy terrain. Eight more warriors clad in fur coats had arrived on their massive caribou, and three other saddled caribou stood close by to rescue us. Yes, they'd arrived just in time to keep my absolutely incredible massage from reaching a very happy ending.

I sucked in a breath and hissed it out through my teeth. At least the cold was distracting me from all that. My nose went numb almost instantly, and the ache in my ribs and hips flared as if the bruises had been waiting for permission.

"You'll need these," Kai said, and held out a gray scarf and hood. His fingers brushed my jaw as he tucked the scarf around my neck and over my nose. His knuckles grazed my cheekbone and lingered just long enough to register heat through the cold. He then pulled the hood down to cover my ears, and his thumbs pressed briefly at my temples to seat it.

Every place he touched buzzed.

"Thank you." My voice was muffled under the wool. He seemed to care for me right now, but I hated hot and cold actions. He needed to make a fucking decision. He was the king, for holy sakes.

His eyes flicked to my mouth, then away. "You will be of no good to our court if you die."

Wow. Who said romance was dead? Clearly, they hadn't met King Grouchy of Hot and Cold. Benefiting his court was the only reason for me to be alive, but at least that reminded me where I stood with him.

Maybe he wanted to keep face in front of his men, but still...I wasn't fond of it, especially after how intense that massage session had gotten. That definitely hadn't been just a normal physical encounter, and I refused to be anyone's secret or side piece. He'd have another thought coming to him if he believed that.

"We'll head directly back to the castle." He approached his caribou and leaped onto its back, even though it was about as tall as he was at the shoulder.

I blinked, impressed despite myself. He'd made that look so easy. "You certainly know how to handle yourself." I set my gloved hands on my waist and glared at him.

The corner of his mouth twitched, but his gaze slid to me, slow and pointed. "You'll ride with me to ensure your safety. Do you need help mounting the caribou?"

Heat sparked in my belly despite the cold. *Nope. Down, girl. How long has this cheetah been kept in her cage?*

"Don't worry. I know exactly how to mount a beast." I winked as Kai's posture tightened, then I studied the caribou to determine how I could do this without looking like an idiot. I was not just going to grab onto its neck and drag myself up. Last time I'd mounted one by myself, I'd jumped off a boulder.

"I could offer the lady a boost," said a guard who suddenly popped up beside me.

"That won't be necessary." Kai waved him away. "Hannah, if you can't get up here in the next two minutes, I will lift you myself."

Challenge accepted. I walked to the edge of the snowy circle. It looked as if there was something helping support the barrier that kept the storm from getting closer and the snow from drifting as high, based on the depth of the snow and how it changed beyond the circle.

"What are you doing?" Kai scoffed. "You're supposed to get in the saddle, not go for a stroll."

My attention landed on a bit of gray stone poking out of the snow at the edge of the circle. I brushed off a little of the snow on the mound to confirm it was a boulder, and then walked back to the caribou.

"Finally, let's quit wasting time." Kai lifted his chin like he was the boss of me.

I ignored him and, with a cheeky smile, I approached the caribou, took hold of its bridle, and tugged it forward. "Come on, baby boy. Wanna help me real quick?"

"What—" Kai startled, stiffening in the saddle as the caribou snorted and followed me forward.

The soldiers watched, faces all but covered beneath the hoods and scarves, though I glimpsed their widened eyes.

I guided the caribou to the boulder, stepped onto the rock, and jumped up. I landed awkwardly and folded over the caribou's neck, practically sliding into Kai's lap with my butt in the air.

Great. So much for dignity. Now they can all see how tight my britches are.

He stiffened against me, and muted murmurs of amusement sparked from the guards. Huffing and grunting, I wiggled and tried to navigate my way into a seated position, but the old bruises flared and complained with a vengeance. The front of my face pressed into the caribou's neck and then against Kai's thigh. "Just a minute."

He sighed, then grabbed me by the shoulders and lifted me easily as I swung my legs into position. He groaned, "You're going to injure yourself again. Be still."

His hands adjusted me with infuriating efficiency, settling me in front of him with my back pressed to his chest, my legs pressed against his, and his arm wrapped around my waist to hold me steady. My ass was positioned directly over his crotch.

It was more intimate than I'd expected. I swallowed hard.

"Would you prefer to walk?" His breath ghosted warmth against my ear, and I hated how much I didn't hate it.

"Point me in the right direction, and I'll figure something

out." I straightened my shoulders as the caribou huffed, its breath steaming in the air. My body still pulsed with desire from that massage, and the warmth radiating from him was already seeping through my bones.

His arm tightened around me as he spoke in a voice so low only I could hear it. "I'm sure you could."

The traitorous heat in my belly and the pulse in my core made me want to melt against him. He was acting secretly hot toward me again, but to everyone else, it would seem like nothing was happening between us.

Not that I wanted him bragging about me either, but I wanted something other than *this*. I rolled my ass over his crotch, wanting to mess with him the way he was messing with me.

Both his posture and his dick hardened. He squeezed me slightly harder, then tugged the reins with the hand not holding me. "Move out," he called to the soldiers. "Keep an eye out for ice prowlers. The last thing we need is a fight."

Ugh. It didn't feel right to tease him if there were threats nearby.

The group fell into formation around us, and the caribou took off, hooves crunching through the fresh snow in a steady rhythm. When I glanced back to see our progress, the two men who had gone into the cabin to prepare it for the next visitors had returned and mounted two of the three remaining caribou. The third trailed after them, in case an extra was needed, I supposed.

We had no sooner passed the boulders and the barrier than the wind picked up like a wild creature, and everything became far brighter. The wild wintery landscape stretched out in every direction. It was a stunning expanse of white broken only by dark spears of rock and the distant smudge of mountains against a pale sunny sky that made everything glitter. The cabin itself had vanished as if swallowed up by the snow, and our trail vanished after we had gone on for several feet. That had to be due to the wards he'd spoken of.

When I glanced over my shoulder, I realized most of the men were squinting, and I wasn't. It was bright, but the light didn't hurt my eyes. I didn't have to squint at all, and I could make out every dip and crevice. Maybe that wasn't as normal as I'd thought. An uncomfortable tension settled in my stomach.

Kai's chest was a wall of heat against my back, and I found myself leaning into him despite my irritation. The scarf helped block some of the wind, but nothing could fully stop the cold from finding every gap in my clothing. At least, the boots were doing their job, and my toes were still attached, which was more than I could say for my dignity after that mounting disaster.

The ride settled into a slow but punishing rhythm that worked its way straight through my bones as the caribou shoved their way through the snow path. Each step rolled my hips forward and back against the saddle. My breath steamed against the wool of the scarf with every exhale, and the deep ache in my ribs spread outward with a soreness that flared whenever the animal shifted.

Kai stayed silent behind me, but his arm remained firmly at my waist and became a steady restraint that kept me upright when fatigue made my spine want to sag. Heat bled through his coat into my back, just enough to make me painfully aware of where his body ended and mine began.

I adjusted once, trying to ease the pressure in my hips, and felt his grip tighten a fraction. He anchored me without comment and scooted back in the saddle a little, which helped me support myself so that I didn't have to use as much of my own strength to hold myself up.

The wind rose and fell with gusts sliding under the edge of my hood and down my collar. My nose ached, then burned, then went numb again. I flexed my toes inside the oversized boots, grateful for the stuffed socks even as stiffness crept up my legs. Snow hissed under hooves, and the soldiers moved like shadows at the edges of my vision, their formation shifting subtly with the terrain.

Time stretched thin and brittle. The steady forward motion blurred into sensation after sensation, but at last, jagged and dark stone walls rose out of the white ahead of us. We were nearing the Eastern Wall Gate. The sight pulled a knot tight in my chest that loosened only when we drew closer, and the gates stood open like iron teeth parting to let us through.

Yesterday, I was desperate to get away, but today I just wanted to get inside somewhere and never experience snow again.

A rider broke from the group and surged ahead with his cloak snapping in the wind. The sound of hooves echoed off stone as we passed under the archway. Inside the city, the air felt different, and I shivered. The cold cut deep but steadier, and the snow was packed hard beneath us. Faces turned, and movement rippled along the inner wall. Calls went up, announcing that the king had returned.

Excitement bubbled inside me. Soon I'd be able to stretch and move, and maybe even have a bath. My chest tightened with hope for that, but then my thoughts turned to Olen and the others, including the mother and her son. With all this cold and snow, I hoped they had found shelter.

The damage from the attack was in the process of being repaired. Scaffolding clung to one stretch of road like a skeletal brace. It reminded me that Olen's house had been thoroughly destroyed by the wyvern, and now Kai knew he had hidden me. A flash of concern shot through me. It was one more thing Kai and I would need to talk about once we were alone together.

The caribou slowed as we entered the inner courtyard of the castle. My muscles protested the change, with stiffness flaring as the animal came to a halt. Kai's arm tightened again, holding me upright. I sucked in a breath through clenched teeth and let it out slowly. Somehow, the air no longer seemed quite as cold.

Kai pushed his hood back and removed his scarf. The wind no longer blew hard against me, and something about the stillness in the yard made me wonder if perhaps this place had enchantments as well, to reduce the cold.

Ashren strode out from the far side, his gaze sweeping the group before landing on us. His coat was dusted with snow but open as if he had thrown it on over his robe and trousers.

Kai swung down in one smooth motion, his boots hitting stone with a solid thud. His hands came up for me without hesitation.

"I can do it." I started to slide down as well, but my body was stiff from being in this position so long. My boot caught on the edge of the saddle as I tried to swing my leg over. The world tilted sideways, and a sharp gasp escaped as I pitched forward. "Fuck!"

"Whoa." Kai lunged forward and caught me before I hit the ground. His hands clamped around my waist, and he lowered me the rest of the way. The impact jarred my sore muscles, but I stayed upright. The memory of his hands on me in the cabin shot through me, unwelcome.

"You need rest," he said gruffly. His irises had turned completely violet, and his pupils were blown wide.

Electricity shot through my core, and I couldn't tear my gaze from his. As much as I didn't want my heart broken, I wanted that closeness and heat that I'd experienced with him. The tugging in my chest strengthened, becoming a deep and agonizing ache. Everyone always left or betrayed me. Why did I want to be with him so much? The thought of being apart from him hurt in a way that made no sense. "Thank you," I managed, my voice rough.

He didn't answer. His hand lingered at my waist, his fingers pressing through the layers of fabric with a warmth I could feel even through the cold. But then he shook his head and pressed his lips together, and his expression returned to unreadable. A muscle in his jaw ticked.

"Thank the Fates you're back! The flare was a great help. Far better than sending out multiple search parties." Ashren's voice sliced through the courtyard.

Disappointment slashed through me as Kai released me and stepped back. He turned away from me to face Ashren. "The storm was fierce, but it passed swiftly. All is well?"

Ashren drew closer. Beneath his coat, he wore an elegant gray robe with velvet trim, silver embellishments, and a simple belt with a silver buckle. "No further attacks and no indication of what the Night King hoped to accomplish, aside from your death. The reconstruction has begun. Scouts haven't found signs of any other breach. You have two more reports that will require your attention, including a request for aid from Silver City. There have been some disputes that will require your attention sooner rather than later." He came to a halt a few feet away and clasped his arms behind his back. When his gaze fell on me, he offered a slight smile. "Hannah, I am pleased to see you survived."

"Me too. Somehow it seemed better than dying." I folded my arms over my chest and tucked my gloved hands against my torso.

Ashren's slight smile grew a little. "May I assume she has not returned as a prisoner?" The way he asked the question made it clear he knew the answer.

Straightening his shoulders, Kai pressed his lips into a thinner line. "She is a guest, and she will be staying with us. She is to be placed in the guest room nearest mine, and whatever she needs will be provided. She is also to have full access to the library and the archives so that she may learn all she wishes about the Day and Aurora Fae." He spoke in a clipped, clear tone as if I were an item on his to-do list.

"Of course." Ashren tipped his head forward and looked at me with his warm charcoal eyes. "Whatever you require. Is it acceptable if Thea assists in her care at this time? We would not wish to overstep."

I bit back the urge to grin. I *knew* I liked Ashren. Even if he kept his manners polite, there was an underlying expression and sincerity in them. He seemed like the quiet guy who wasn't so much shy as he was contemplative, and who knew precisely how to get under his brother's skin.

"Yes. Thea may assist." Kai's tone remained solemn. "As I said, see to it she has everything she requires."

Ashren gestured toward the stairs, and we began walking as he continued speaking. "The wyvern is recovering well. He's quite strong, and he appears untainted by the enchantment. Additionally, there is the matter of Olen. He is currently being held, but I do feel it important to note that he was aiding some of the vulnerable citizens at the time of his apprehension, even if he did assist in a prisoner's escape."

My heart tightened. Neither of them was looking at me, so I cleared my throat. "That isn't accurate, at least, not if you're talking about me." I held my hands up as Kai looked at me, his brow furrowing.

"Hannah." He said my name in an exasperated tone while arching his brow. "I am well aware that you were hidden in his larder. Had the wyvern not attacked, I would have found you. Do you think me a fool?"

"No, I was definitely there." I matched his pose and lifted my chin. "But he had no choice. I took him hostage and threatened to kill him if he betrayed me." Though I wanted to look between Kai and Ashren to see if either believed my story, I remained focused on Kai. He was the one I had to convince.

This was a lie, but it was an essential one. Olen hadn't asked to have his home destroyed or volunteered to help me. I'd broken into his home, and he'd gone above and beyond to give me aid and then to help others. Even if my judgment of men was shit, I knew Olen was a good one. "He didn't want to betray you. He's loyal and good. He even warned me that what I was doing was wrong and dangerous, but I didn't listen. I thought you were going to kill me or keep me locked in that prison to freeze to death."

I placed a hand on my heart, hoping Kai would soften some. "*Please.* I'm willing to stay here as we bargained, but I ask that you don't punish someone who showed me genuine kindness, even though I'm sure I scared him half to death."

His nostrils flared, and he closed his eyes. "He still should've told me of your presence as soon as I entered the house."

"Olen lost Isabella." I turned to Ashren in surprise. "If he feared for his life, then he wouldn't be comfortable telling you about Hannah. Not only that, but what would punishing him say to your people after seeing how heroic he was?" Ashren lifted both hands.

Tension spiked as soft flakes of snow drifted down. My butt wanted to get inside, but I couldn't throw Olen to the hounds... or the wyverns. I wasn't sure which one was more vicious, since nothing made sense here, but I guessed either worked.

Kai tensed then sagged while his jaw worked. Ashren looked between Kai and me while Thea appeared at the top of the staircase, her expression incredulous, as if she'd caught my plea. Her arms were folded over her chest with her hands tucked into her long, blue velvet sleeves.

With a long sigh, Kai looked back at me. "Did he harm

you? Demand anything of you?" He asked these questions softly and with a look in his eye that made my breath catch.

"He was a perfect gentleman." I raised a hand to put on his chest and stopped myself. "And—he said he had a mate." I wasn't sure what that meant, but it had sounded important when he'd said it to Kai earlier.

Ashren offered a slight shrug. "Isabella was his world. No one will ever replace her for him."

Kai's expression shifted, and something unreadable passed behind his eyes. He glanced at Ashren, then back at me. "Very well. Olen will be released without punishment. But he will be watched." His voice carried a warning edge that made it clear this was as much mercy as he was willing to extend. It was as much as I could hope for.

The knot in my chest loosened. "Thank you." The words came out softer than I intended. Part of me had feared he would still insist on some draconian punishment.

He gave a curt nod, then turned toward the stairs and gestured at Thea. "Hannah, you are to go with Thea. She will escort you to your guest chamber and ensure you have all you need. Ashren, are the reports fully prepared from all the outposts and agents?"

I reached out to touch his elbow and then let my hand drop to my side. "Wait. Can I speak with you in private about something else?" The words were out before I could stop them, but I needed clarity. "It's important."

Kai hesitated a breath, then turned back to me. "No, Hannah," he said firmly, his eyes violet though his voice remained flat. "That won't be possible."

CHAPTER 22

Hannah

Shock ran through me, and my spine went stiff. I swallowed hard and tried to collect myself. Surely I'd heard him wrong.

Yet, the *no* repeated in my head like an echo. The way he'd said it—so simple and cold—shook me to my core. I wanted to talk about what had happened, but I'd be damned if I was going to beg. That wasn't who I was.

My chest constricted, and fear clawed my throat as if I were on the verge of losing something precious. I hated the tears that pricked along the backs of my eyes. Fuck me. I wasn't weak. Yet, the words spilled out of my mouth anyway. "It's *important*."

Kai motioned for Ashren to go on and said, "Make sure the reports are ready for me, and have the attendants prepare for my journey. I'll read them before I leave for Silver City."

My heart locked in my chest. I hated myself for even trying to plead with Kai. Who even was I anymore? I pressed my lips into a tight line. "I could talk with you while you're preparing to go."

Ashren hesitated, then bowed slightly. He started up the

staircase, pausing only to speak to Thea. Thea nodded slowly, though she did not look at him.

Kai waited until Ashren was out of earshot, then stepped closer, lowering his voice as he leaned in. "Hannah," he said softly, his pupils wide and his irises all violet. "What happened was...intense. But it was a biological reaction to closeness after a near-death experience. I have given you my word that I will ensure you end up where you belong. You are under my protection." His hand started to lift as if to touch my face, but he drew it back.

Then, he squared his shoulders as he stepped away. "Trust me. When I wish to pursue an actual physical relationship, there will be no doubts. I am not a man who is shy to admit what he wants. But right now, we both have other matters that require our full attention. Make the most of your time here. I will return in a few days. Perhaps in the next week or so, and we will speak then."

He was talking to me as if I were a child. Rage burned hot and bright within me.

When he stepped back and looked at me, I forced the anger into the center of my chest and gave him the sweetest smile I could muster. "Oh, please don't trouble yourself. I understand completely. I'm just a woman. It was wrong of me to assume that I could take up your time. I misunderstood. Silly me."

He frowned and canted his head. His hands moved to his belt as he studied me and then stepped back. "I appreciate your understanding." He turned and walked up the stairs.

When he neared the top, he slowed as if debating whether to look back. Then he shook his head and continued. He murmured something to Thea that I didn't catch and disappeared at the top.

Thea smiled faintly before her gaze returned to me. She stepped down the stairs into the open air of the courtyard.

Her long, straight red hair was tucked behind her ears, and the snow began to fall again, catching on the bright strands. "Well, Hannah...you're going to be trouble, aren't you?"

Annoyance flared through me, and I prepared for what was likely a lecture. As much as I liked her from our minimal interactions and appreciated her kindness, the last thing I needed was to be put in my place. "Maybe. Is that a problem?"

She stopped before me and shook her head. I noted she was about half a head taller than me. Her smile broadened, then pulled crooked. "Not as long as you're the witty kind. Let's get you inside. You look like you could use a hot meal, a hotter drink, and the hottest bath your skin can stand."

Tears pricked my eyes again. As much as Kai had dumbfounded me, she was doing the same but in the opposite direction. "I wouldn't say no to any of that." A knot formed in my throat, and my voice thickened.

Her ginger hair was not quite as dark a red as Aunt Maureen's, but something in her manner reminded me of my great-aunt, especially the way Thea had spoken just now.

She brought a hand out from where she'd tucked them in her sleeves and gestured toward the staircase. "Come along then." She climbed the stone stairs with the easy grace of someone who had walked this path a thousand times, her long blue skirt trailing over the steps. "As soon as you were spotted on your way back, I guessed where he would want you placed, so I took the liberty of having your room prepared."

"How did you know?" I frowned. The way she'd said it was like a hidden joke, and I *hated* being kept in the dark.

"Psh." She scoffed and cut her eyes at me. "It was obvious. The guest quarters, right next to his, of course. Just as surely as he has returned to his study and to pack the same things he always does on these trips."

I followed her, my sore legs protesting every step. The stone was slick with a thin layer of ice, and I had to focus to keep from slipping in the oversized boots. "You seem awfully confident about that." And very close too. A spark of jealousy flared within me.

"I've known Kai and Ashren for a long time."

As we passed through the heavy wooden doors, I decided to get to the point. "Are you involved with him?"

"Kai or Ashren?" The coy tilt of her head and arch of her brow was startlingly playful, as if she were daring me to specify who I was asking about.

My eyes narrowed before I could keep the jealousy hidden.

She giggled and shook her head. "Kai is like a brother to me. A brother who has attained great power and responsibility and now carries an even greater weight on his shoulders. Ashren is not like a brother to me in *any* sense. But if you would like me to tell you more of Ashren, I am happy to. Or I could discuss Kai."

My stomach somersaulted, and a sour taste filled my mouth. I didn't want to think about Kai right now. The bastard king was even worse than I'd imagined. Our last conversation replayed in my head, and heat filled my cheeks.

Warmth seeped through my coat and into my spine, but not enough to loosen my legs. My thighs still felt carved from wood, stiff and aching with every step I took. I rolled my shoulders once, trying to coax blood back into places that had gone half numb during the ride. "What do you think I should know, in general?"

She shrugged and glanced over her shoulder. When she noticed she was a few strides in front of me, she slowed her pace. "I'd tell you that the people here are tight-knit because we have lost so much. And there are formalities, rules, and orders because they provide structure, but under it all, there is far more. Kai clings to structure, and he likes everything to be done his way. He despises handling multiple things at once."

Instead of continuing toward the broad central hall, she

veered down a narrower corridor tucked between two pillars. The ceiling lowered slightly, making the space more intimate. Decorative metalwork traced the walls here, dark iron shaped into twisting vines and frost-petaled flowers with their edges catching the low magic-light. Deep blue and silver tapestries woven with abstract scenes of snowfields and shadowed trees at dusk in the mountains hung between sconces. The air smelled of clean linen, spicy cologne, pine, and resin.

"So he's particular." Nailed it. He was a stickler and had a rod shoved up his ass.

"Oh yes, very particular, even when we were young." We reached a door, and she opened it and waved me to the staircase beyond. "This is a side staircase, and it's the easiest and quietest route to the bedrooms from this side of the castle. Just as many stairs, but fewer interruptions, better spaced steps, and much closer than if you take the main staircase." We continued to climb, and she glanced back with a knowing smile. "There's another staircase like this on the other side of the castle, if you're coming from that direction. You might not be glad of the steps right now, but I bet you'll thank me once I show you what I set up in the washroom."

My heart skipped a beat. "Just promising me a hot bath makes me want to kiss you."

She laughed, the sound echoing off the stone around us. When we reached the landing, she guided me through the next door. The decor on the third floor was far nicer than on the first. Carved beams arched overhead, the dark wood etched with frost motifs that shimmered as I moved. Thick, patterned rugs softened the floor, muffling our steps. Doors lined the hall. Most of them were closed, but a few were cracked.

We took a turn to the right at a junction of the halls.

Thea patted my arm. "You're going to do fine here. I heard Kai say that you're welcome to visit the library and the archives. You'll enjoy them, I think. I love the library at sunset. It has the most beautiful view."

She spoke as if she'd known me all her life. Kai had said that she was from the Day Court and had lost her people, aside from a few survivors. Something twinged inside me. I'd lost mine as well and felt out of sorts. "I look forward to it."

Several servants bustled toward us in blue and gray uniforms, their arms laden with crumpled clothes and what looked like cleaning supplies. Their footsteps quickened as they moved away from the end of the hall where two large double doors stood open, spilling warm light into the corridor.

Thea guided me to a door on the right side of the hallway. "This is your room. I think you'll find it quite comfortable—"

My feet carried me forward without permission, drawn toward those open double doors like iron to a lodestone. I knew with absolute certainty whose room lay beyond. It was just a gut instinct, but then again, he had said he wanted my room to be next to his.

"Hannah, that's Kai's room."

"I figured." I stepped over the threshold and stopped.

The bedroom was regal but simple. Deep shades of indigo with silver accents caught the fading daylight from tall windows. A massive four-poster bed dominated one wall, its dark wood carved with the same frost-petal motifs I'd seen throughout the castle. The bedding was crisp and perfectly arranged, not a single wrinkle marring the deep blue coverlet.

Bookshelves lined another wall, the books organized with obsessive precision—spines aligned, heights graduated, everything in its proper place. The desk and bureau on the other wall were also perfectly ordered. A trunk sat open near the foot of the bed, partially packed with neatly folded clothing. Kai's scent permeated everything in this space, wrapping around me like phantom arms and making my stomach twist.

Thea stepped in alongside me. "The servants will be back in a moment to finish the packing. He likes the sleigh completely ready to go before he even goes down to the stable so he can work to the last minute."

I nodded but didn't budge. Anger fueled me as I glanced around, deciding exactly what I wanted to take from him.

Thea looped her arm through mine and leaned in close to my ear. "The one good thing about him being so orderly is that he always notices when something is missing or out of alignment. I'll steal something of his from his study to let him know we aren't happy with him. Something small. He'll know why I did it."

My eyes widened. Was that a Day Fae tradition? What were the chances of someone else having a tradition so similar to my family's? It had to be because of the fae connection.

She smiled as she pulled me back. "Come on. Let's get you to your room. You'll feel much better after a hot bath."

I couldn't sense my body as I followed her out of the room toward my own. "You don't have to take something. I don't want you to get into trouble."

She shrugged and pushed open the door to my room. "Oh, it won't be the first time I've done it. I steal certain things so he knows that he's done wrong and that it's me. He won't punish me. The worst he'll do is grumble and glare. Maybe demand extra precision or something. But honestly, aggravating him is half the fun."

I entered the room and froze.

Softer shades of blue and lavender swept across the space, the colors blending like the sky at twilight. The bed was smaller than Kai's but no less elegant and was dressed in pale violet linens with silver embroidery along the edges. The furniture was simpler, too—a wardrobe of light wood, a writing desk positioned near the window, a cushioned chair by a small fireplace where flames already crackled. The motifs here were all dusk, with crescent moons and stars carved into the head-board, woven into the rug beneath my feet, etched into the frame of the mirror on the wall. No frost. No ice. Just the gentle promise of evening.

"This is beautiful," I breathed, stepping farther inside.

Thea beamed. "I thought you might like it. The dusk rooms are my favorite. They're warmer somehow, even though the colors are cool." She crossed to a door on the far wall and pushed it open, revealing a washroom beyond. Steam curled through the doorway, carrying the scent of something floral and clean. "The bath is already drawn, but if you need more hot water, just turn the tap on the left. The aqueducts run beneath the castle, and there's an enchantment that heats the water as it flows. Just don't add sulfur if you happen to have any."

"Why would I have sulfur? Wait." I stared at her. "You have hot running water?"

"Of course." She laughed a little. "Life would be a wretched misery without it. And I don't know what minerals and additives are common for you. You aren't from around here."

A laugh escaped me. "Where I come from, that's considered pretty advanced plumbing. I guess I'm just relieved. I figured we'd have to heat up the water and haul it up here. Don't worry. I don't have sulfur."

"Well, if times become dire, we might. For now, though, we are blessed by Fate." Her expression softened as she studied my face. "Rest. Enjoy the bath. I'll have food sent up, and if you need anything at all, just pull the cord by the bed. Someone will come. And...as far as things you should know, I would tell you that Kai protects those under his care. That includes everyone in this kingdom. He is, however, an enormous ass when it comes to articulating his feelings."

A startled laugh escaped me.

She dipped her head forward and smiled. "Please enjoy your bath. I'm sure I will see you soon." She squeezed my arm gently before slipping out, the door clicking shut behind her.

I stood alone in the quiet room with the crackle of the fire and the distant murmur of castle activity the only sounds. The steam from the washroom called to me, promising relief for muscles that felt like they'd been beaten with rocks. But there was one thing I needed to do before I could truly relax. Something that tugged at me, and I already knew exactly what it was.

Needing to move before the servants took Kai his trunk, I cracked my door open. Footsteps grew fainter, as if someone had just come and gone. There was no sign of anyone here now.

As much as I appreciated Thea's offer to steal a little something to let Kai know her feelings, I needed to do something myself. But what I took wouldn't be something innocuous. I'd do it Aunt Maureen's way. I needed to make sure he knew it was me and that it stung.

I slipped out of the hallway and past the open double doors of his room. The trunk was still half packed, and I lifted the clothing to check for items inside. I wouldn't take something that would hurt him, even though he deserved it. As I scanned, I found his weird gray boxers underneath a cloak.

A wicked idea occurred to me.

I removed all his boxers and then darted back to the door and shut it. Then I slid off my boots and pants before shimmying out of my light turquoise panties. I pulled my pants back on and tucked my panties where his boxers had been.

I beamed. That ought to send a message. If he wasn't going to talk to me, at least I knew he'd be thinking of me. Refusing to talk to me was a bitch move anyway, so he could just wear these panties instead of his boxers.

Cackling inwardly, I scooped up his boxers and my boots,

ran back to my room, and closed the door. I shoved his boxers under my mattress and stripped down. Within seconds, I immersed myself in the hot water, soaking up to my neck.

My muscles relaxed, and my anger faded. I'd get justice soon, which made me feel even more settled.

The long soak definitely improved my mood, and Thea was true to her word about sending me up a hot meal: roasted chicken with parsley potatoes and mashed turnips with green herbs that looked like rosemary and tasted like chives. Little hand pies with a red jelly inside that tasted like a mix of blueberries and peaches for dessert.

After the bath and food, I curled up in the bed. Things hadn't ended the way I'd hoped with Kai today, but I'd gotten some satisfaction.

I fell fast asleep.

The following day, Thea took me to the library. It was two stories tall with a vaulted ceiling painted a deep midnight blue and dotted with silver stars. Tall windows lined one wall with tinted glass in soft shades of amber and rose that filtered the dying sunlight into warm pools across the stone floor. The view showcased the snow-covered mountains beyond the castle, and as Thea had promised, the sunset would be stunning. I could already imagine the peaks looking as if they'd caught fire in the golden glow.

This place was gorgeous. I could live here and die happy. Who needed King Grouchy Butt? Not me. That was for sure.

The walls were filled with bookshelves holding heavy leather-bound and cloth-covered books throughout. Rolling ladders on brass tracks provided access to the higher shelves, and scattered throughout the space were reading nooks. There were two alcoves tucked between shelves, each with a large window seat, and six deep armchairs were positioned in the center of the room around a glass-enclosed firepit.

For all my best intentions, though, I couldn't stop thinking of Kai. He made everything more difficult just by existing. Maybe I was capable of murder after all.

Each day, Thea checked in on me regularly to make sure I ate, and she took me around to meet the other occupants of the castle. I enjoyed my conversations with her and Ashren, and she always seemed to know just how long to stay before I needed time alone. She had an uncanny knack for pulling out books of interest and sharing stories that made it feel as if we'd known each other for ages. And, every day, she gave me at least one update on Kai and what he was doing, even though I pretended I didn't care. Because, you know, I didn't.

After four days, she informed me he was returning from Silver City. "He'll probably be here after the third bell past midnight," she said from the doorway. "I think he's eager to return. Perhaps he wishes to talk with a certain someone."

"Well, good for him. I'm sure they won't be available." I forced a neutral expression as I sat in the window seat with a large book about portals and their magic, trying not to buy into her shenanigans. I knew what she was up to. She couldn't fool me.

I debated telling her what I'd done with the panties but decided against it. That truth would come out soon enough, and Kai couldn't blame anyone but me.

"Of course. I'm sure you'll find something in the next eight hours to occupy yourself with." Thea grinned and stepped away, pulling the door shut behind her.

A moment later, the door clicked open again. Damn, she was persistent. I'd give her that.

I kept my gaze fastened on the page, studying a diagram that looked like something out of a biochemistry class I'd failed. I didn't understand it, but I wasn't even going to act semi-interested in Kai's return. "Still not going to be available, Thea."

"Not even for a little chat? I heard you were asking about me," a friendly, familiar voice said.

My head snapped up. "Olen!" I shoved the book aside and climbed to my feet.

He stood in the doorway, his red-brown curls tousled and his brow furrowed, though he was smiling. He wore a heavy black cloak and simple black garb underneath, but his smile was as warm as it had been when he'd told me about his brother and his perspective on following the law.

"Hannah." He crossed the library in four long strides and held out his hands. There was a dark bottle in one and two cups in the other. He set them on the small table near the window seat. "It seems you're not a prisoner anymore."

"Well, at least for now. There's always tomorrow." I hugged him. His cloak was damp, as if he'd just been outside, even though there was no snow on him. I rolled my eyes. "We came to an *arrangement*."

"I'm glad. I've been worried for you." He hugged me tight, then stepped back with his hands gripping my shoulders. "I didn't know you'd been asking after me, or I'd have stopped in sooner. But repairs on the wall and managing other damage have occupied most of my time. We had to rebuild some of the towers to the south, as well as one of the outposts."

"They said you were busy, and you did lose your house." I wouldn't have been surprised if he blamed me for that since Kai had followed me to him and the berserker wyvern had followed Kai. "Do you have somewhere to stay?"

"Yeah. That's all sorted... more or less." His lips trembled slightly, and the lines in his brow deepened. He stepped back to the table. "It's all working out as well as it can, though with the war and all...times are hard." He uncorked the bottle and poured the dark liquid into the wooden cups. "But we didn't get to finish our drink last time, and I thought we should at least do that."

"You came all this way to share a drink?" I laughed and pushed the book to the center of the window seat. "You didn't have to do that."

"I was just...it meant something that you asked after me. And I wanted to make sure you were all right." He set the bottle down and handed me the cup. "Between all that and dealing with the royals, let's say I haven't had much rest. In times like these, we do what we must."

"You don't have to tell me. I know all about those royals." I glanced at the drink, and an odd sort of twinge passed through me. My thumb brushed the rim of the dark wood. Something was off. "Are you all right? I mean...I know you lost your home, but...other than that?"

He shook his head, then raked a hand through his hair. A wry laugh escaped his lips. "Well, the house situation hasn't helped. A lot of memories were lost in the destruction, but it wasn't your fault. And...I'm aware that the king is not pleased with my actions, just as I'm aware I have you and his half-brother to thank for not being imprisoned or worse. But, all things considered, I'm well. Though I doubt you'll see me much after this."

I rolled my eyes. "He's a dickwad."

His mouth twisted, and he shook his head. "Can't say I know what that means, but you're probably right." He lifted the cup. "To the end of the war."

I would at least enjoy this moment with my friend while I had time left. I lifted mine as well. "To the end of the war." I downed the drink, and a burn settled deep in my chest.

"Well, sometimes we need a little kick." I swallowed hard, the burn settling into a deep haze. Clearing my throat, I set the cup down on the table, my hand heavier and clumsier than it should have been. The warmth from the brandy spread through my chest and into my limbs, but it wasn't the pleasant buzz I expected. Maybe drinking an unknown liquid in a fae land wasn't the best idea. "That's... that's strong stuff."

"Blackthorn brandy." He filled both our glasses again, chuckling. His expression looked pained, though. "Aged twelve years." His thumb pressed harder against the rim. "Kicks like a caribou."

My legs wobbled, and I grabbed the window seat to steady myself. The burn seemed to be spreading throughout my body.

Olen didn't laugh, but he didn't reach out to help me either. He just studied me with his cup still in his hand. "You're the one who actually gave me the idea for this," he said softly. "It was very clever, really. When the Night King told me what I had to do, it was ironic that I realized *you* had inspired the perfect plan. I could never lace clovefall whiskey with anything. It's not possible. But blackthorn brandy...well, that burn will hide anything."

The room tilted sideways, and the bookshelves blurred into smears of leather and gold. "You bastard!" Or at least that's what I tried to say. The world tilted, and I tried to steady myself, scream, or do anything.

A strange look of sadness twisted on his face. "I'm sorry, Hannah. I truly do like you, and I admire your spirit. This is the last thing I wanted to do, but I have no choice. The Night King can't be stopped, and the only way anyone in this court will survive is..." He trailed off as he bowed his head. "Just let go, Hannah. You won't remember anything. You won't feel anything either. I made sure of that. No matter what they do, you won't suffer. I'm sorry. This is the best I can do."

I fought the pull, clawing at consciousness like a drowning woman reaching for the surface. My fingers scraped uselessly against the window seat cushion, my nails catching on embroidered thread. The library blurred around me. The stars on the ceiling spun like a carousel gone mad. Bookshelves melted into rivers of leather and gilt. Then my knees buckled.

I didn't feel my body strike the floor, but when I looked up through the haze of my vision, I saw Olen stooping beside me. He brushed the hair from my face. "Sleep, Hannah."

Kai...

Darkness claimed me.

Want to continue Hannah and Kia's love story, click here to read book 2, The Steel of the Wicked Heart.

Want to read a romantasy where wolf shifters get kidnapped and taken to a fae land to compete in a ruthless bridal competition for the aloof Shadow Prince, click here to read Bonded to the Fallen Shadow King, book 1 in the Of Fae and Wolf Trilogy.

About the Author

Jen L. Grey is a *USA Today* Bestselling Author who writes Paranormal Romance, Urban Fantasy, and Fantasy genres.

Jen lives in Tennessee with her husband, two daughters, and three miniature Australian Shepherds. Before she began writing, she was an avid reader and enjoyed being involved in the indie community. Her love for books eventually led her to writing. For more information, please visit her website and sign up for her newsletter.

Check out her future projects and book signing events at her website.
www.jenlgrey.com

Also by Jen L. Grey

The Fae Spark Trilogy

The Curse of the Frost King

The Steel of the Wicked Heart

Rejected Fate Trilogy

Betrayed Mate

Cursed Magic

Wicked Fate

Of Fae and Wolf Trilogy

Bonded to the Fallen Shadow King

Claimed by Shadow and Blood

Forged by Heart and Claws

Fated To Darkness

The King of Frost and Shadows

The Court of Thorns and Wings

The Kingdom of Flames and Ash

The Forbidden Mate Trilogy

Wolf Mate

Wolf Bitten

Wolf Touched

Standalone Romantasy

Of Shadows and Fae

Twisted Fate Trilogy

Destined Mate

Eclipsed Heart

Chosen Destiny

The Marked Dragon Prince Trilogy

Ruthless Mate

Marked Dragon

Hidden Fate

Shadow City: Silver Wolf Trilogy

Broken Mate

Rising Darkness

Silver Moon

Shadow City: Royal Vampire Trilogy

Cursed Mate

Shadow Bitten

Demon Blood

Shadow City: Demon Wolf Trilogy

Ruined Mate

Shattered Curse

Fated Souls

Shadow City: Dark Angel Trilogy

Fallen Mate

Demon Marked

Dark Prince

Fatal Secrets

Shadow City: Silver Mate

Shattered Wolf

Fated Hearts

Ruthless Moon

The Wolf Born Trilogy

Hidden Mate

Blood Secrets

Awakened Magic

The Hidden King Trilogy

Dragon Mate

Dragon Heir

Dragon Queen

The Marked Wolf Trilogy

Moon Kissed

Chosen Wolf

Broken Curse

Wolf Moon Academy Trilogy

Shadow Mate

Blood Legacy

Rising Fate

The Royal Heir Trilogy

Wolves' Queen

Wolf Unleashed

Wolf's Claim

Bloodshed Academy Trilogy

Year One

Year Two

Year Three

The Half-Breed Prison Duology (Same World As Bloodshed Academy)

Hunted

Cursed

The Artifact Reaper Series

Reaper: The Beginning

Reaper of Earth

Reaper of Wings

Reaper of Flames

Reaper of Water

Stones of Amaria (Shared World)

Kingdom of Storms

Kingdom of Shadows

Kingdom of Ruins

Kingdom of Fire

The Pearson Prophecy

Dawning Ascent

Enlightened Ascent

Reigning Ascent

Stand Alones

Death's Angel

Rising Alpha